An intriguing story about God's working out His will, from Abraham's idol-worshipping father to a modern day Messianic Jewish family. Tightly written and fast-paced. The ending will leave you wanting Book 2.

—**Brandilyn Collins**, bestselling author of over 30 books, including the Seatbelt Suspense® novels

From a criminal investigation in Manhattan to the birth of Abram in ancient Ur, Jerry Jenkins weaves together a tale of drama and suspense that will draw you into the lives of two families separated by 4,000 years of history yet sharing remarkably similar struggles of faith. *Dead Sea Rising* combines the thrill of a whodunit with the moral and political intrigue of the ancient, and modern, Middle East. But be prepared. Once you begin, you won't be able to stop until you reach the final page!

—**Dr. Charlie Dyer**, Professor-at-Large of Bible and Host of *The Land and the Book* radio program

This inescapable adventure kept me turning pages thru an explosion of unforgettable intrigue and passion as only Jerry B. Jenkins can pen.

—**DiAnn Mills**, Christy Award winning author

I don't know whose books you might read. At our dinner table, we often discuss whichever Jerry Jenkins book one of us is devouring. His dialogue is equal to the best of Nelson DeMille, his storylines equal to the best of John Grisham. But Jerry Jenkins books are on another level. And now *Dead Sea Rising* . . . Wow! This book may be the best of Jerry Jenkins. And that, my friend, is saying a lot!

—**Andy Andrews**, *New York Times* bestselling author of *The Traveler's Gift* and *The Noticer*

From the first few pages, *Dead Sea Rising* offers suspense and drama, making you wonder how this fascinating story originating in Manhattan finds its mysterious roots deep in the Middle East. True to Jerry's style, the reader is quickly carried forward, drawing you into the intrigue of ancient Mesopotamia. If you love history—especially biblical history—this is a fun and fascinating read!

—**Joni Eareckson Tada**, Joni and Friends International Disability Center

Dead Sea Rising is a page turner! No one does biblical fiction like Jerry Jenkins!

—**Karen Kingsbury**, bestselling author

DEAD SEA CONSPIRACY

A NOVEL

JERRY B. JENKINS

DR. CRAIG EVANS, BIBLICAL CONSULTANT

WORTHY
PUBLISHING

New York • Nashville

Copyright © 2021 by Jenkins Entertainment, LLC

Cover design by Gearbox
Cover images by Shutterstock
Cover copyright © 2022 by Hachette Book Group, Inc.

Worthy
Hachette Book Group
1290 Avenue of the Americas, New York, NY 10104
worthypublishing.com
twitter.com/worthypub

First Edition: August 2022

Worthy is a division of Hachette Book Group, Inc. The Worthy name and logo are trademarks of Hachette Book Group, Inc.

The publisher is not responsible for websites (or their content) that are not owned by the publisher.

The Hachette Speakers Bureau provides a wide range of authors for speaking events. To find out more, go to www.hachettespeakersbureau.com or call (866) 376-6591.

Library of Congress Cataloging-in-Publication Data
Names: Jenkins, Jerry B., author.
Title: Dead sea conspiracy : a novel / Jerry B. Jenkins.
Description: First edition. | New York : Worthy, 2022. | Series: Dead Sea chronicles
Identifiers: LCCN 2021053695 | ISBN 9781546014225 (hardcover) | ISBN 9781546002185 (ebook)
Subjects: LCGFT: Novels.
Classification: LCC PS3560.E485 D44 2022 | DDC 813/.54—dc23/eng/20211105
LC record available at https://lccn.loc.gov/2021053695

ISBN: 9781546014225 (hardcover), 9781546002185 (ebook)

Printed in the United States of America

LSC-C

Printing 1, 2022

To Moon, a treasured friend

The greatest friend of truth is time.
Error is always in a hurry.

—

Vance Havner

Therefore from one man [Abraham], and him as good as dead,
were born as many as the stars of the sky in multitude—
innumerable as the sand which is by the seashore.

—

Hebrews 11:12 NKJV

DEAD SEA
CONSPIRACY

PRELUDE

From Book 1 **DEAD SEA RISING**

Archaeologist Nicole Berman's father, Benzion, explains a photograph of a beautiful young Asian woman, Bian (Charm) Nguyen, that Ginny, his wife of forty years, discovered among his keepsakes…

Eleven West, Mount Sinai Hospital, New York City

"Sure you want me here for this, Dad?" Nicole said. "Seems it should be between you and Mom."

"I want you here," her mother said. "Whatever this is, you ought to hear it too."

Her dad nodded. "I'm just sorry I never told you, Ginny. You told me about your previous relationships—"

"Which didn't amount to much. So this was a relationship?"

"It was."

"In Vietnam?"

"Yes."

"Did you love her?"

"I thought I did…well, yes. I did. And hard as it is even for me to believe, while it was deep and meaningful and special, especially at that time in my life, I can tell you honestly, even at its best it was nothing like

I

what we have, Ginny. I can't deny Charm and I were in love, but I don't want you to ever think it holds a candle to—"

"I've never doubted your love, Ben. It just gave me pause to find that picture and wonder. And to learn she was someone so special to you and I have never heard of or about her…"

"That's all on me. I regret it and I'm sorry. Sorry for not telling you. Sorry for hiding the box. Sorry for leaving it out where you could stumble onto it."

"Did you sleep with her, Ben?"

"May I tell you the story from the beginning?"

Ginny nodded, and he told her everything, leaving nothing out…

"I never saw her, talked to her, heard from her, or wrote to her ever again…I was relieved when my father told me that the proxy scholarship from the foundation had been used by Bian (Charm) Nguyen at Saigon National Pedagogical University. All I know is that she graduated. I don't know where or when or if she ever used her teaching degree or even whether she's dead or alive."

Nicole's mother's eyes were full. She reached for him and he took her hand. "She sounds like a wonderful woman."

"But I was lost without you," he said.

"Who knows how receptive you'd have been if you'd never met Charm? I'm curious enough to maybe look her up myself some day. She opened your mind, developed your heart."

"It shouldn't surprise me you'd be so good about this," he said. "Forgive me?"

"Of course. But there had better be no more secrets."

"Promise."

CHAPTER 1

Mada'in Saleh, Saudi Arabia
May 23, 2019

Conflicted.

How else could Nicole Berman describe herself on one of the most pivotal mornings of her life? As the first woman, and certainly the first under the age of forty, to be awarded a permit to serve as lead archaeologist on a dig here, she should have been euphoric. And, in many ways, she was.

But Nicole had hardly slept the night before. During her fourth day of this visit to the Middle East, she welcomed more than forty members of her team to the King Faisal Hotel in Al-'Ula, twelve miles south of the dig site. There she oriented them regarding the next few weeks, including the fact that at the dig site, women could wear shorts and informal head coverings, like caps—but that in the hotel and everywhere else, they should honor the customary modesty of the country.

Many from this team she had worked with before, but more than half were new, including nearly all the volunteers. Most hailed from the States, but about a quarter of the team came from other countries. She was proud of the diversity, not just ethnically, but also in seasons of life. Volunteers ranged from late teens to senior citizens, including one robust couple in their eighties.

She urged team members to call her Nic and reminded them she would not see them at the next morning's buffet breakfast, but would wait for them at the site. That prompted one of her favorite volunteers to rise—Indian-born detective Pranav Chakrabarti, a forensic technician with the New York Police Department's Crime Scene Unit.

"A thousand pardons!" he began with the charming lilt that still favored his native language, despite twenty years in the States. He introduced himself as Nicole's bodyguard and informed the team, "I've been cleared by the Saudi government to carry a weapon—a nine-millimeter Glock, if you must know. This young woman has two doctorates. Two! That's two more than most of us. So if in my presence you refer to her as anything less than *Doctor* Nic, I'm liable to whup you upside your head."

That perfect icebreaker seemed to endear Detective Chakrabarti to all. Nicole felt in good hands with him, but he was also part of the reason for her foreboding. She'd met him months before when he helped investigate the attempted murder of her own mother in Manhattan. Ginny Berman had been a patient at Mount Sinai Hospital for weeks while the NYPD's Senior Services and Domestic Violence Unit painstakingly uncovered the attack related to Nicole's bid for this Saudi dig.

Despite that someone clearly did not want her here, with the support of both her mother and father, Nicole would not be dissuaded. Her mission was that important.

Her mother slowly, finally, began to rally, and it appeared she might be discharged. But one morning Nicole and her father were summoned from the Berman Foundation offices to the hospital by Kayla Mays, the petite midtwenties Black administrator who had proved most kind to the whole family.

"Kayla tell you any more than she told me?" Nicole asked her father in the back seat of a staff car.

He shook his head. "Has to be good news though, right? Your mom's been adamant about getting out of there."

"Hope so," Nicole said, but she wasn't as optimistic. News of her mother's release shouldn't require their presence until it was time for her to leave.

When they arrived a few minutes later, Nicole found beautiful Kayla's cheeks wet, and she seemed unable to look Nicole in the eye. Her mother's doctor pointed her and her father to chairs in a small conference room. Kindly yet directly, he said, "There's no easy way to break this to you, but your wife and mother took a sudden turn for the worse this morning and passed less than an hour ago."

Impossible, Nicole thought. "She was perfectly fine last night! What happened?"

Benzion stood quickly. "I want to see her."

"Let's let them make her presentable, and—"

"Right now," Ben said.

Nicole had shared her father's urgency but now remained haunted by the pained expression she found on the face she had come to cherish over the years—as if her mother had fought for a last breath. There had been no signs of trauma or danger for days. Nicole couldn't make it compute, and her father seemed on the verge of a breakdown. "How does something like this happen?" he asked the doctor, his voice constricted. "No warnings from all these machines?"

The surgeon flipped a page on her chart and turned it toward Nicole. "Alarms were triggered," he said. "And a nurse reached her within thirty seconds. She called a Code Blue, and the crash cart and team arrived inside another thirty seconds. They tried everything…"

The bottom of the chart read "2 of 3 pages," but when Nicole reached to peek at the final page, the doctor said, "Miss Mays herself can corroborate these notes" and she let it go.

Nicole found herself grateful that Kayla had been with her mother. "Was she conscious?"

Kayla nodded, clearly struggling to speak. "Well, not at first. I checked on her, like I did so often—"

"And we appreciate that," Nicole said, fighting to control her own emotions. "She was so fond of you."

"And you know how I felt about her. She appeared to be asleep. Then she opened her eyes and seemed to struggle."

"Struggle how?" Nicole's father said.

"Her eyes grew wide and she seemed to plead with me without speaking. I asked if she was all right, and that's when the machines started beeping. I wanted to help, to do something, but as I reached for her, a nurse burst in and elbowed me out of the way—which was a relief. I'm sorry, so sorry."

Nicole tried to take comfort in the fact that her mother did not die alone, that a friendly face was nearby, but she anticipated sleepless nights as memories flooded her. It encouraged her to know her mother had heard the good news about Nicole's approval to lead the Saudi Arabia dig, after having insisted on updates about it every day. But that too just reminded her heavily how she depended on her mother's interest in her life and how she cherished their daily interactions.

Nicole had been unable to mourn her mother the way she needed to, as the bulk of the funeral planning fell to her. More than once she caught herself with an urge to call or text her mother, and she often called Kayla just to talk about her. Nicole hated learning firsthand what was meant by the phrase *dark night of the soul*. She suffered through too many to count.

Her father was also a wreck, and he immediately announced he would not join Nicole for the dig—at least not at first.

"You sure, Dad? Don't you need something to distract you—"

"I don't *want* to be distracted, Nic! I have to know how this happened. I'll be no good to you or anyone else until then. Don't you need to know, too?"

"Well, sure, and I'm devastated. But we both know it's going to turn out to be some freak aneurism or something that couldn't have been avoided. And knowing anything more is not going to bring her back."

"So humor me," he said. "I can't let this go."

Nicole knew her father well enough to accept that, though she wanted him along for her first lead job. Well, he'd get there as soon as he could. And it wasn't as if she was among strangers. Detective Chakrabarti had begged to volunteer and endured a lengthy vetting process by the Saudis before being allowed to come *and* also to carry a weapon.

And Kayla had expressed interest in Nicole's profession the day they'd met, telling her she "almost majored in archaeology myself." She stepped up—at her own expense—when two volunteers dropped out at the last minute. Nicole believed she would make a perfect personal assistant. She'd keep her close, counting on her organizational skills and detail orientation to allow Nicole to concentrate on the work itself.

So before dawn on the first day of the dig, Nicole met both Kayla and Detective Chakrabarti in the lobby of the King Faisal Hotel. With Pranav driving and Kayla in the back seat of a rented Land Rover, Nicole played navigator and directed him first to a McDonald's drive-through and then on to the site.

"That may be the last less-than-healthy meal we'll have over here," Nicole said.

"Hope not," Kayla said.

Nicole had flown over early, as was her custom, and spent the previous three days at the site, thrilled afresh at the stunning rose-red beauty of the place. Gleaming edifices hewn out of the rock transformed from deep ruby in the bright sunlight to breathtaking pink hues as the skies changed throughout the day. It reminded her of the magnificent palettes of ancient Petra in Jordan with its jaw-dropping array of colors. Here, however, the massive works of architectural art had been carved from separate monoliths, rather than from great and largely connected cliff faces. She arranged with a couple of trustworthy locals her father had recommended to keep an eye on the dig site after-hours when the usual security staff was off duty.

Nicole had also supervised local workers she paid to remove enough debris and large rocks that would have impeded ground transportation and the camp setup. She had ordered two storage sheds full of tools and equipment and a trailer to serve as the temporary office, connected to power for computers, a refrigerator, water, drainage, and air-conditioning.

Now, at the perimeter of the site, Chakrabarti stopped at a checkpoint manned by a uniformed guard wearing a UN helmet. Nicole leaned forward and greeted him.

"Morning, Doctor," the guard said. "And who do you have along today?"

While he examined their credentials and the ID badges encased in plastic dangling from lanyards around their necks, she informed him that the rest of the team would arrive by bus by five thirty a.m. The guard noted that the detective had been cleared to carry a weapon and asked to see it. He hefted it carefully, keeping the muzzle facing away. "This is what NYPD carries, eh? Took a little training there myself a few years ago."

The guard seemed to study Kayla longer than Pranav, which didn't surprise Nicole. Kayla was striking enough to give both men and women pause, though Nicole expected more decorum from the guard. She cleared her throat and he seemed to cover. "You know, Ms. Mays, that you can burn just as severely here as your teammates. You from Africa?"

"Manhattan," Kayla said flatly. "It's right there in my papers."

"So it is," he said.

"And yes, I'm old enough to be aware of the sun."

The guard waved them through.

"Didn't expect to see the UN here," Chakrabarti said.

"Oh, yes," Nicole said. "UNESCO has hundreds of locations like this all over the world. They call 'em heritage sites."

"All digs?" Kayla said.

"Not all. Anything the UN considers significant, culturally or scientifically."

"Nice to know I'm not the only one looking after the place," Chakrabarti said. He and Kayla seemed unable to take their eyes off the ancient porticos looming in the predawn.

"Mind the path, Detective," Nicole said. "You'll have plenty of time to take this all in. It's well known for its 131 rock-cut monumental tombs."

He slowly passed a parked flatbed truck laden with a crane and pulled up to the site. Nicole asked for a few minutes alone. With Pranav and Kayla waiting in the vehicle, she strode through the area, scoping out where she would have the volunteers mark off and begin digging the four 20-foot-by-20-foot squares and erect sunscreens over them. Already sticky as dawn broke over the horizon, she could tell the day was going to be a broiler—frankly the way she liked it. Yet while she didn't want anything to dampen the thrill of this achievement, something kept her from exulting.

How Nicole wished her mother were alive to rejoice with her, maybe even join her. Imagine both her mom and dad involved in such a monumental life moment.

On the other hand, with neither of them here she wouldn't have to defend against charges of nepotism. No question she felt uniquely privileged to have been born into the family of the Berman Foundation. But she had also paid her dues since she was a teen, volunteering for digs and learning everything there was to know to qualify for this assignment. And she had also earned those doctorates.

Nicole would ask the detective to shoot a picture of her here once the sun fully rose. Maybe he'd enjoy shooting something other than a crime scene.

Still that feeling was there...

Conflicted.

CHAPTER 2

Ur of the Chaldees
Four millennia prior

King Nimrod's right-hand man, Terah, should not have been surprised at his wife's resolve. Belessunu had said she was going to do this, and now she had actually taken their boy and sojourned, on her own, toward his ancestors. Terah had been seventy when the lad was born, and ten years later he suddenly felt every day of his age.

The loneliness was not new to Terah. Belessunu and young Abram had lived in a cave for the first decade of his life, but at least Terah stole away to visit them every day or two, as they relied on him for food and oil and other necessities. Like the king, Terah sought the comfort of concubines, but they did not live with him. They rarely even stayed the night with him, and he was left feeling hardly comforted at all.

Now he not only spent his nights alone as before, but he was also left without loved ones for succor. Loved ones. At least he loved them. He had given them myriad reasons to not love—or trust—him.

But now he missed them both—terribly. And he dared not send anyone to check on their well-being on the road, for there was a reason they had been hiding for so long. No one could know that little Abram was alive and well.

King Nimrod himself had plotted to kill their firstborn son, convinced by his stargazers that the baby was a threat to the throne. In heated discussions with his pregnant wife, Terah had actually referred to the prospect of a male offspring as a curse.

That was something a man could only try to take back but which his wife would also never forget—like so much else Terah had said and done in the wake of Abram's birth. Such as substituting a trusted servant's firstborn for his own and presenting him to the king to dispose of as he wished. Terah might as well have murdered the infant with his own hands. Even Terah's closest confidant had taken his own life over having allowed Terah to commit such evil and participating in the tragic deceit.

But Terah and Belessunu had fundamentally been at loggerheads with each other long before they had been blessed, or cursed, with a child in their dotage. She put up with the concubines he occasionally visited—whom he justified by saying he was relieving her of the entire burden of his cravings. Belessunu had confronted Terah on how he'd drifted from the worship of God to believing in every pagan deity known to man—including his own king. Nimrod referred to himself as Amraphel and considered himself divine, along with all the gods of nature.

Terah had been so immersed in his worship of many gods that he had taken to crafting graven images of dozens of them, including his favorite, Utu the sun god. Travelers from near and far knew of Terah's skill and enterprise and frequently stopped to buy graven images from him.

Belessunu, who had married him when he too believed in the one true God of the Hebrews, Yahweh, made clear she had no patience for his devotion to a pantheon of deities. And as the time had drawn near for the birth of their first child, she had even claimed to speak to Terah under the authority and with the very words of the Spirit of the living God.

She spoke with such conviction that at times Terah believed she was indeed speaking for the Lord Himself, maker of heaven and earth. And yet Terah remained committed to gods represented by the very images he crafted with his own hands. Belessunu told him she had become convinced he was irredeemable, especially after the sacrifice of an innocent servant's even more innocent child and then telling the grieving parents he had failed in a heroic attempt to protect the baby from wild animals...

Terah couldn't help but love his own son and always looked forward to visiting Abram in the cave. But every encounter with Belessunu devastated him. He could not seem to reach her, to soften her view of him, to return to any measure of the love they once knew. And she made plain to him that she would raise Abram in the tradition of his—and Terah's—forefathers: worshiping the one true God.

Belessunu needed Terah only for sustenance. No one else could be trusted to know her or the boy's whereabouts, so no servant could deliver them food or oil for their lamps. That gave Terah reasons to visit, satisfying his need to interact with his son. But Belessunu had become more than a stranger. How dare she? She seemed an enemy, eager to taunt him by having Abram recite what she taught him every day.

The boy would talk of midnight forays from the cave, when there was little danger anyone would see them. "I look to the heavens," the lad would say, "and Mother tells me of God, who created it all."

"No mention of the gods of the sun and the moon and the stars?" Terah would venture.

The boy would laugh. "Mother said you would say that! Those so-called gods were conjured by mere men who don't believe in Yahweh. But where were they when our ancestors were protected from the great flood by God Himself?"

Terah scoffed. He knew the story, of course, as the accounts of everyone's forebearers—Noah's sons Shem, Ham, and Japheth—had been passed down through the generations. But what made the tales of Yahweh true and the narratives of his gods not true? Yet Terah dared not counter Abram's training for fear of kindling the wrath of his wife.

And the last thing he wanted was for her to break into recitations of the ancient holy books in that voice she claimed came from God Himself. Besides, King Nimrod's belief that Terah had proven his devotion to the throne by sacrificing his own son had solidified Terah as his most trusted aide. He had put Terah in charge of building the tower to heaven that would become Nimrod's eternal shrine.

Why Belessunu could not be proud of him for that assignment, Terah could not understand. She clearly did not believe Nimrod was divine in any fashion. And she told Terah that the fact that he was a murderer made her finally accede to young Abram's pleadings and, when he had turned ten, she prevailed upon Terah to buy her a camel and set out to introduce the boy to Noah's son Shem himself. "He will tell Abram everything about the ark, the flood, and the promises of God."

Terah had tried everything in his power to dissuade her, trying to scare her with the dangers of being seen, found out, attacked, raped, killed. "It will take you months to get that far north along the Euphrates!" he wailed. "What will you do for food, provisions, protection?"

"God will provide. He always has. He has fed us lo these many years through you. Imagine! He should have stricken you dead for your sins."

"How can you take my only son from me?"

"You exiled both of us with your evil scheme."

"But God promised he would be—"

"Oh, now you believe in the one true God?"

"I'll believe anything you want if you will not expose Abram to such an impossible journey."

"Terah! You cannot be shamed into returning to God. You must come to him with a contrite heart. But even then He may not forgive you. Who knows how long it takes for His patience to run out?"

"I will never see you or the boy again!"

"You will see us in the afterlife," she said, "but only if you truly repent and turn back to the God of your youth."

CHAPTER 3

Mada'in Saleh, Saudi Arabia

Nicole paced the dig site in the faint light until the bus labored up to the checkpoint behind her. She faced the rising sun and bowed her head, whispering, "Hear O Israel! The Lord our God, the Lord is One. Blessed is the name of His glorious kingdom for all eternity. And you shall love the Lord your God with all your heart, with all your soul, and with all your might. And these words which I command you today shall be on your heart. And you shall teach them to your children, and speak of them when you sit in your house, and when you walk by the way, and when you lie down and when you rise up."

She peeked back past the Land Rover to where the guard boarded the bus. His checking everyone's documents would give her time for a picture. She signaled Kayla and Detective Chakrabarti to join her. "I want a shot of just me in front of where the dig squares will be," she told Pranav, "with the cliff in the background. Then can you set up to shoot us all, you two included?"

"Of course," he said, unpacking his case. "But if you can wait three or four minutes, the sky will be brilliant, and look at those clouds. They'll be pristine."

He proved right, and as the sun fully emerged, the cliff and the clouds seemed to burst in 3-D relief from the cerulean sky. Pranav set his camera on a tripod and positioned Nicole, peering through the range finder and adjusting his settings. He shot a couple of times as she smiled sweetly, then told her, "Show me what you're really feeling right now."

She felt grateful, which her smile had displayed. She also felt excited, fulfilled, confident, and if she could ignore everything else in her life, perhaps she could playfully mug for the lens. Nicole pushed her floppy, wide-billed hat back on her head and spread her feet. Arms akimbo, she pasted on a closemouthed grin as if she alone were in charge. Which she was.

"Perfect!" Pranav and Kayla said in unison, and Nicole burst into laughter, unable to hold the pose for even one more picture. She jogged to Pranav to see the shot on the back of his camera and almost didn't recognize herself. She knew it was due to the skill of the photographer, the quality of his equipment, and his genius in waiting for just the right light—a morning version of most afternoons' golden hour. But still the result stunned her. Overcome, she managed, "You must send that to me."

How her mother would have loved this picture! And how it would thrill her father. Just enough mirth showed in her eyes to prove the pose was a tease, but the shot was no less fabulous. Here was a woman at the top of her game, owning her new role and in fact owning the entire site in one of the most beautiful places on earth.

By the time the bus rumbled into position behind the trailer and the rest of the team disembarked, Nicole had pulled a couple of index cards from her pocket. She peeked at them to remind herself of all she wanted to cover with the entire group. After Pranav shot the predig team photo, she would open with an unapologetic pep talk to set the tone for the entire project.

She was as ready as she had ever been.

CHAPTER 4

Ur

Terah had been supervising the tower project at Babel for years, and proud as he had once been to have been handpicked by the king for this singular role, he now found himself in the pit of despair. With his wife and son away, no one remained to share in his glory—not that they ever did anyway.

Belessunu made no secret of her disdain for Terah's dastardly actions—despite that he had spared their only son. Yet Terah held to a modicum of hope in that when she spoke of his need to return to his devotion to the one true God, he detected a certain longing in her voice—as if she believed God might actually answer her prayers. Sometimes, in the wee hours of his loneliest nights, Terah himself sensed in the depths of his soul a glimmer of hope that something within him might change. Could the prayers of his beloved reach far enough to change the very mind of God about him? But by morning, after torturous attempts at even a few hours of sleep, he settled back in to his reliance on the gods he fashioned with his own hands—and justifying his every act, heinous as each was, with the knowledge that he had rescued his own son from the most powerful enemy in the land.

But Terah was coming to know himself. Could the man who so recklessly caused the spilling of innocent blood really prove so cunning that he could take credit for keeping this most dangerous secret—the very existence of Abram, the king's greatest threat? Was the boy's safety not really under the purview of God Himself? Little about the scheme seemed all that crafty in retrospect, and myriad vulnerabilities in it could and should have easily exposed Abram—and Terah—to King Nimrod. That the king—tall and broad and revered throughout the land as a mighty hunter—bought the idea that Belessunu had abandoned her husband upon the death of their son—and that Terah had been able to maintain the ruse for ten years already—seemed a result of God's protection, not his own wiles. Careful as he had been for the entire time, how was it possible that apparently not a soul ever noticed and reported his visits to the cave every few days to the king?

One night in bed, staring at the ceiling, Terah felt the God of his wife—and his ancestors—seem to impress something deep on his heart. "Did you not think I could protect your child from the king?"

Oh, misery! Unable to trust the one true God, who had promised his firstborn son would become the father of nations, Terah had taken matters into his own hands. The result had made of him a liar, a murderer, alienated from the wife of his youth, estranged from the very heir he had saved, and hopelessly separated from the one true God.

The one true God. In his heart of hearts, he knew the Lord, knew the folly of worshiping and depending on gods of wood and stone. The question was whether he had damned his own soul. As the full weight of his sins grew within him, his conscience plagued him every second of every day. Every decision, every consultation with the king or the tower foremen, carried with it the private torture of seeing himself as God saw him.

Though progress on the edifice was ahead of schedule, King Nimrod had grown increasingly impossible. Terah had the hired workers and conscripted the slaves who produced more bricks and hauled them higher and higher, but the king had fallen ill and worried aloud that he might not see the culmination in his lifetime. He insisted on being transported to the highest point of the tower so he could instruct Terah exactly where to position the massive statue of himself that should have already been completed.

Beyond that, he had decreed that no one but the royal historians were to refer to him by his given name, but rather, everyone was to call him only King Amraphel—the moniker he had given himself to proclaim his deity. Under that name he had invaded Canaan along with other rulers under the leadership of the king of Elam. The coalition had triumphed over Sodom and other Cities of the Plain in what had become known as the Battle of the Vale of Siddim.

"Is my image finally finished?" King Nimrod asked as four aides hefted him—in his royal chair—to the tower site and began the arduous incline. A half dozen others trailed closely, some armed.

The structure had already reached nearly half its projected elevation of more than a mile and a half. The plan had been to simultaneously fashion a massive statue of King Amraphel, arms outstretched, so it would be ready to be transported atop the project when the tower reached its full height in a few years. "The plans are finished," Terah told him, "but no, construction has not yet begun because of your—because—"

"Because I did not like the rendering! It looked as if I were blessing the entire region, as if I were some benevolent ruler bestowing grace and peace on all my subjects."

Precisely, Terah thought. *Who wouldn't want to be memorialized that way?* But he said, "I understand, my king."

"Do you? I am not so sure."

"You have well explained it to me, oh great Amraphel. Your visage and posture are to be triumphant, that of a respected, admired—"

"And feared!"

"Yes, and feared king."

"King, ruler, and god!"

"I understand."

"And so why has the sculpting not begun?"

"We await a rendering that pleases you."

"Fetch the artisan in charge."

"He is not on-site today, my sovereign. He's at work in his—"

"Did I ask where he was, Terah?"

"You did not."

"Did I order you to fetch him?"

Terah bowed, nodded, and signaled an aide. "We will deliver him with dispatch."

Why did the king have to be this way? Could any man possess more than Nimrod enjoyed? Absolute power. Ultimate reign. A wife of youth and beauty, not to mention a dozen fetching concubines. And yet Nimrod so jealously defended his throne that he refused to refer to Ninlia—nor did he allow anyone else to—as the queen. She wore royal apparel and even a crown, and at times sat in the throne next to his at court in Shinar, where she even bore a scepter. But he made clear at every opportunity that she was not royal by blood and certainly not divine.

As the entourage slogged higher and higher up the ramps encircling the core of the monolith, Terah felt abruptly overcome—as if God Himself were again trying to speak to his soul. Could it be? Plain as day, as when his own beloved Belessunu spoke for the one true God in that haunting voice, Terah heard something within that bore the ring of truth: "The king's self-given name does not mean what he thinks it means."

What was Terah to do with such a message? He tried desperately to ignore it, averse as he was to more conflict. But it had been so clear! "Oh, great king," he said, "tell us again of the name you have chosen for yourself. What does it mean?"

King Nimrod wrenched around and seemed to search Terah's face. "How kind of you to ask!" He addressed his entourage. "Should you ever wonder how I choose my top aides—in this case my very top—you would do well to remember this very question. It evidences devotion and worship, does it not, Terah?"

"My intention is plain," Terah said.

"*Amraphel* simply means 'a god who dwells with mortals.' While my destiny is in the heavens with Utu and my other fellow gods, I have deigned to remain below and rule my loyal subjects for as long as I am granted breath."

The sycophants grunted their apparent approval, and Terah added his own murmur—just as it seemed God spoke silently to him again. This time it rang so clearly Terah would not have been surprised if others also heard it. "*Amraphel* means 'he whose words are dark,' and for his blasphemy, he shall surely die. I am the Lord your God, and I have spoken."

Terah had not an iota of doubt he had heard from the God of his forefathers. But why? He had strayed so far and stood guilty of so many abominable acts…Had the creator really addressed *him* when He said, "I am the Lord your God"? Could He be Terah's God…in spite of everything?

As important, what was he expected to do with this knowledge of the true meaning of the king's new name?

The four men bearing the king's chair often had to step near the edge to avoid laborers, carts, and animals moving up and down the ramp that circled the massive creation. King Nimrod seemed to grow more impatient every time, snorting, sighing, shaking his head. "Why are we moving out of the way of slaves? Does no one here have a voice? Must I myself command these peons to make way for their god? You there! You! Face me!"

The two men in front shifted the poles resting on their shoulders and turned.

"I did not say stop!" the king screamed, addressing the man on the right. "I said to face me!"

The one on the left turned back to the path, causing the other to mince step sideways to both keep moving and yet still face King Nimrod. That caused the entire litter to dip and the king to nearly pitch from his seat. He cursed. "The next time we encounter anyone coming down or passing us on the way up, command them to make way for their king!"

The man, looking petrified, nodded and attempted to bow, which made the king lurch only farther and desperately grab the pole to remain upright. "You're useless! Terah, replace this man!"

With a glance and a nod, Terah assigned another to take the man's place. The original turned ashen and began apologizing.

"Silence!" the king shouted. "Terah, who has a sword?"

Terah peeked back at the others. "Two are armed, my king."

"I want this man's head."

"Oh, surely—"

"Did that sound like something other than a command from your god, Terah? Or must I demand your head too?"

After all he had done for Nimrod and what the king had just said in praise of him…

Terah looked to one of the swordsmen, who appeared stricken. The other drew his blade. "I would be honored to serve my king this way."

Terah flooded with rage. Did Nimrod expect him to have a man executed, right here right now—for such a trivial offense? Despite all the evil Terah himself had committed to save his own son, he could do no more of this. He would not give the command.

"What is your wish, sir?" the swordsman asked him.

"Not my wish," Terah said. "Answer to your king."

"You heard me," Nimrod said. "I want this man's head."

"No!" the chair bearer screeched. "I will do anything you ask, my king!"

Nimrod twisted again and glared at the swordsman, as if to ask why he was not acting. The man advanced on the victim, who skipped out from under the pole, causing the chair to drop and dump the king onto his back in the dirt. "Kill him!" Nimrod shouted.

The guard swung his weapon and opened a gash in the man's shoulder as he tried to dash away. The second blow, to the middle of the man's back, sent him over the side.

"Forgive me for not producing his head, my king."

CHAPTER 5

Mada'in Saleh

Nicole could hardly believe the change in her own psyche once the group photo had been taken and she addressed the team at the site itself for the first time. It was as if she had become an entirely different person. Oh, she had been thrilled to be awarded her dig permit and granted such a unique role. But she was here now, and this was real. The entire endeavor rested on her shoulders.

Somehow she set aside her grief over her mother and her disappointment at the absence—at least for now—of her father. Not only had she overcome the huge odds against her—youth, gender, and inexperience—to get the Saudis to approve her, but she would also have to prove to her own team that she was up to the challenge. And that meant from the get-go.

Her height proved an advantage. No one could refer to her as the "little woman." But she had to work on her volume and tone. Though rarely deferential—especially when she knew she was right—Nicole could be soft-spoken. Well, not now, not here—not during the dig. She held up both hands, and when some on the periphery continued to chat, she hollered, "Listen up! While I want you to become family, when Mama talks, you listen! Put on your big-kid pants, do what you're told, and we'll have some fun. It won't be easy. In fact, there'll be days, maybe even today, when you'll wonder what you've gotten yourself into. But no one forced you to come. So I expect you to see this through."

Nicole glanced at her notes. "Sometime over the next few days you may notice me consulting with a newcomer. His name is Dr. Samir Waleed, a retired Saudi archaeologist we at the Berman Foundation have known for years. He'll serve as my codirector here, and, frankly, his name on the application contributed in a large way to our gaining approval. Dr. Waleed won't be here every day, but when he is, I would ask that you not speak to him unless he approaches you. He's all business, an introvert.

"I've also been informed that we can expect an observer. It's some sort of a political requirement and will be a gentleman named Nasim Qahtani, head of the National Museum in Riyadh. I know nothing more about him but will introduce him when he arrives. His job is to keep an eye on things—whatever that means—on behalf of the Saudis, so I shouldn't have to tell you to be nice to him at all costs. We have nothing to hide, so feel free to show him anything he asks to see, but do refer any questions to me."

Nicole introduced her square supervisors, including Suzie Benchford, a Scandinavian she had worked with on several previous digs. Suzie was a broadfaced blonde with rosy cheeks who had somehow learned to speak English without an accent—and in a plainspoken manner Nicole had come to value. Suzie was anything but needy, but rather independent and a self-starter.

Nicole dug in her backpack for a recent issue of *Biblical Archaeology Review*. "Where you stand right now—this very locus—is known to your colleagues around the world. If you're not reading *BAR*, you should be, and if you haven't read this piece, find it online and read it before you go to bed tonight. And by the way, bedtime should be early. I'm not coming around to tuck you in, but, trust me, you're going to be exhausted after working till about one p.m. today."

She ran through an extensive housekeeping list, including congratulating everyone for remembering their trowels, kneepads, and sunscreen.

She pointed out where all the other equipment lay—handpicks, flashlights, compasses, tape measures, hoe-like tools, buckets—and assigned each person to their respective dig square. "You'll work five of every seven days for the next six weeks, a very few of you in the trailer office, but most in the ground.

"You newcomers see the supply of lime-yellow tennis balls? We cut them as necessary to cover exposed metal spikes, the tent pegs driven into the ground to support the poles for the shades. Those two or three inches of metal aboveground presents serious tripping hazards, so each will be capped with a ball. You'll find yourself grateful for these if one keeps you from gouging an ankle or tripping headfirst into a deep square."

Someone asked what the flashlights and headlamps were for. "We're not working predawn or long after noon…"

"Right," Nicole said. "But once we're down a few feet, you'll see why you need the lights. The canopies protect us from the worst of the sun, but they also create shadows right where we need to see most clearly. And speaking of that, the loose walls of earth and stone that result from digging are called baulks. Some of you have been assigned to place sandbags around the tops of these to prevent erosion and collapse. I can't emphasize enough the importance of this. Do *not* stand on the bags or lean over the squares. That's treacherous. As we get deeper, we'll use sandbags as steps and eventually use ladders."

"I don't see any shovels," someone called out.

"And you won't," she said. "The larger picks—mattocks, we call them—are for breaking ground, then you'll scrape with the small hoes and trowels and scoop the soil into buckets. Use baggies for glass and bone, envelopes for coins."

Nicole pointed out that on every dig day, coffee and Danish would be provided for the entire team—herself included—at the hotel at four a.m. "Be on the bus no later than five so we arrive here before dawn. More coffee and water will be available here, and we'll begin work at first light." Certain volunteers would erect the sunscreens to cover each of the four dig squares and an area where tables would contain assorted special equipment, like Ground Penetrating Radar detectors, a compressor, pneumatic tools, paperwork, charts, records, and even a food preparation area.

"By around nine thirty you'll be more than ready for a more substantial breakfast. We'll provide watermelon, olives, cucumber, flatbread and pita bread, tomatoes, and peanut butter. Eat and drink more than you think you need. Heat stroke and dehydration are common and dangerous, but they're also avoidable—something we aim to preclude at all costs. You need the electrolytes found in the cucumbers, tomatoes, and olives. By midday it'll be well over one hundred degrees Fahrenheit, which is why we quit no later than one. Believe me, you'll be ready to be done by then, as I expect us to excavate tons of material each day.

"Now, you newbies need to know this: Real-life archaeologists spend as little time as possible in the field like this. Digging is expensive, not to mention destructive. The majority of my work following this dig will take place in a lab where I'll analyze data, write reports, and interpret our findings. Digging can be fun and fascinating, but the work can also be slow and exacting. It can take months to examine thousands of tiny, nearly identical artifacts. But that's precisely what you're here to dig up for me."

Nicole paused for effect, then waved everyone closer and spoke more quietly. If they had to strain to hear her, so much the better. "You need to know I'm here for one reason, and it may not be one you'd guess. I'm more than just curious about this area and its history and what we might find. I'm here because my father fascinated me with tales of the Dead Sea Scrolls when I was a child. Now, I know we're a long way from Qumran, where the scrolls were found. But they remain the reason I pursued this profession.

"You may have your own reasons and goals, and while I'm interested in you and your résumé, frankly I care more about my outcome. So let me tell you specifically why we're here: Last time I dug here, I uncovered a rare find that could prove historically pivotal. Without saying more than I'm allowed to, it was a fragment that—provided I can find more of it—could change the face of the Mideast conflict as we know it."

Nicole let that sink in and enjoyed the looks on so many faces. "Now let's get those screens erected so your supervisors can show you exactly where and how to start digging."

A tall, ruggedly handsome Asian with pale eyes, who looked to be in his forties, raised a hand. "What could possibly—?"

"I'm not ready to talk specifics, but—"

"Well, how do we know what we're looking for?"

"I promise I'll get to that. For now let's just say my dream—my goal— is to prove that the centuries-old divide between Muslims and Jews, and ultimately Christians, is based on faulty history."

"Wow," he said, a hint of a smile showing perfect teeth. "No small task. I don't want to be a nuisance, but can you tell us that at least *you* know what you're looking for?"

"Well, of course," Nicole said.

"And at some point you'll tell us? Or aren't you sure you trust us yet?"

He hadn't said this unpleasantly, but he *was* bordering on becoming a nuisance. "I don't want to spend any more time on this right now, sir—"

"Max."

"I'll bring everyone up to speed once we're into the dig, Max." Nicole remembered his name from his application. He came with quite a pedigree, if she was thinking of the right person. Maybe overqualified to be just a volunteer, but she couldn't complain.

CHAPTER 6

Babel

It wasn't as if Terah had not seen violence, especially in the presence of King Nimrod. In fact, Terah himself had initiated enough that he should have been hardened to it. But something rocked him about the capriciousness of this callous murder. The farther they climbed the great tower, the more disgusted he became—with both the king and with himself.

When hoofbeats approached from below, he assumed it was the sculptor of the king's image and prayed the man had thought to bring a fresh rendering of Nimrod looking the way he wished to appear. If he arrived with only more excuses, he might easily face the same fate as the hapless chair bearer. But the donkey that clopped into view bore not the sculptor, but the wife of the slain man. She dismounted and stood before the king, forcing his carriers to halt.

"I demand to know what happened! How does my husband, who served you faithfully—and with pride—for so many years, wind up dead at the base of the tower?"

"So my message reached you, dear woman?" the king said.

"Your message? No! Someone recognized my husband's body! What was your message?"

"I dispatched a courier to get word to you of your loyal husband's unfortunate demise. We were forced to the edge by a load of fresh brick and he lost his footing, poor soul."

"Liar!" the woman screamed. "I saw his body! His shoulder and back had been ripped open!"

"He must have hit rocks on the way d—"

"The sides of the tower are smooth! He was clearly attacked by a swordsman and driven to—"

"Terah!" Nimrod said. "Did this woman call her king a liar?"

"She did."

"Then why do you just stand there? Mete out justice! She must also die!"

Terah found himself willing to perish before he would execute this innocent woman. But before he could call out Nimrod for his blatant lie, the woman keened, "I'll save you the trouble!" and leapt off the tower.

"Now let's move," the king said. "No more delays."

CHAPTER 7

Mada'in Saleh

On a rock outcropping overlooking the dig, with sunshades in place and everyone noisily busy, Nicole barely suppressed a whoop and a holler that would cost her any respect she had built. She loved the cacophony of dig sites, but especially this one—her own. With at least ten volunteers working each of the four squares, it was clear they were having fun getting to know each other, sifting soil for artifacts, laughing, and shouting for more buckets.

Not all was perfect, of course. "Take a lesson!" Suzie Benchford called out from Square One, where she sat fanning one of the volunteers and pouring a bottle of water over his head. "Everybody be careful and hydrate! This sun is no joke!"

Nicole found herself curious about the attractive Asian who had posed the questions earlier. She scanned the site for him before asking Kayla where he might be.

"Oh, believe me, I noticed him too," Kayla said. "He's a volunteer doubling as your IT guy. He's in the trailer."

The temperature inside was not likely even ten degrees cooler, but to Nicole it felt like a freezer. She'd spend as little time there as possible and keep an eye on which volunteers and staffers seemed to look for reasons to get out of the heat. Such breaks could become addictive, but not to the kinds of workers she preferred.

She found the man in question wrestling with a box on his desk in front of a laptop computer. "Opening presents?" she said.

"Sorry?" he said, quickly standing.

"Nothing, sit. Just looks like Christmas morning—"

"Never did Christmas," he said, settling back in. "That was just for the few Christians where I come from."

"And where is that?" She reached for his badge. He flinched and stiffened. "Pardon me," she said. "May I?"

"I could just tell you."

"Fair enough. I apologize."

Nicole silently chastised herself. Few Americans would have found her move an invasion of their personal space, but she reminded herself to think twice before treating everyone the same here.

"Rith Sang from Cambodia," he said.

Nicole cocked her head. "Thought you said Max."

"I did. Please call me Max."

"Why not Rith?" she said.

"Max is just easier for westerners," he said.

She had detected a hint of tonality more common to Asian countries other than Cambodia, where the nationals usually spoke English in more of a monotone. Nicole hadn't memorized everyone's particulars, but some of Max's vitae came back to her. "You're the International U. grad. Phnom Phen. Master's."

"Archaeology, yes," Sang said. "But I'm what you call a double threat, I think."

"Also a techie."

"Exactly."

Nicole couldn't quite get a quick read on Max. His questions outside had not been unreasonable, and he had not seemed contentious. Plus he had exhibited no frustration when she put him off. But neither had he offered his hand when he introduced himself, and she now detected a tinge of defensiveness. Maybe she had caused that with her cultural gaffe. Could she win him over? His résumé had made him a no-brainer selection—especially with his computer savvy.

"May I sit?" she said.

He squinted. "You're the boss, Doctor. You can do what you wish."

She pulled up a chair. "My reputation is in your hands, Max."

"How so?"

"Because of your training, I can bounce things off you that others may not understand. And I rely heavily on the internet for research, documentation, all that."

He nodded and gestured toward the box. "You'll like this, then. Satellite dish I'll put on the roof before the sun makes it impossible to be up there."

"Did the drone arrive?"

"It did. I assumed that was for you."

"Oh, no," Nicole said. "I was hoping to ask Detective Chakrabarti to use it to get a bird's-eye view of the entire site. Amazing what you can learn from that."

"I have experience with drones," Max said. "There's a bit of a learning curve."

"I thought of Pranav only because he's a photographer, but there's plenty for him to do—including keeping an eye on me." She paused, looking at Max. "So…if you're willing?"

"Tell me what you want shot and I'll get to it in a day or two. For now I've got to get this dish assembled and up."

She stood. "I'll leave you to it, then."

"But you wanted something, didn't you, ma'am?"

Being called *ma'am* was as quaint as his having stood for her. "I did! Just wanted to get back to you about what we're looking for here."

CHAPTER 8

Babel

Terah wondered what was happening to him. As King Nimrod's entourage slowly set off again, to him they appeared ashen. Had they ever considered revolting, seeing fellow citizens plunge to their deaths—one at the behest of the king and the other a suicide that should also be credited to his account—now was the time. And Terah would have applauded them, rewarded them! Had they opted to pitch King Nimrod over the side from three-quarters of a mile up, he'd have sworn by every god of the heavens that it had been simply a tragic accident.

Would they do the same for him if he hurled his own eighty-year-old body against the king's transport and sent him flying? How tempting! Yet innocents might be lost in the effort, and Terah was finished with all that. Why? Because in spite of everything he had selfishly perpetrated in the name of justice for his family, the very God he had mocked, flaunted, and turned his back upon continued to speak to his inner being. "Vengeance is Mine" so clearly came to him in that moment that he nearly went to his knees. Terah wanted the Lord to repeat it, to promise He would see to Nimrod's demise.

For the first time in years, Terah felt genuine emotion. He bit his lip to keep from whimpering, silently promising God that as soon as he was back in his own chambers, in private, he would seek Him, beg His forgiveness, strive to be reunited with Him.

"Do not mock the Lord your God."

"I'm not!" Terah cried within. "I won't! You'll see I'm sincere!"

"What I require of you may prove too much to bear."

"I deserve anything you inflict upon me!"

"Begin by standing up to your king."

"How? Give me courage, Lord, strength!"

"My strength is sufficient."

Clopping hooves and the squeak of wheels made Terah turn. The guard who had murdered the other at the king's command hollered, "Beware there! Keep clear of your god and king!"

The entourage bearing Nimrod slowed and edged to the side. "Do not give way!" the king screeched. "Make them go around!"

But a two-wheeled cart driven by a royal soldier and bearing the court sculptor skidded to a stop behind them. The artist leapt out and prostrated himself. "O great Amraphel, my king!"

"'And my god,'" Nimrod urged.

"And my god! Forgive my delay!"

"You're past forgiveness, sir," the king said. "Unless you have an image that pleases me."

"If I may rise and show you…"

Nimrod pressed his lips together and nodded, as if bored beyond words. "Did you notice carnage below?" he asked with a casualness that sickened Terah.

"I did, my king—and god!" the artisan said as he scrambled to retrieve a stack of clay tablets from the cart. "They fell?"

"Tragically," Nimrod said, seeming to idly study his hands. "Everyone involved in this endeavor must take great care to protect himself. You would not want to meet the same fortune, would you?"

"Of course not, my king and god."

"Come, come. Show me."

The man was clearly petrified, and the tablets proved unwieldy. It seemed it was all he could do to keep them from sliding against each other and dropping. He approached Nimrod and raised a knee to help support the bundle, finally moving to the top of his stack an image that looked freshly etched. Terah peeked over the man's shoulder to see a rendering of King Nimrod standing with his legs spread, feet planted firmly, arms outstretched, gazing down as if upon his kingdom. Indeed, if such a structure were manufactured and placed at the top of the tower when both were completed in a few years, it would appear the king had the entire world under his purview.

The question now, naturally, was whether the artist had captured the fearsome expression Nimrod desired. The king reached for the tablet and held it in both hands before his face. His visage looked formidable and terrifying, the way the craftsman must see his king in his nightmares. Why anyone would want to be portrayed in such a manner, Terah could not fathom.

"And the size of this in finished form?" Nimrod said. "Original specifications?"

"So massive it will take years to construct and will have to be transported to the top in sections. And yes, when it's assembled, it will be visible from miles and miles away. Now should you find the expression too severe, my master, know this remains a work in progress and I can—"

"No! No! A thousand times no! I have waited far too long as it is. And you have captured me the very way I want to be seen."

"Oh, thank you! Thank you, my—"

"Now stop blubbering and get it finished. Terah, how long before the tower is complete?"

"We're on pace for three years from now."

"Can my statue be completed by then?"

The artist cocked his head. "I should think it possible. Let me check with my—"

"Oh, I'm sorry," the king said, his sarcasm obvious. "You misunderstand my question. What I'm asking is whether you're willing to risk your life by not having it done in time to coincide with the completion of the tower."

"Yes! Of course! I mean, no! No risk of that, my king. None whatso-ever. It will be done, ahead of schedule!"

The king yawned. "Stay with us. We're going to the current high point. There I will strike the pose of your statue and everyone here will have the privilege of kissing my feet."

"An honor!" the artist said.

Kiss his feet? That Terah could not do, would not do, and God con-firmed it in the depths of his soul. For the next half hour, as he trudged behind Nimrod's chair, he desperately sought the Lord for an escape. "My king," he said finally, "I'm seeing some materials that appear to be misdi-rected, so I must see to them if I may beg your leave. We can't afford to fall behind..."

"Of course," King Nimrod said. "But don't walk. Take the cart."

Terah left the cart at the palace in Shinar and made his way home, in one way relieved but in all other ways downhearted. How long could he escape the king's demands, and when would it become obvious he was no longer loyal?

Despite that it was the middle of the day when he arrived home, he threw himself down onto his sleeping mat, weeping. "Wretched!" he wailed. "Beyond forgiveness! Am I beyond hope, oh God? Redeem me! Forgive me! Set me on the right path!"

"My anger still rages over you," the Lord impressed upon him.

"As it should! If I cannot be restored, take my life and spare me this misery! I can no longer bear it!"

"I will not take your life. But you may choose to take it yourself when I make known to you what I require."

CHAPTER 9

Mada'in Saleh

"Doctor Berman, I didn't mean to badger you into telling me anything you're not prepared to share with everyone."

Nicole studied Max. What a conundrum. She prided herself in her facility with languages and dialects but had to confess that didn't make her as sensitive as it should have to varied ethnicities and cultures. Her father was a natural, able to put at ease anyone in the world within minutes of meeting them. She had already offended Max's sensibilities and now found herself puzzled by his approach to conversation.

Nicole felt much more comfortable interacting with Middle Easterners and Europeans. She found Asians' unfailingly polite directness interesting. Max seemed a dichotomy. He pushed for specifics while insisting he didn't want to be favored.

She could have appreciated the courtesy, but it made her defensive somehow. Nicole felt the need to reestablish her authority. "I tell what I choose to tell to whom I choose to tell it."

"Well, all right then," he said. "What do you Americans say? 'I'm all ears'?"

She smiled. "That's what we say. Your English is remarkable."

He waved her off. "A prerequisite for the ambitious from just about any-where in the world. You're hopelessly behind globally without mastering it."

"And that's you, ambitious?"

"I won't deny it."

"What's your ambition?" she said.

"To get you to stop talking about me and tell me what it is you want to tell me."

Nicole laughed. "Well played. But indulge me. I hope to assemble a very small, tight, inner circle here. I want to be open with the whole team, but with a select few I need to be able to be vulnerable—discuss doubts, fears, challenges, gain honest input. You might qualify."

"Should I be flattered or worried?"

"What would worry you?"

"How quickly you seemed to conclude this about me," Max said.

"You ask good and valid questions, and you seem unintimidated."

"You *do* intimidate me. But my questions were obvious, on everyone's minds, or I wouldn't have raised them."

"But you did, that's the difference. Why didn't a dozen hands go up, people talking over each other, demanding to know what I meant?"

"Human nature," Max said. "You had established your authority, which made them trust you. They didn't want to seem to challenge you, especially right from the beginning."

"That didn't stop you."

"I apologize if I seemed to—"

"No, Max, that's what I'm saying. You pushed, but you were wholly respectful and direct. I like that. Need that."

"So you're inviting me into your inner circle?"

"Maybe. Being on the front end of my internet exposure puts you in a strategic place. But I'm only thinking about this, so you should be too. I won't force you."

"And meanwhile you'll see if you can trust me with a little information?"

"Precisely."

"I hope to prove worthy."

"I won't keep you, because you need to get that dish up. But how much do you know about the Bible?"

"More Old Testament than New, if that's what you're asking. Mostly refer to it for history and geography."

"So if I said that a century or two after the time of Abraham, this very place was called Dedan, either named after Abraham's grandson—"

"—by his son Jokshan, mentioned in Genesis somewhere, right?"

"Okay, Max, this is spooky. You're that familiar with—"

"Just wanted to be prepared."

"So you know what I'm looking for, what I'm after?"

"You haven't kept it a secret. It was in some of the journals. Not much more than what you said to the group, but it seemed plain where you're headed with this."

"So let me ask you this, Max. You think Abraham's grandson Dedan—by Jokshan—was named after the city, perhaps even born here?"

He shrugged. "Never considered that. But even if you could show that Mada'in Saleh is ancient Dedan, somehow linked to Abraham and his grandson, what would that mean to this dig?"

"Think about it. Wouldn't the mere fact that another site here may link with a figure in the Jewish Bible make Muslims uneasy?"

He paused and seemed to study her. "Pretending to speak for Muslims would make me uneasy."

"Humor me, Max. I won't tell anyone."

"Well, I suppose Muslims might worry that archaeology might confirm the Jewish version of the story, so to speak."

"For the same reason the Islamic Authority over the Temple Mount in Jerusalem doesn't permit archaeological investigation there. They insist that no Jewish temple ever stood on that site, and they certainly want no evidence that would prove them wrong."

Max seemed to grow nervous, almost as if he felt he were intruding on Nicole's time. But it was she who had initiated this conversation and was keeping it going. She winked at him. "You have my permission to respond before I let you get back to your dish," she said.

"Well," he said, "knowing you're Christian, I would guess you find their position obstinate and anti-intellectual. What do they have to fear?"

"I am not only Christian, but I'm specifically a Messianic Jew."

"I'm aware."

"You are?"

"Your background is well-documented. Why do you think everybody wanted to join this dig?"

"Surely not because of my faith…"

"Ask around. That had a lot to do with it. With everything else you had going against you, it shows courage."

"Maybe foolhardiness," Nicole said.

"Maybe."

"Is that what attracted you?" she said.

Max hesitated. "I just like a challenge," he said. "And it's clear you do too."

CHAPTER 10

Ur

On his bed, the sun piercing the curtain to illuminate the entire room, Terah sensed the newly familiar nudge inside, as if God were about to impress something upon his heart yet again. He knew it had to do with the idols.

Terah slowly rolled off the mat and trudged to the main room, where four dozen of his intricate carvings stood in neat rows on a table. Even he was impressed by his handiwork, his love for and devotion to these gods evident in his attention to detail. He never discounted his wares, pricing them high for the sojourners who traveled many miles to select from among them.

For so long the idols had distracted him, even after he'd tried to communicate with the God of his forefathers and believed he had somehow succeeded. Still he had refused to abandon these graven images, finding some strange comfort in consulting them, praying to them. But they meant less than nothing to him now. As he settled on a bench where he could see all of them at once, they seemed to mock Terah. Their dead eyes and visages, either smiling or benign, appeared imbecilic to him. Worse, they clearly interrupted whatever faltering communication he had tried to reestablish with God.

Though the Lord had clearly spoken to him on the tower in the presence of the horrid king—whom he had also once worshiped—Terah now felt dead inside. "God, speak to me! Save me from myself! Am I beyond salvation?"

If he expected some relief, some mercy in light of that cry, Terah could only despair. If anything, it became clear God had become angrier with him. Of course He had a right to be, because of all the evil Terah had perpetrated, but was there no remedy, no respite from the Lord's judgment? It seemed not, because Terah grew more and more agonized as he slouched, staring at the idols he had fashioned with his own hands. When he developed an overwhelming urge to vomit, he leapt off the bench and burst outside, doubling over under the portico.

There he wretched so violently that he was driven to his hands and knees. He felt as if his bowels had been ejected through his throat. And in that ghastly state, limbs quivering, tongue burning, his own stench forcing dry heaves, God chose to speak to Terah yet again.

"Along with all the heathen who make images, you are useless. Your precious creations can neither see nor know, or they would be shamed. Who forms a god that profits nothing? All like you should be mortified and fear the Lord your God. You carve an image and fall down to it. You'd be better off to burn it and warm yourself. But, no, you pray to it and say, 'Deliver me, for you are my god!'"

"I repent!" Terah cried. "I repent!"

"A deceived heart has turned you aside. All who worship idols will be disgraced along with you, a mere human who claims you can make a god. Stand in terror and disgrace. Stand, Terah!"

Terah rocked, trying to get his feet under him, but he was paralyzed. "Lord, forgive me, I cannot!"

"You imported sheets of silver and gold from afar to make your idols. And some you dressed in purple cloth as robes."

"Never again, Lord! Never again!"

"You have disgraced my name by revering other gods before me—idols that have no breath or power."

"Tell me what to do, oh true and living God of creation!"

"I should harden your heart so you are unable to turn to me! You have defiled your dwelling with these abominable frauds. As long as they remain, I shall never dwell with you."

"Lord God, do not harden my heart! I will do whatever you command."

"I, the Lord, have spoken."

"Do not depart from me! Have mercy on me! I entreat you not to torment me!"

Feeling returned to Terah's limbs, so he tried again to rise. But all he could manage was to collapse prostrate, sobbing. "Tell me, Lord," he whimpered. "What would you have me do?"

But it was clear God had left him.

Rage rose within. Furious with himself, he labored to sit up, the acrid residue of his own innards assaulting his nostrils. Finally able to stagger to his feet, bracing himself against the wall, Terah felt as if he'd run a long distance, something he hadn't been able to accomplish for years. He slowly moved to the door and peeked in.

What's this? His idols had been scattered. Not one stood in its original spot. It was as if someone had swept most of them off the table, and the ones remaining had toppled and rolled. Several lay in pieces on the floor. Seemingly from everywhere, unseeing eyes met Terah's. Had anything been left in his stomach, he'd have vomited again. He continued to silently plead that God would show him what to do, but the Spirit of the Lord no longer impressed anything upon him.

Yet Terah knew what he had to do. He was eager to utterly destroy these idols, every last splinter of each one. The question was whether it would do any good. Had God hardened his heart so he would still be unable to fully repent? He felt such deep remorse that he feared God had hardened His own heart against hearing his remorse.

How could he know? First things first. Clearly, the Lord would not again visit Terah in the proximity of the idols. Terah painstakingly made his way about one hundred yards beyond the house to his livestock pen. Wedum, the tall, thin servant who had been with him since his teens and was now in his thirties, used a long branch to keep a goat from annoying the cattle.

Every time Terah saw the man, he was reminded of Mutuum, who had served alongside Wedum for many years before the tragedy ten years ago. Though the slightly older and shorter man lived with his wife and three remaining children only a few miles down the road with many other servant families—including Wedum's—Terah had hardly seen him since, catching a glimpse of him from afar in the market but a handful of times. Whenever he asked Wedum about Mutuum, the man fell mostly silent, saying only that his former work partner was still grieving the loss of his infant son after all these years, despite that his wife had borne him two more children.

It had been Mutuum's newborn Terah pretended was his own and whom the king had had slaughtered, believing Terah's offspring was a threat to the throne. Terah had then told Mutuum and his wife that the child had been attacked by wild dogs while in his care and that he himself had suffered serious injuries in a heroic but failed effort to keep them from devouring the baby.

Though no one had reason not to believe the tale, Mutuum could not face Terah again and went to work for another government official.

"You look pale, Master," Wedum said now. "Are you well?"

Still fatigued to his fingertips and toes, he sighed. "I need you to help me gather dry twigs and brush for a fire."

"You have no embers in the house?"

"I'm building the fire here, in the pen."

"I can build it just before dark, sir. You need not trouble your—"

"I have need of it now, Wedum."

"In the middle of the afternoon? Where are the animals to go?"

"They'll keep their distance."

"They certainly will! And think us mad, building a fire under a blazing sun."

Terah started by finding cakes of dried dung that crumbled in his hands.

"Oh, sir! You must not soil yourself with that! I will find kindling."

But Terah thought it fitting that what he planned to burn be fueled by dung. The flint would ignite it as quickly as straw.

"Are you planning to sacrifice one of the animals, Master?"

"Not unless the Lord God tells me to."

"Then may I ask, why a fire?"

"I am repenting of my idol making, Wedum. They all must go."

"I wouldn't dare burn any gods," Wedum said.

"I wouldn't either, if I still believed they were gods."

"You no longer believe? But what about your business? A man passed a couple of hours ago, asking if yours was the home of the idol craftsman. He said he would be back in a day or two to buy some."

"They will be only ashes by then."

CHAPTER 11

Mada'in Saleh

Midway through the second day, Nicole's team finished prepping the excavation areas. Brush and weeds had been cleared, litter picked up, and large surface stones rolled aside. Suzie Benchford and the other three supervisors had measured and staked out their respective squares at the foot of a sandstone cliff that contained the Nabatean artwork and, most crucially, the underlying paleo-Aramaic script Nicole had discovered the last time she'd been there.

By the end of the day, stakes had been driven into the rocky ground and their strings set, the sifting station set up, and the tool sheds stocked, and Max had the trailer fully equipped.

Three days into the dig, Nicole already found herself sleep-deprived, exhausted, and yet ebullient. She believed they were getting closer every day to the find she had dreamed of for years. And her inner circle of confidants had become more than she could have hoped for too. It consisted of Detective Pranav Chakrabarti, Kayla Mays, and Rith Sang, who went by Max. They met every few days before dawn in a private conference room at the King Faisal Hotel, where she bounced off them all manner of issues ranging from how the team was gelling, to what they had found so far, and what they thought of both Samir Waleed and Nasim Qahtani.

The retired Saudi, Dr. Waleed, seemed to have impressed them all with his quiet leadership. The team had honored Nicole's request that they respect his social reserve, and that appeared to have emboldened him to patiently walk them through proper procedures and become all the more productive.

As for Dr. Qahtani, the so-called observer, Kayla's assessment was simple. "Dreamy."

Nicole pretended to dismiss that, but she couldn't deny it. Having expected an older, robed, stuffy cleric from the museum in Riyadh, she had been dazzled by his appearance. Midforties, with a full head of dark hair graying slightly at the temples, he showed up in a late model Jaguar F-TYPE and wore a tailored suit. Nicole had at first blanched at the naïveté of wearing such garb at a blistering, dusty dig site, but he showed enough foresight to also wear rugged construction boots and had gloves sticking out of each pocket of his suit jacket. He also carried the tiniest of umbrellas, not more than two feet in diameter but enough to protect him from the sun.

"You must be the boss lady," he said upon greeting her in only slightly accented English.

He also shocked her by extending his hand. She tentatively shook it, then led him to a small table under a canopy where they could talk in private. He pulled out her rickety folding chair for her and then sat across from her.

"Forgive me, Dr. Qahtani," she said, "but in all my visits here—"

"—you've never shaken a man's hand."

"No, and I was instructed—"

"—in all kinds of Muslim etiquette, of course. You need not worry yourself about any of that with me. In fact, you may call me Nasim if you wish, provided I may call you..."

"Dr. Berman," she said with a wink. "Or Boss Lady is fine."

He roared. "And in all my encounters with American women—including when I studied in the States—I have never been winked at by one."

"Sorry, I'm not usually this—"

"Say no more," he said. "We will get along just fine."

"Then may I assume you're not a practicing—"

"—Sunni? No. In fact, do you know the term *non-madhhabi*?"

"Referring to Islamic studies not limited to a particular sect?"

"Very good, Nicole! More precisely, I'm *ghair-muqallid*, which means I do not necessarily follow a particular tradition but do identify as Sunni Muslim. I'm really closest to what you might call unaffiliated."

"All that to say you shake hands with American women."

"Exactly. Listen, I'd love to meet everyone, but I can't stay long today. I'm driving all the way back to Riyadh today, but I wanted to connect with you and tell you not to fret over my role. Fortunately I have other business in Al-'Ula over the next several weeks, so I'll drop in here as I'm able. I do respect the Muslim weekend, so you won't see me on Fridays or Saturdays. And when I am here, I will stay out of the way as much as possible, though you will see me take copious notes. I have to earn my pay, as you Yanks are so fond of saying."

"May I ask to whom you report?"

"The government, naturally, but more particularly the Department of Antiquities and Museums."

"Of course."

"And I have done my homework," Qahtani said.

"I'm sorry?"

"You should be," he said with a smile. "I know your subversive reasons for being here. You're the evil Iron Lady from America determined to show the entire Muslim world that we have it all wrong and that Abraham and Ishmael were anything but enemies."

Nicole could hardly breathe. How could she possibly succeed if the very observer she'd been assigned knew everything from the get-go? She found her voice breathy, weak. "But personally you don't care…"

"Because I'm unaffiliated, right! And truly, I don't care. But I can't promise my superiors feel the same."

"So you won't tell on me, is that what you're saying?"

"Of course I will!" he said, still grinning. "You think I know what you're up to and they don't?"

"I appreciate your transparency, Doctor, I really do, but—"

"Nasim, please!"

"—Nasim. But then how in the world—?"

"Were you approved in the first place?"

"Yes! And do I have a prayer of—"

"—succeeding? That's entirely up to you. It depends on whether you find what you hope to find. Even rabid, devout Muslims, Sunnis of the highest order, aren't entirely closed-minded. They have brains too. American intellectuals have no monopoly on scholarship. What do you suppose my superiors might do if they are shown the evidence you long to produce?"

"Suppress it. Banish me? Ruin me? Or worse?"

"Make you a victim of Sharia law? Behead you?"

"Don't think I haven't considered that!"

"You'd have been a fool not to. And yet here you are. That impresses everyone. My advice would be to give this your best, your all. Let me put your mind at ease. You're entirely too prominent, too well-known, to fear some audaciously severe treatment by Saudi Arabia. Humiliated? Maybe. Slandered? Of course. Your work torn asunder by more degreed leaders than you could count? Yes. But at worst you will be deported back to your comfortable position at your father's foundation only a little worse for wear."

"Oh, that's all?"

"What did you expect? Professional courtesy?"

"Based on how I've been treated so far."

"Surely you didn't expect that to last, given your aim, your goal."

"I expect opposition, sure."

"And you'll get it. But not from me. I have to say I admired you long before today. Oh, you puzzled me, confounded me, maybe made me wonder about your sanity. But Boss Lady, you're in the Margaret Thatcher category."

"Maggie?" Nicole said. "She's way before either of our times."

"Yet you know as much about her as I do! We're both historians, aren't we, at heart?"

"She's why you referred to me as the Iron Lady?"

"If the shoe fits."

CHAPTER 12

Ur

"You're wanting to burn all your idols, Master?" Wedum said.

"Please help. I am feeling my age today."

"How will you get them all out here?"

"Let me worry about that! I'm going to need a lot of wood."

"But, sir, do I serve you best by gathering more or by taking the cart and fetching the id—"

"For now just do as I ask, please!"

"Of course, Master. But may I ask one more question?"

Terah straightened and glared. "What?!"

"Might I have one or more of them, as you plan to destroy them anyway?"

"Whatever for?"

"I have always admired your work. And I do believe in the gods, even if you no longer do."

"The one and only true and living God requires this of me, so no, none of my idols will be given to anyone. Most of them are in pieces as it is."

"Pieces?"

Terah told him what he had discovered.

"Someone invaded your house while you were outside? How could they?"

. "It could have been only the Lord Himself. And it's not the first time He took vengeance against my idols. He is a jealous God."

Wedum moved outside the pen and soon returned, his arms full of dry twigs and branches. While situating them just so over the crumbled dung, he said, "I hope you will not forsake your artistry in light of this. My children still enjoy the animals you carved for them so many years ago."

"They do? I had forgotten about that. Yes, I should think I could still carve, if that's what you mean. Just no more idols."

Soon the pile of kindling stood nearly as tall as Wedum. "This will make more fire than you need, Master."

"It must blaze long enough to reduce every idol to ash. Get the flint so I can get it started before I fetch them."

Wedum produced the flint, but Terah insisted on starting the inferno himself, painfully squatting, then kneeling to reach the dung under all the kindling. Resting painfully on his elbows, the old man struck the pieces together half a dozen times before one of the sparks dropped into the manure and began to glow. Terah dropped the flint stones behind him and crawled even closer to delicately blow on the fledgling flame. It quickly spread and grew, igniting the waste, finally reaching the smallest twigs.

The fire released the stink from the excrement, and Terah lay on his belly and breathed it in. Somehow a smelly fire seemed just right for the task. *This is what my life has come to. Top aide to the king flat on my face in the dust at the base of a burning pile of manure.*

"Master!" Wedum shrieked. "Get out! Your hair is afire!"

Terah swiped at his head with both hands, feeling the heat, but that left him unable to back away from the growing blaze. Wedum grabbed him by the ankles and dragged him to safety, using the hem of his own garment to smother the flames in Terah's hair.

"Thank you, my friend!" Terah said. "For a moment there I wondered if God required me as the sacrifice."

Wedum did not appear amused but sat shuddering. "We must back away even more," he said. "As I feared, this is going to be too big for your purposes."

"It looks just right to me," Terah said. "Help me up."

With Terah bracing himself against an aging post, Wedum rolled a wood cart to the opening of the pen. "I will harness a goat to pull it—"

"No, I must do this myself. I can pull it both ways."

"Oh, let me, sir! Especially on the way back, loaded with idols."

"You may not understand this, Wedum, but I insist. It will be hard, but it seems it's all part of my penance. I am repenting of creating these worthless objects, and worse, worshiping them, praying to them as if they had ears. Just let me do this."

The animals skittered as far from the fire as possible, crowding the rickety fence. The entire pile blazed now, flames shooting into the sky. "I will try to keep them from stampeding," Wedum said. "You don't need to lose livestock too with all this."

"I would deserve it, but yes, thank you. Do protect them."

Terah had forgotten how heavy even the empty cart could be. Usually Wedum or another servant used it, and almost always with an animal towing it. It had been years since Terah had used it at all. And once he lifted the front tongue from the ground and held it at his waist behind his back, he found he could not make the cart roll.

"At least allow me to push to help you get underway," Wedum said.

"Very well. But then let me go on by myself."

"But how will you get it started for the trip back, once it is full?"

CHAPTER 13

Mada'in Saleh

"Walk with me a moment, if you would," Dr. Nasim Qahtani said, rising and snapping open his tiny umbrella and tipping it toward Nicole.

"Oh, I'm fine," she said. "I'm used to the Saudi sun by now."

"It makes you radiate, if I may say so," he said, making her self-conscious about wearing shorts. "But I'm sure you know to be careful—sunscreen and all…"

"Hat, shades, everything," she said. "I spend most of my time out of direct sunlight."

"But not all your time, obviously," he said, sounding a little too appreciative, but because of his sunglasses she couldn't tell exactly where he was looking.

When they reached his Jaguar, he handed her the umbrella and sat in the car long enough to start it and get the air-conditioning running. "Want to join me so we can finish our chat out of the sun?"

"No thanks," she said, "if I can stay under the umbrella."

"You may," Qahtani said, stepping out again. "In fact, why don't you hang on to that for me? I have another at the other site I'm visiting over the next few weeks."

"If you're sure."

Nicole wondered if he would use the umbrella as an excuse to stand close to her, but he surprised her by keeping his distance. "And feel free to use it as you wish," he said. "Make the rest of the team jealous."

She chuckled. "I'll store it for you in the trailer. Now I should be getting back to—"

"Sure, just let me get a handle on a few logistics so I don't need to bother you next time I'm here."

Bother me? "And when might that be?"

"Monday for sure. Now tell me, may I assume you're a literalist?"

"That depends…"

"Oh, Nicole, I know you're intelligent enough to know when your Christian Bible is historical as opposed to figurative, but—"

"But do I think archaeology can prove Genesis is historically accurate?"

"Exactly. And what do you know about this very location and how important it is to Islam?"

"Well, I know it became prominent to Muslims as early as the eighth century."

"Very good," Qahtani said. "Now tell me, is it not your aim to discover enough here to somehow connect Abraham and his descendants in a way that supports Genesis rather than the Qur'an?"

She hesitated. "Let me say it this way, Doctor: I'm not intentionally pitting the Bible against the Qur'an. But I do plan to follow the archaeological evidence, yes."

"Do you see how that could create a problem, for the Saudis and for you?"

"Of course, and I won't deny that I come with certain hypotheses and, I'll admit, even hopes. But I have zero idea what I will in fact find."

"So you're not jumping to conclusions?"

"What kind of researcher would I be if I did that, Doctor?"

"I'm not going to get you to call me Nasim, am I?"

"Sorry. I'll try to remember, but it doesn't feel right just yet."

"All right, Nicole, listen. I must be off, but I hope I've allayed your fears of my getting in the way of your efforts here."

"You have, actually, and I appreciate—"

"But I need to be entirely up front with you. Let me tell you what I believe the real worry is among my colleagues and, more important, my superiors. Finds here at what you well know is ancient Dedan might appear to confirm the primacy of Isaac and his descendants, as opposed to Ishmael and his descendants. The people I answer to hold firmly to the doctrine that Abraham's true son of blessing and promise was Ishmael, the father of the Arabs."

"And not Isaac," Nicole said, "the father of the Jewish nation."

Dr. Qahtani stepped even more directly into the sun and had to shield even his sunglasses with a hand. He faced Nicole directly. "We've known each other only a few minutes," he said. "And already I admire your mind and what I can judge of your character—among other things."

She felt her face flush and hoped it didn't show. "Well, likewise, but you don't really kn—"

"Lest there be any doubt, Nicole, you need to know that the mere possibility that discoveries here, right in the backyard of the birthplace of our religion, could lend support to the Jewish version of history and would rock the Islamic world. Many Muslims would be willing to do anything to prevent that. Anything."

Nasim, looking every bit as somber as he sounded, slipped back into his car and lowered the window.

"See you Monday," Nicole said with a tentative wave.

"I very much look forward to that," he said.

Nicole kept the umbrella overhead till she reached the trailer where Max looked up from his monitor.

"You all right?" he said.

"Why wouldn't I be?"

He shrugged. "You look a little shaken, that's all."

"Just some stuff I need to bounce off the team."

"You just missed Kayla."

"Oh?"

"She sneaked in here when your guy showed up. You'd have thought she was a schoolgirl, spying on you two through the blinds. Said you seemed pretty familiar with each other, but you'd not met him before, had you?"

Nicole shook her head. "He's easy to talk to."

"And so are you, so you two must have communicated well."

"Better than I expected."

"Want to talk about it?"

"Not really. Well, not yet anyway. But let me ask you something. Would this excavation be worth it, provided I find what I hope to, if it turns this entire region on its head?"

Max sat back and entwined his fingers behind his neck. "You're just considering that now? You made clear to us, the inner circle anyway, exactly why you're here. You think if you succeed, the people in this part of the world are going to be happy about it?"

"But I would never reveal anything without hard, scientific evidence."

Max grinned. "Forgive me, boss, but when has that ever made a difference to anyone? I proved to a friend once that his girlfriend was cheating on him. That won me my first busted lip."

"Seriously? What was your proof?"

"I was an eyewitness."

"Lesson learned?"

"Hardly," Max said. "I was also the culprit."

CHAPTER 14

Ur

The hundred yards back to the portico protecting Terah's entrance from the relentless sun seemed more like a hundred miles. Once the cart began to move, Terah started quickly, only to almost immediately slow and pace himself. "Keep adding to the fire, Wedum!" he called over his shoulder. "I want it at its peak!"

When, finally, he reached the house, Terah labored to turn the cart around on the stone pathway before his door, trying to give himself the best chance of getting underway again once he had loaded it. He was careful to maneuver it in such a way that he wouldn't have to try to nudge it over even a small obstacle.

Inside, Terah started by cleaning up the mess on the floor around the table. More than once he had to take a break and sit, exhausted by bending his bulk at the waist and stretching to reach fragments of idols that had fallen and rolled. After half a dozen gasping trips to the bed of the cart, he had made little progress. But even after another break he hardly felt better. In fact, he grew hungry. Little surprise after having retched seemingly everything inside him. But what would the Lord God of his forefathers think of his taking a respite from this task?

To reach every last scrap on the floor, Terah crawled on his hands and knees and reached far under the table. Part of him didn't mind the grueling effort. It was a price he was more than willing to pay, and he wanted this task finished once and for all. The fragmented idols felt like so much trash to him that not one of them—not even his favorites or the most beautiful—held any appeal or engendered an iota of regret about his plans for them.

Oddly, however, the more he hefted them, arranged them in his arms, and delivered them out to the cart, the further he felt from God. It shouldn't have surprised him, he knew, because the Lord had told him he would never again speak to him in the presence of the idols. He could only imagine how abandoned he'd feel when hauling the whole load back to the livestock pen.

Eventually all that were left remained on the table. Terah wondered how many trips outside he had left in his ancient knees and hips. He grabbed a large leather satchel from the kitchen and began stuffing it with idols and pieces. It was all Terah could do to hoist it over his shoulder and totter to the door. He had to lean against the frame and catch his breath, finally able to wobble to the cart and dump the contents into the bed.

Though God had seemed to forsake him, Terah still got a heavy impression in his heart that the bag itself had been defiled. So he tossed it into the cart as well.

Now, would he be able to tow the load all the way back to the pen?

Not a chance.

First he tried pulling the cart from under the portico the way he had dragged it there. He couldn't budge it. Then he lifted the tongue off the stones, set it in place, and tried pushing from the back. There he got a hint of the full weight of his cargo. He couldn't even make the cart shake. Though it was the last thing he wanted to do, he stepped out into the sun, cupped his hands around his mouth, and bellowed, "Wedum!"

The man came running. But even with both of them pushing and pulling and grunting, the cart barely jiggled. "Let me get a goat," Wedum said. "Or even a cow."

"All I want is to get it started," Terah said. "I still must deliver it. The fire appears at its peak. Will it last?"

"You have plenty of time."

"All right, fetch a goat. If one can help us get rolling, I'll take over."

Wedum looked dubious but jogged back.

The goat appeared to fight the servant all the way, almost as if he knew what lay ahead. Wedum struggled to attach him to the tongue of the cart. Even with the two men pressing their entire weight against the back, the animal's hooves slipped on the stones as Wedum hollered at it to go. Finally the cart began to roll and Terah breathlessly said, "Loose him! I'll take over!"

"You'll never be able to make it, Master!"

"Let me try!"

But Wedum had been right. In the end it took the three of them to muscle the cart all the way to the fire. When they arrived, Wedum freed the goat to scamper back to the others while Terah clung to the side of the cart, chest heaving.

"Let me empty it," Wedum said. "I'll be sure everything gets into the fire."

"No! You don't understand! I must do this myself."

It took Terah longer to unload the bed than it had taken him to fill it, and he had to stop every few minutes to catch his breath. He was grateful Wedum at least gave up trying to help. Trouble was, Terah could get within only several feet of the conflagration and had to throw the idols and pieces of idols with all his might. For fragments that didn't make it, he had to shield his face with his tunic and scurry in, toss them, and quickly escape. Shortness of breath was one thing, but now he felt tightness in his chest, then real pain.

Still, every time Wedum approached, Terah waved him off. "If you insist on helping, just throw more wood on the fire!"

"That's what your idols are, Master! You have all the fire and heat you need!"

When he had finally finished, Terah bent and planted his palms on his knees and breathed deeply for several minutes. The pain in his chest eventually dissipated, but the tightness remained much longer. When he could finally straighten, he felt dizzy and sat with his back to one of the wheels on the cart. From there he watched his handiwork burn and burn. *If you were really gods, you would save yourselves.*

Wedum stood by the far side of the pen, just outside the fence, and appeared to stare at his master. "I can tell this is making you happy," he said.

"More than you can imagine," Terah said, feeling he had taken the first step on a long journey.

When the last idol was ash, God impressed deeply on Terah's heart, "You have only just begun."

"What more can I do, Lord?" Terah whispered.

Wedum must have thought him mad, talking to himself, and busied himself with the animals. And when he was able to get closer to the fading fire, he slipped in and swept embers and unburnt twigs atop the pile. By late afternoon the fire belched white smoke rather than black, and Terah pleaded with God again to tell him what he should do.

"The goat has been defiled. Sacrifice it to Me."

"Wedum, do you have a blade?"

"Of course."

"Purify it in the fire and make the blaze big again, enough for a sacrifice."

Wedum looked puzzled and appeared to wait for an explanation.

"The goat!" Terah said. "When the fire is ready again, bring me the blade and the goat."

"It's a male," Wedum said.

"It's all right. This will not be a typical sacrifice. It has been defiled."

Wedum looked shocked. "By pulling the wagon?"

"Yes! Hurry! I must obey the Lord!"

"Your god is telling you to do this?"

Terah glared at the man. It was unlike him to question his master. Wedum looked miserable as he knelt to first hold the blade of his knife over embers. He waved it cool and tossed it to Terah. And he mumbled as he added to the fire yet again.

"What are you going on about?" Terah demanded.

"Have I too been defiled? I pushed the cart. What if your god tells you to sacrifice me too?"

"Nonsense!"

"But what if he does? You apparently never question him!"

"You are correct! But God loves mankind."

"Even if we have been defiled?"

"Just do as you're told! You are not in danger."

CHAPTER 15

Al-'Ula, Saudi Arabia

That night at the King Faisal Hotel, Nicole hoped for an early bedtime. She finished entering copious notes into her laptop, ordered room service, and was dressed for bed when her room phone rang.

"Hey, this is Max. Sorry to bother you."

"No bother. What's up?"

"I was hoping to see you at dinner. Wanted to follow up on your comment about wanting to bounce things off the inner circle after your meeting with Dreamy."

She told him she was done for the day. "Sometimes I just need a break from being on for everyone. Know what I mean?"

"Sure. Sorry."

"And please don't call Dr. Qahtani that, Max. And I'll mention that to Kayla too. You both know how important it is to maintain a sense of decorum and seriousness around him. As open and friendly as he's trying to be, he's also a truth-teller, and frankly he has me rattled."

"How so?"

"Let's just say he clarified the potential consequences here."

"Surely that was no surprise, Chief. Nobody with a brain like yours would dream of digging in the Muslims' backyard without knowing—"

"That's exactly what he called it—the backyard of the birth of their religion."

"—so what's new?"

"Guess I expected him to be a little more circumspect. More diplomatic."

"He tried to bully you?"

"No! That's just it. It was as if he were commiserating with me, trying to protect me."

Max snorted. "You know better than that. Pretending to be on your side?"

"Basically, he's unaffiliated."

"Is that right?" Max sounded genuinely surprised. "His bosses know that? How can you work for the government here without buying into—"

"He identifies as Sunni, but in name only. Of course, he was born and raised here, so he knows how to act and what to say. It wouldn't surprise me if his superiors don't know."

"Or he's just playing you."

"To what end?"

"Hoping to make you overconfident? Hoping you'll get sloppy? Maybe trying to get you to reveal more to him than you might otherwise? Listen, any chance we could chat this through face-to-face?"

"Tonight?"

"Yes."

"No. I'm ready for bed, Max. And I don't want to appear to divide the inner circle. Show favoritism."

That elicited silence too long for Nicole's comfort. He seemed to affect a humorous tone, just this side of genuine. "But you do favor me, don't you, Nic— Dr. Berman?"

"Good night, Rith."

"Oh, come on, I haven't crossed a line, have I? You're not even going to call me Max anymore?"

"Max, hear me. I'm just maintaining boundaries. You know I talk to you in more depth about a lot of things because of your training. And, yes, I'm fond of you. But I've known Kayla and Pranav longer than I've known you, and I'm trying to build trust among us all."

"I know, Nicole. Just wondering if I'm supposed to be offended yet."

"You're not! I'll text the circle and we'll meet for breakfast as usual. You'll get all your questions answered then."

"And stop calling you after-hours…"

"I'm always glad to hear from you, Max."

For the first time since the dig officially began, Nicole found herself unable to immediately drop off to sleep. After a grueling morning in the sun, she had tried to relax at the pool. But she found that impossible with everyone else on the team trying to do the same but finding reasons to chat. By dinnertime several days in, she was usually fighting to keep her eyes open and wound up sleeping soundly. Now she lay on her back in the darkness, eyes wide open. And speaking of first times, it seemed like two decades ago that her mind raced with thoughts of a man. After a disappointment in love, she had resolved to become the best scholar she could be—and she succeeded. She had barely dated for years and didn't allow herself to stress over it. Her brain seemed to have enough bandwidth to earn two doctorates, more than enough to occupy her time.

Yet here she lay, six thousand miles from home, near the spot of a potentially life-changing professional achievement, and all she could think about were two men in their midforties. Ironic that Kayla had nicknamed one Dreamy. He was, of course, but how could she dream about him if she was unable to sleep? Anyway, dreaming about Nasim Qahtani was the last thing she wanted to do. Dashing though he might be, and as Islam-neutral as she could hope for—at least for someone in a position so strategic to her endeavor—she could never, ever, allow him near her radar of personal interest.

First, naturally, she refused to believe or trust his attempt to set her mind at ease about his intentions. Someone seemingly well connected in Saudi Arabia had been behind the attempt on her own mother's life in Manhattan—which eventually succeeded. And if, as he said, extremists might do anything to thwart Nicole's efforts here, how could she be sure that did not include Nasim himself?

Part of her wanted to believe him wholeheartedly, but that was naïve. What were the odds he could really become an ally and protect her from detractors? What a gift—which could come from only God Himself—if she could come to trust Nasim, become his friend? And who knew? She had been raised by a Messianic Jew and his Gentile wife who had never wavered from their evangelistic bent. Her parents had never been shy about sharing their faith with anyone.

Diplomatic, sure they were. Both developed international sensibilities and decorum that endeared them to people of all ethnicities and faiths. But still her parents had always found ways to inject spirituality and their own faith journeys into cordial conversations. They were rarely successful at proselytizing, but it didn't stop them from trying. And even those who might have been offended, or should have been, usually came to admire both Ben and Ginny for their forthrightness.

Nicole had long felt inadequate as a witness. She chose her spots and didn't shy away from her views, but she couldn't claim to be as winsome a defender of her faith as her parents. And all that pondering made her only imagine the possibility of actually persuading Nasim to consider the claims of the one true and living God—and His Son—on his life.

Nicole turned over and threw off all but her sheet, finding the air-conditioning less than effective. *What a joke. Do I really want to win Nasim for Jesus, or for me?*

Worse, she couldn't push Max from her mind either. Was it possible she favored him for more than just his training and background? He appeared no closer to being sympathetic to Christianity than Nasim did, but, unlike Nasim, Max even fell short of being unaffiliated with some sect. She was impressed with the way his mind worked—and not just from a scholarly standpoint. He was way more than book smart. His ability to reason philosophically reminded her of her dad.

How was it possible that Max—Rith Sang—was still single?

And why did she care?

Nicole forced herself to think about the next day. The team—supervisors and volunteers—seemed to be becoming family. Codirector Samir Waleed had them humming along harmoniously, as far as Nicole could tell, allowing her to concentrate on the bigger picture. She frequently checked in on all four excavation squares and was most encouraged by what the team was finding, especially in Suzie Benchford's northwest quadrant. Nicole had used her trowel and brush in all four holes, but she would concentrate on Square One until she closed in on what she was hoping for.

She would share this with the inner circle over breakfast and debrief them all on her encounter with Dr. Qahtani. She had to wonder if Max was at all jealous of him. But why would he be? Max had not exhibited other than professional interest in Nicole, though clearly Nasim had bordered on the inappropriate more than once.

Nicole chastised herself for letting these men invade her mind to where she couldn't even drift off, despite an early morning staring her in the face. Until she did.

CHAPTER 16

Ur

Terah stood by the cart and with his thumb gingerly tested the blade Wedum always kept sharp. It would make quick work of the goat, assuming Wedum could get him to Terah. But when he approached it, the animal skittered away, bleating and causing the rest of the livestock to cluster at the far end of the pen. Wedum wended his way through cows, sheep, and other goats to corner it, then grabbed it by both short horns, pulling it past the fire and out to Terah. It took all his weight and strength to drag it close.

Terah reached for the goat, planning to wrap one arm around its head and slit its throat with the other.

"You will not be able to hold him, Master! He's heavier than I am."

"I need to do the killing anyway," Terah said. "Steady him."

The goat clearly seemed more terrified of the cart than the knife and fought to escape. Wedum deftly pivoted around the animal's head and straddled it, settling onto its back with his feet firmly planted on the ground while still holding firmly to the horns.

"Tilt his head back," Terah said, and as soon as he did, Terah deftly slashed the throat and stepped out of the way of the gushing blood. The goat's last bleat was stifled and it staggered beneath Wedum before flopping and bleeding out.

Terah tried dragging it into the pen but got only a few feet from where it had fallen. "I know you want to do this yourself," Wedum said, "but—"

"Yes, I need your help."

Terah pulled the carcass by its head while Wedum lifted the other end. They muscled it to the fire and swung it atop the flames. "I hope that satisfies your god," Wedum said, backing away and sitting by the fence.

Terah sat next to him, as exhausted as he had ever been. "I hope so too."

But almost immediately, God spoke silently to his heart.

"My anger burned violently toward you because of your idols. But that pales in comparison to my rage over the stench of your deeper sins."

"Deeper than praying to false gods?" Terah said aloud.

Wedum quickly rose and moved away.

"Yes!" the Lord continued. "Deceit! Your lying tongue nauseates me—and the murders you used those lies to hide."

"I murdered no one!"

"The blood of the baby remains on your hands! I also hold the blood of Ikuppi to your account! You have much to rectify."

"But, Lord, if I am guilty of murder, what can I do to rectify it?"

"Start with Wedum."

"Wedum? I have been nothing but good and generous with him since I've known him!"

"If you don't make things right with him, I will turn my back on you."

God fell silent and Wedum looked petrified. "What does your god want with me? You promised I was in no dang—"

"You're not! He wants me to make things right with you, so let me seek Him on this and—"

"You have nothing to make right with me, Master, please! I want no part of—"

"Silence! I need to listen to the Lord!"

"I want to go home, to be with my wife and chil—"

"Go! You can work longer tomorrow. And I will talk to you then."

"You'll be all right here? You don't need me for anything else?"

"Go!"

"Speak to me, Lord. Show me how I have violated Wedum and I will do or say whatever you require."

Silence.

Terah sat miserably in the dust, the fire dying but still making him pour sweat. The animals seemed to eye him warily from the far end of the pen. A trail of the goat's blood led from the edge of the fire back to the wheel of the cart where Terah had slain it. *So this is what I've come to,* he thought. *Second in command in the kingdom, sitting in filth trying to appease my God. My God. Yes, that's what I want Him to be.*

"But will you have me, Lord, or have I run beyond the reaches of your love, your mercy, your forgiveness? Have I done too much, sinned too greatly for too long…?"

"You cannot escape Me," God said.

"I don't want to escape! I want to return to you!"

"You have not loved or served me since you were a young man."

"I know, and I repent! I throw myself before you!"

"You have much to answer for."

"Show me what I can do! Try me! Purge me of my sin! I don't deserve—"

"No, you do not deserve My long-suffering. You do not even see your offense against your servant."

"How can I convince you I want you to show me? I will do anyth—"

"Does he know you have deceived him?"

"Deceived him about—?"

"Does he believe your lies about Mutuum's baby? About your own son? Your wife? Your friend Ikuppi?"

Terah hung his head and wept.

CHAPTER 17

The King Faisal Hotel, Al-'Ula

To reach the private breakfast room by four a.m., Nicole left her room at 3:55, her backpack stuffed as usual. At that time of day, if she ran into anyone on the elevator, it would likely be one of the other three in her inner circle. But today she found Pranav Chakrabarti leaning against the wall across from her door.

The detective had proven most delightful to work with, businesslike and anything but intrusive, yet always seemingly cheerful. Customarily he first connected with her at breakfast and drove her and Max and Kayla to the site about ten minutes ahead of the bus carrying the rest of the dig team. For the rest of the day, he usually hung back but never let her out of his sight. He had agreed with her that he need not shadow her at the hotel, though an app on his phone monitored where she was at all times.

"'Morning, Pranav," she said. "Problem?"

"Not yet."

"Uh-oh."

As they headed for the elevator, he said, "I just wanted to alert you that I may have to violate your no-phone rule during breakfast."

"Oh?"

"Both your father and Detective Wojciechowski have been in touch with me and may have more information for me soon."

George Wojciechowski was head of the New York Police Department's

Senior Services and Domestic Violence Unit and had handled the investigation into the attempted murder of Nicole's mother. But that case had been closed since the perpetrator had apparently committed suicide.

"They've been in touch with you this morning?"

"Yes, ma'am."

"What time is it in New York?"

Pranav glanced at his watch. "Coming up on nine p.m."

Nicole's mind raced. "About what? Surely there's not more foul play suspected in my mother's death…"

"You know I would never keep anything of significance from you, Doctor, but I really must wait until I have more information."

"Don't go all formal on me now, Pranav, please. You mentioned my father. Does whatever's going on mean his coming will be delayed even more?"

"Possibly, and as soon as I know more, I'll tell you."

"Pranav—"

"Please, D— Nicole, trust me to do what I feel is best for everyone. I'm merely informing you that should I appear busy with my phone or even have to step away to take a call, it's only because this could be important."

"But is everyone all right back home?"

"No one is in imminent danger."

She studied him. "You're not putting my mind at ease."

"I'm not trying to, ma'am. As for here, I will protect you with my life."

"Well, I certainly hope it doesn't come to that."

"So do I."

Max and Kayla sat waiting in the small breakfast conference room, and Max stood—as he always did—when Nicole, or any woman, entered. It impressed but also embarrassed her and she didn't know how or if to respond. Neither did she know if this was Max's idea or if he was following Pranav's lead. Today, of course, the detective entered with her, but previously he had done the same. This morning Max seemed to avoid eye contact with her and said nothing. That was unlike him, and she worried she had offended him on the phone the night before.

"Lots to talk about," she said, as she urged Kayla to go first at the buffet where they each filled their plates and returned to sit. Nicole bowed her head briefly and prayed silently, as did Pranav.

Kayla raised her hand. "May I ask a completely off-the-wall question?"

"Of course," Nicole said, "but you know you never need to raise your hand. And we are a little pressed for time this morning."

"I know, but I'm just curious what you and Detective Chakrabarti are saying when you, you know, bless the food or whatever it is you're doing. My family always prayed out loud, but…"

"Well, I'll let Pranav speak for himself, but as you know, I'm what's called a Messianic Jew, so usually I say a Jewish prayer."

"Interesting!" Kayla said. "Like what?"

Nicole shrugged. "Today I said, 'Blessed are You, Lord our God, king of the universe, who brings forth bread from the earth.'"

"Beautiful. And you, sir? A Hindu prayer?"

"Oh, no, dear," Pranav said. "I thought you knew I was a Christian. My prayer is always different, but I usually thank God for life, for my family, for the day, for my salvation, and for the food."

"Nice," Kayla said. "We were Christian too, but we didn't go to church or anything. My mom usually did the praying."

"You say you *were* Christian?" Pranav said.

"Yeah, I'm not really anything now. Whatever somebody believes is good with me."

"Maybe we'll get a chance to talk about that some time," Pranav said with a smile.

"Oh, believe me, I know where you're coming from, and I've heard it all before—many times."

Pranav's phone vibrated and he stood quickly with an apologetic look. Nicole nodded and he hurried into the hall.

"Detective Chakrabarti cleared that with me already," Nicole said. "I needed to make an exception today."

"Why?" Max said. "Something up?"

"Nothing to speak of—yet." Nicole was relieved to hear anything out of Max.

"So," Kayla said between bites, "your text said we were going to talk about Dreamy…"

"My note said 'Dr. Qahtani,' Kayla, and I know you're just kidding amongst us, but I'm going to ask you to refer to him by his title and real name even in private."

"Really?"

"You're fully aware of the customs here, and you also know how pivotal Dr. Qahtani is to our mission."

Nicole was struck by how dramatic Kayla looked even when pouting. She had pasted on a mock scowl and let her shoulders droop. "Okay, Mom."

"Thanks. I did have an interesting meeting with him, on which I'd like to debrief you all, but let's wait for Pranav. But then I'm going to have to hurry."

Nicole kept watching the clock, determined to still leave the hotel ahead of the bus. But when Detective Chakrabarti returned he looked grave. Naturally she was dying to know what was going on in New York, but she had to get to the subject at hand. "All right, so my meeting with—"

"Terribly sorry," Pranav said, sitting quickly and scribbling on a notepad as he spoke, "but I must—"

"You may keep doing what you're doing," Nicole said, "but I need to—"

"No, you don't," he said, still writing.

That was so unlike him that Nicole was stunned nearly to silence. "I'm sorry?"

"I deeply apologize, ma'am, but you really must see this first."

CHAPTER 18

Ur

"I *have* deceived Wedum for all these years! What must I do to make things right with him?"

Silence.

"Lord, please! I cast myself at Your feet! What can I do?"

Silence.

"I am in misery, oh God! I miss my wife, my son…"

Silence.

Terah rolled to his side in the filth of the livestock pen as the fire continued to burn itself out. He buried his face in his arms, wailing. "I miss You too, Lord! Have mercy on me!"

Silence.

Terah lay sobbing for what seemed like hours, finally persuaded God had abandoned him for good. He deserved it, he knew. His evils loomed ever over him and sickened him. But why then had the Lord told him to destroy the idols and sacrifice the defiled goat? Terah knew that had been just the beginning of his penance, but he was willing to endure it all— whatever it was.

"God, I am at the end of myself! Starved as I feel, I will never eat another morsel if You have left me. Come what may, I will lie here until I starve to death. I rest only in Your promise that my son shall become an exalted father."

Silence.

So this was how it was going to be. Terah's final wish was that he would go quickly and that Wedum would discover the next morning merely his wasted body—like that of the goat. But a man couldn't actually starve to death overnight, could he? Terah didn't mind the misery. He didn't merit or expect anything else, though he dreaded the setting of the sun and that he might shiver till it rose again.

The knife! That was the answer! He hadn't given it back to Wedum, had he? What had he done with it once he had used it on the goat? Left it in the wagon? On the ground? He felt the pocket of his tunic. Yes! He had idly slipped it there. He could cut his own throat and put an end to his wretchedness in minutes.

Terah sat up and steadied himself, letting a bout of dizziness clear. And now he had an even better idea. He would gather more kindling and stoke the glowing embers until the fire roared again. When he believed it was sufficient, he would stand on a rock as close to it as he could bear, leaning as far as he could manage, pull the blade as deep across his neck as possible, ensuring he would tumble into the flames. He would sacrifice himself! If that didn't convince the one true God of his remorse, nothing would.

Weak, spent, aching all over, Terah felt strangely energized by the task he had assigned himself. Had he gone mad? Of course he had. God had talked to him. He had talked to God. Of that he had no doubt. But now the Lord had made clear the conversation was over. Belessunu had made plain that she and the boy would not take him back unless he returned to the God of his forefathers. But now that was up to the Lord himself. Terah was more than willing, but clearly God would not have him. And so he foresaw nothing else to live for.

He somehow mustered the energy to fill his arms with kindling three different times and add it to the fire. It roared and crackled anew, and Terah found it harder and harder to get close to the blaze. But he forced himself, giddy at the prospect of the freedom from a decade of agony. Nothing could be worse than being at enmity with the almighty God.

The flames leapt to the sky again and Terah felt blisters rise on his cheekbones. He found just the right rock to place before the fire. He would stand on its edge so he could fall only forward when the deed was done. He pulled the knife from his pocket and held it to the far side of his neck. He teetered and had to step down twice before regaining his balance. Sparks and ash landed in his hair and beard, and he welcomed the pain.

Just as he was about to dig and draw the blade across, the sky turned black and a gust of wind and snow blinded him, swept him off the rock to the ground, knocked the knife from his fist, and blew out the fire, as well as the flames in his hair and face. Terah lay unmoving, certain he had been thrust into an afterlife where he would be eternally tormented by frigid squalls. He opened his eyes just in time to see the giant flakes melt and hear them hiss as the smoke dissipated into the heavens.

And finally the Lord spoke again. "Do not lay a hand on yourself, for now I know that you fear Me and are willing to die for your sins."

Terah leapt to his feet, free of pain or weakness. His sweat had dried and he felt clean. Even his raiment, now spotless, seemed to shine. He breathed in the pure, cool air and felt refreshed as the sun reappeared in a cloudless sky. "Lord, what have you done?"

"You know."

Not only did Terah know, but it was also as if God overwhelmed him with insight, knowledge. After all his pleading to be shown what he could do in response to his depravity, he now knew. He was to start with Wedum, as the Lord had instructed. He felt compelled to seek him out this very day, wholly confess his deceit, and intreat Wedum's forgiveness. But also, as he had been warned, that was only the beginning.

Terah somehow knew that before he even dreamed of satisfying his ravenous hunger or retiring for the night, he had more accounts to settle. There was the wife of his friend and confidant, Ikuppi, who must be told of Terah's role in the man's suicide. Yadidatum, the midwife he had forced to collude with him in deceiving both the king and the parents of the slain child.

This all had to be done at once, including his confession to Mutuum and his wife. Would they, could they, ever forgive him? That was no matter. Truth was all that mattered now.

The question was what might become of this truth? Terah would confess to Wedum, Ikuppi's wife and children, Yadidatum and perhaps her son, and Mutuum and his wife. This would all take place in the servant settlement a few miles away, but the news of it would soon sweep the entire compound. How long before it reached the palace in Shinar, the court, the king? Terah could not even imagine Nimrod's fury. He would learn he had been lied to, tricked by his most trusted aide into slaughtering the wrong newborn a decade before.

Worse, he would realize that the threat to his throne remained in the form of a ten-year-old he had never seen. That meant a death sentence for Terah and Abram. Except that God had promised the boy would be an exalted father. Terah could still not fathom what that meant, but he now knew his God was powerful enough to protect his son and fulfill that promise.

As for his own life, he no longer cared. Once he had fulfilled all the requirements of trying to rectify his dastardly past, he would have to evade King Nimrod. And what better way to do that but to set out after his wife and son? He couldn't wait to reunite with them.

CHAPTER 19

The King Faisal Hotel, Al-'Ula

Detective Pranav Chakrabarti folded a note and pushed it across the breakfast table to Nicole.

Cannot talk here. Mention no names. Same at dig trailer.

She looked up sharply at him while trying to hide her alarm from the others. "Let's, ah, let's not try to cover anything in the short time before we have to leave. We'll get back to this later."

"Oh, man!" Kayla whined. "Thought you were gonna tell us about Doctor—"

"And I will," Nicole said. "But I want to be at the site when the rest arrive, so bear with me."

"What's going on?" Max said.

"Just a little behind schedule," she said. "We'll be fine if we leave on time."

Detective Chakrabarti ignored his food and continued to write. As he folded another note, he said, "Might not be quite as hot today as yesterday. Not supposed to reach a hundred and ten."

"Oh, wow," Max said. "Sounds like a cold front."

Pranav slid the note to Nicole.

I need to sweep the Rover for bugs or a tracking device, or we can't talk during the ride either.

Nicole nodded again, and he left.

"All right," Max said, "what's happening, and why all the sec—"

Nicole held a finger to her mouth and said, "It'll be nice to turn the AC down a tick in the trailer today, huh?"

Max cocked his head but at least appeared to know to be quiet.

Kayla mouthed, "Do I need to be scared?"

"I'm excited about today," Nicole said. "Square One should reach a new strata."

Max and Kayla seemed to freeze, clearly catching Nicole's drift.

"Eat up," Nicole said cheerfully. "Don't wanna run out of gas midmorning."

On the way out of the hotel, Kayla said, "All right, what is this?"

"Outside," Nicole mouthed.

"You're scaring me," Kayla whispered.

As soon as they reached the parking lot in the predawn darkness, Nicole stopped and brought the other two up to speed on Pranav's notes.

"He thinks the place is bugged?" Max said. "Guess we should have thought of that. But what does that say about the hotel phones? I don't even want to think about what we may have talked about."

"What about our rooms?" Kayla said. "And where's Pranav now?"

"Making sure the car is clear. We may have to talk out in the open from now on."

When they reached the Land Rover, Pranav helped load their backpacks into the rear. "So?" Nicole whispered as he slammed the hatch.

"Nothing so far," he said, "but let's not risk anything till I can do a thorough search."

They rode to the site chatting about nothing. Nicole worried they sounded like amateurs inventing innocuous small talk and would sound suspicious to anyone monitoring them.

Kayla whispered in Nicole's ear, "How'm I supposed to respond to the guard?"

"Same as always."

Almost every day the UN guard perfunctorily checked their badges, then he would always say something flirtatious to Kayla. Either he was trying to win her over after offending her the first day or this was his modus operandi.

Kayla invariably responded with something snarky but had always seemed careful not to cross a line. Nicole worried that if she reacted differently today, especially if the car was bugged, whoever was listening would notice.

Today the guard began by kibbitzing with Pranav, greeting him boisterously. "Shoot any terrorists lately, Detective?"

"Not this week," Pranav said, a little too loudly but smiling. "But I'll be ready when the time comes."

"Ha! I'll bet you will!"

He lowered his head to look into the back seat, where Nicole and Kayla always sat. Kayla appeared to meet his eyes and look away, expressionless. "Our young friend not quite awake yet?" the guard said.

She turned back. "Not your friend," she said brightly. "But I'll tell your wife I ran into you."

The guard roared. "You can't tell my wife anything! Even I can't!"

"Very funny."

"No, I wouldn't say that," he said, still laughing. "See you when you leave when I can get a better look at you in the daylight."

"Oh, good, then you'll be able to see me sticking my tongue out at you."

The guard slapped the door. "Good to go, Chakrabarti! You all have a profitable day!"

"That might have been a bit much," Nicole whispered.

"Sorry! I don't know what to do."

Pranav parked near the trailer and said he needed to get in and sweep it.

"I should go in with you," Max said. "If we're being watched, it'll look strange if I don't."

As the men entered, Nicole and Kayla strolled several feet from the Land Rover. "I'm not good at this cloak-and-dagger stuff," Kayla said.

"You'll be fine."

The sky was still black when Pranav emerged from the trailer and joined them. "Just like with the car, I found nothing yet. But I wouldn't take any chances talking in there. I mean, don't all of a sudden stop talking at all about Dr. Qahtani, but don't be judging him or saying anything about your finds here that you're not ready to share with the government."

"Got it."

"Mr. Sang is really curious, but I convinced him that if the four of us were seen huddling here, that wouldn't look right either."

"Good," Nicole said. "I'll find a place and time to update him. But first you and I have to talk. Where can we do that?"

"I'll let you know."

"Ooh, can I come?" Kayla said.

"No," they said in unison, and she laughed.

"I'll be in the trailer," Kayla said.

CHAPTER 20

Ur

The late afternoon sun no longer bore the sting it had earlier, and Terah was struck with the difference in how his property looked. Whatever God had done to him—and of course it felt personal—had affected the entire area. The moisture from the melting "snow" flakes, now drying in the sun, made even the cart look new, pristine. From where he had slain the goat, the trail of blood to the fire was gone, somehow swept away or covered by the briefest of sandstorms.

Even the livestock pen looked tidy, the animals appearing to have been unaffected by the squall. Their coats and even hooves had been washed clean, and now they separated from each other, except for the young nestling against their mothers. Even the usual expansive dung piles had been obliterated. Fresh, clean animals, no longer skittish or wide-eyed, idly roamed from the far end of the pen and milled about.

Most bizarre to Terah, not an iota of residue remained from the fire. It was as if all of his and Wedum's labor in building it, starting it, reigniting it not once but twice, had never occurred. Terah felt an urge to get going, so he opened the gate. Normally some of the animals—usually a bull or a couple of cows—would follow and try to slip out with him. Now they didn't seem to even notice. He secured the gate and started for the house, which—for the first time in years—didn't seem such a laborious journey.

He felt twenty years younger and covered the hundred yards in under a minute.

That was enough time, however, for Terah to realize that after his obligations were met that evening, he dared not return to his home. As soon as the news of his confession spread, King Nimrod would send troops to seize and likely kill him—or torture him until he revealed the whereabouts of his son.

He decided to fill a pack with foodstuffs and load it into his chariot. But almost immediately his conscience stabbed. Neither the chariot nor the steed were really his. They belonged to the king and came with Terah's role. What was he to do? He certainly would need the food, no matter what. Yet as he began to fill a sack, God spoke to his heart. "Walk empty-handed."

Walk? Terah thought. *And take nothing? But how will I—?*

"Behold, I, the Lord your God, come with a strong hand, and I will feed you like a shepherd feeds his flock."

"But how—?"

"I who sit high above the earth and stretch out the heavens like a curtain, can bring rulers to nothing."

"You will keep King Nimrod from—"

"I am the everlasting God, Creator of the ends of the earth. I neither faint nor grow weary. I grant power to the weak."

"I know, Lord! You already have!"

"You shall run and not be weary, walk and not faint."

Terah hated himself for it, but still he hesitated. How could he be so weak of faith when he had no doubt the one true God of the heavens had spoken to him? *I am to walk all the way to the servants, and then, what, try to overtake Belessunu and Abram on foot? They are so far ahead by now.*

Silence.

Terah could not imagine anything but fully trusting God and obeying. If his cowardice in any way caused the Lord to withdraw, that would only devastate him. He hurried out the door empty-handed before he had time to reconsider. There sat his chariot with the horse tethered nearby. What would become of the animal? *Should I refill the feed and water buckets?* No, he decided. The God who had told him to walk alone would take care of the animal too.

The sky grew pale as the sun dipped low on the horizon, and Terah found the walk invigorating, despite dreading what he had to do. He ran over in his mind a thousand times the various responses he expected. It would require a miracle alone to keep these people from killing him. What he had done at their expense was detestable, incomprehensible. Oh, he would tell them why he felt he'd had to do it, but nothing justified his having destroyed their lives for his own ends.

After less than half a mile, he drew within sight of the servants' village, still strangely without the fatigue he would have suffered even earlier in the day after a walk like this. Now he slowed, realizing he would pass their guards—half a dozen men bearing swords, shields, and spears—assigned to keep out strangers and dangerous beasts. They would recognize him, as would anyone in Nimrod's kingdom, but Terah had not visited here since the day ten years before when he had announced the death of Mutuum's baby.

"Is that you, Terah?" one of the men called out as he approached. "To what do we owe this honor? You look younger than ever!"

"Spare the compliments," another spat. "Accident or not, he could not protect an innocent, a newborn, one of our own."

"You are right, my friend," Terah said. "I was of all men a failure. I have come to visit my servant Wedum and his family."

"He is expecting you, knows you're coming?"

"He does not."

"I'll fetch him," one of the young men said, and ran off.

"Tell him I am eager to visit!" Terah called after him.

"He was at your place all day," the skeptic grumbled. "Why didn't you talk to him then? Does he not deserve some time for himself?"

"Indeed he does. But I have private business with him."

"Most families are eating just now. Can't you smell it?"

"I certainly can." The aroma of baked bread, frying vegetables, and sizzling meat rekindled his hunger. But he would not eat until he had done his duty, even if it meant offending by refusing an offer.

Wedum appeared alarmed, jogging to Terah. "What is it, Master? You have need of me?"

"No, my friend. I just need to speak with you, and your wife if she is available."

"She will soon be putting our youngest to bed, but come, have some dinner and we will soon be free to speak."

It was not easy for Terah to refuse the food, for Wedum's wife was known as one of the best cooks in the settlement. Once she put the baby down and busied the other children outside, she and Wedum and Terah sat in the front portion of their tent, open to the air with only a fabric awning above.

"What has brought you all this way?" Wedum's wife said. "Did you walk?"

He nodded. "It was manageable."

"Well, you look no worse for it. Are you sure I can't get you some—?"

"Thank you, no. I have come to confess something to your husband and beg his forgiveness."

Wedum's eyes grew wide. "Oh, no, sir, this is highly irregular. You are not to lower yourself before your servant, even if you are guilty of an offense—which I assure you, you are not."

"But when the Lord God of creation feels otherwise, which of you am I to obey?"

CHAPTER 21

Mada'in Saleh

Nicole appreciated Detective Pranav Chakrabarti's ability to read people and situations. She valued his quiet wisdom and skill when he'd been brought in on her mother's case, but she had also been frankly worried when he expressed interest in taking a sabbatical and volunteering for the dig team. She made sure he was assigned where his expertise could be put to the best use, but would he fit in?

With most of the team he proved a friendly and gregarious presence. But he also proved to be all business when circumstances called for that. The sparkle in his eye would dim and the quick smile disappeared. That was the Pranav she encountered today. She sat with him under a sunscreen about midway between the excavation squares and the trailer where Max worked—the same place she had sat with Dr. Nasim Qahtani.

It wouldn't be long before the sun would peek over the horizon and start warming the site. But for now Nicole enjoyed the milder air on her skin. Just about anywhere else, the high eighties before dawn would be considered hot, but here that was still at least twenty degrees cooler than it would be by late morning. "All right, Detective," she said, "spill."

Chakrabarti said he had first heard from his NYPD boss, Detective George Wojciechowski, during the wee hours of the morning. "He woke me, of course, but I quickly reminded myself that New York is eight hours behind us, so it was only about eight in the evening there."

"And working that late isn't new to W, is it?"

"Don't I know it. He made me feel at home, calling in the middle of the night. Anyway, he was just leaving a meeting with Dr. Berman—the other one, I mean—your father. I have to confess, ma'am, I was at first confused, because Detective Wojciechowski seemed to have two things going, and he was trying to inform me of both at the same time."

"Start with the part that involves my dad."

"Well, they both do, since your father is hoping to get over here sooner rather than later."

"But one of these has to do with my mother, right?"

"It does, I'm afraid."

"I know Dad didn't want to leave until he figured out how my mother's health could have failed so quickly when she was almost ready to be released. But I don't think either of us suspected anything criminal that would involve Wojciechowski again. Were we wrong?"

"You were. And so was I. I felt the same way you did when I heard the news of your mother. I sincerely thought it was a bad break, a cruel irony after all she had been through." Chakrabarti riffled through the pages of his thick notepad. "Her attacker, the Bulgarian housekeeper—I had her name here..."

"Teodora Petrova," Nicole said.

"Right. Ms. Petrova had connections over here, of course, but once her effort failed, we all thought your mother just needed to be protected until she could heal."

"And she was well on her way, Pranav! Otherwise, I never would have come when I did. She insisted I stay on schedule, and her doctor assured me she would be released well before I left. So what happened?"

Chakrabarti referred to his notes again. "Well, after Petrova apparently committed suicide, we hoped whoever was behind her would be satisfied that they had made their point. But neither did we want to be naïve. They could easily have found a new hit person. That's why we beefed up security at the hospital and arranged for constant monitoring of your mother, should she be released back to her apartment and your father wanted to come over here."

"He never would have left her without protection."

"Once she passed, we worried about even more carefully protecting you and your father. With you here, we still worried someone might try something with him."

"I know, and both he and I are sorry for how we reacted to that."

"Overreacted, I'd say," Chakrabarti said with a smile.

Nicole nodded. "But since they hadn't scared me out of coming, what would be the point of threatening him? Did someone try something with him? Is he all right?"

"It's more complicated than that, ma'am. The NYPD was satisfied your mother had died of natural causes, until…" The detective flipped a few more pages. "Mount Sinai's security personnel reached out to us. Their insurance company, after reviewing the case, concluded that the hospital might be vulnerable to legal action."

"From…?"

"Your father."

"Why? Dad would never—"

"They were suspicious of the final documentation on your mother's chart. Something didn't add up. She'd been fine. Actually better than fine, for almost two weeks—her vitals virtually normal all day and all night. That's why everyone was so optimistic. Then she died, virtually without warning. And the autopsy found she died of heart and respiratory failure."

"But doesn't that happen frequently with elderly patients?"

"But she'd been out of the woods, as they say, for more than ten days. Suddenly her heart, respiration, and blood oxygen levels plummet? The ME concluded that this thrust her into atrial fibrillation. Her pulse skyrocketed to nearly two hundred beats a minute and, in essence, destroyed her heart."

"So the medical examiner thinks…?"

"Homicide."

"But who? Why?"

"Well, we know why, ma'am. The same motive behind the original attack."

"So the Saudis, or whoever, *did* replace Teodora…"

"It looks that way."

"But with all that security, how did they get to her?"

"Are you sure you want to know?"

"Of course!"

"They combed all the CCTV footage, everybody's comings and goings…"

"And?"

"And it all pointed to an inside job."

"No."

"Come, Doctor, you're much too intelligent to be closed-minded."

"But we know everybody inside! I know every nurse, every doctor, even every aide."

"Or you think you do. Everything points to one person—the last to see her alive."

"You're not saying—"

"I'm just telling you what was told to me, ma'am."

"Impossible."

"That's not what Detective Wojciechowski thinks. He's already been in touch with the Department of Justice's Office of International Affairs. They handle extradition requests. They're going to ask the Saudis to arrest and hold Ms. Mays until Wojciechowski can come and get her."

"I don't believe this. There's no way…"

"We can't say a word to her, ma'am, or to anyone else, until all this gets sorted and she's apprehended."

"Pranav! It makes no sense! She loved my mother. And my mother loved her."

The detective held up a hand. "Detective Wojciechowski has also asked me to examine her application to volunteer here too."

"That's easy. She told me the day we met that she had minored in archaeology and would love to come on a dig someday."

"I've heard that story before—I think from both of you. But I'm to look into why two volunteers backed out the same day—late in the process. That's what freed a spot for her, isn't it?"

Nicole sat shaking her head. She could not make this make sense. "You said Wojciechowski had two things going. I hope the other explains why you're so worried about bugs in the hotel and the car and the trailer."

He nodded. "Interpol tipped off New York." He looked over her shoulder. "Oh, the team is here."

Nicole turned. The bus's interior lights were on, and the guard was making his way from the front to the back. "Showtime," she said, rising. "Let's pick this up later."

"I'll be subtle," Chakrabarti said, "but I'm going to keep an eye on Kayla."

"Please."

"I can't ignore the evidence, Nicole."

"No, I know. I meant please do keep an eye on her. And I'll keep her close too, running errands for me and all that, so everything seems normal. You going to the trailer?"

"I can," Pranav said. "But I don't like losing sight of you either."

"Just ask Kayla to join me as I welcome the troops. I'll be right here."

CHAPTER 22

Servant Settlement, Shinar, Ur

Terah couldn't miss Wedum shooting a glance at his wife. "I suppose you must obey your god, Master. But respectfully, you know I worship all the gods, as you did for so long. You were such an example to me—"

Terah held up a hand. "I apologize, Wedum, but I did not come to be praised. I have failed you in a most evil way and am here to beg your forgiveness."

Wedum began to protest again.

"Please, no, my friend," Terah said. "I must ask you to allow me to fully reveal to you my deceit. You'll understand why I am wholly guilty and not even worthy of your consideration. You see, when my son Abram was born…"

And Terah haltingly, tearfully, revealed everything he had done to protect his first and only son when he learned that King Nimrod had been warned his offspring would threaten the throne. Wedum's fellow servant, Mutuum, had named his and his wife's own son, born just two days before Abram, after Terah himself. That had been such a selfless, honorable act that Terah could hardly believe what he was now confessing. He had promised the midwife, Yadidatum, he would intervene with the king on behalf of *her* son—who had been imprisoned for theft and was to have his right hand severed—if she would join Terah in a great lie. But in reality he had given her no choice. Agree, or her son would suffer. Disagree and he would not only leave her son to his fate, but he would also have her killed.

Wedum's wife turned ashen at this revelation and Wedum himself narrowed his eyes and grew stony. He appeared to try to control himself, and though he sat still, his chest heaved and his pulse thrummed in his neck.

"What did you force her to do?" Wedum's wife managed, just above a whisper.

"Only God can give me utterance to admit it," Terah said, wishing he could dig an abyss and pitch himself in. "I made her bring me my name-sake, Mutuum's baby boy, claiming I just wanted to see him." He hung his head. "I took her and the boy to the king, into his very court. Yadidatum remains the only servant ever to have broached the entrance. I presented the baby to the king as my own son and made her say she had delivered him from Belessunu's loins."

Wedum covered his mouth and his wife gasped.

"I offered him to the king as a gift, knowing full well he would kill him rather than allow a threat to his reign."

Wedum's wife rasped, "So he was not devoured by wild dogs…"

"He was not."

"And your own son?"

"Remains safe, hidden."

Wedum spoke through quivering fingers, "Master, that makes you—"

"—a murderer. I know."

"But why?"

"I believed then that I had a reason. And I even believed the plan had been given to me by my gods."

Wedum stood. "Why confess to us? Mutuum and his wife are the victims."

"God told me to start with you. Oh, Wedum, he has opened my eyes to the depths of my depravity and shown me how I have deceived you from that day to this. You had no reason to believe other than what I told you, that Abram had been offered to the king and that baby Terah had been attacked and consumed by beasts."

"Despite your heroic efforts to protect him," Wedum spat. "The king's guard—"

"Ikuppi, yes. Ikuppi even backed my account."

"As did the midwife, right here, when you wailed over what had happened to the child."

"I am responsible for all of it. And all I can do is prostrate myself before you and beg your forgiveness." Terah stood to kneel before them.

"Please, no!" Wedum said.

His wife moaned and shook her head.

"I do not know what to say, Master," Wedum said. "You must fall on your face before your god, and perhaps all the gods of the sky and earth. I am but a man with no power to forgive such atrocious acts."

"Oh, Wedum, I am not asking that you absolve me of the murders—yes, I include Ikuppi's suicide as a death I caused—but rather only for my having lived a lie before you lo these many years."

Wedum turned his back on Terah and stepped to the edge of the tent. His wife stared at the ground, shoulders drooping. Wedum mumbled something, and Terah asked him to repeat it.

"I said I am not sure I can keep serving you."

Terah slumped back down. "My plea remains. If you ever find it within yourselves to comprehend the depth of my sorrow and regret and forgive me for lying to you, I would be forever in your debt. I could not blame you if you abandoned me. I deserve no better. Do what you must do."

Wedum turned to face him. "If I do what I must do, I would bring Mutuum here to hear this from your own lips."

"No, please. I must go to him myself. He dwells in the same place as always?"

Wedum nodded and looked away, and his wife sat sobbing as Terah rose and moved past them, trudging down the path toward Mutuum's tent.

CHAPTER 23

Mada'in

Nicole gathered everyone for a brief pep talk and to inform them that she planned to make the rounds of all four dig squares that day. But she was troubled when Pranav Chakrabarti emerged from the trailer not with Kayla but only Max. She found it hard to concentrate on what she wanted to say when Pranav left Max at the edge of the team, hurried to the Land Rover, and raced up to the exit.

"I'm expecting Codirector Waleed in a few minutes," she said, "and Dr. Qahtani a little later this morning, so you know the drill. Be on your best behavior, and let's get to it."

A middle-aged woman raised her hand.

"Sorry," Nicole said. "I'm kind of in the middle of something and can't take questions just now, unless it's an emergency."

"No, it's fine," the woman said.

As the team dispersed to their stations, Nicole rushed to Max. "Where's Kayla?"

He shrugged. "Got me. Pranav came looking for her, but she'd already left the trailer while you two were out here. Said she needed to tell you something."

"I didn't see her."

"She can't be far. Pranav said he'd find her and asked me to keep you in sight till he got back. What's going on?"

"Nothing, I hope. Here he comes now."

The Rover was moving faster than Nicole was comfortable with, kicking up a huge cloud of dust as Pranav skidded into position near the trailer. "We're good," Pranav said as they approached. "Thanks, Max. I just need to talk with Dr. Berman."

"You found Kayla?" Max said. "Where was—"

"Give me a minute with Nicole, please."

"Sorry," Max said, heading for the trailer.

"What do you mean 'we're good'?" Nicole said. "Where is she?"

"I just didn't know how much you wanted Max to know yet. You and I both saw her go into the trailer before we talked, so she had to slip past us when we were sitting there. The guard says she jogged up to his station shortly after we arrived and told him you were sending her back to the hotel to get something you forgot. She asked him to call her a cab."

"What?!"

Pranav held up a hand. "He asked her why she didn't take the Rover, and she said I needed it this morning."

"You needed it for what?"

"He didn't ask."

"So he called her a cab..."

"Of course he did," Pranav said. "He'd do anything for her."

"You don't think she heard us talking..."

"No. Either she was tipped off by someone that she's under suspicion, or she caught on that I was being briefed. And of course she knew I feared we were being bugged. But I didn't know how to caution only you."

"So she's clearly on the run?"

"Clearly. The question is whether she's trying to leave the country or seek asylum here."

"You have to stop her, Pranav."

"Well, yes and no. If she's headed back to New York, we should be able to track her flight and have someone grab her when she arrives. In that case, I'd just as soon let her go. But I would like to keep her from finding asylum here, because once she does that, this becomes an international incident and the Saudis will protect her at all costs."

"Can you have security at the Faisal detain her till you can get there?"

"The guard said she had her backpack with her, so I can't imagine she would risk stopping back at the hotel for anything. I wish I had time to really scour the hotel, the car, and the trailer for bugs, but that's going to have to take a back seat to my trying to find her."

"She could be anywhere, Pranav."

His phone chirped. "I've got to take this. The cab company was to call with where she was dropped off."

"I'll be in the trailer," Nicole said.

"Tell Max nothing yet," he said, and took the call. "This is Detective Chakrabarti…"

Max spun in his chair to face Nicole as she sat before his desk with a finger to her lips. He looked grave and scribbled as he spoke. "The team seems energized today."

"Yeah, and I am too. Hope to make some real progress. It'll be good to have both Dr. Waleed and Dr. Qahtani here."

Max slid a note to her as they chatted. "Anything to report to Qahtani yet?"

You must tell me what's going on! Outside at midmorning breakfast?

Maybe, she scribbled back. *Don't know much yet.*

"I'm keeping him up to speed," she said. "He's proven easy to work with."

Kayla? he wrote.

We'll find her. Nothing to worry about yet.

"Good. That's good. You never know with local overseers."

I've come to care about you, you know, he wrote.

Nicole squinted at him. "I know," she said. "But Nasim's actually been helpful."

You know what I mean, he added. *As a friend. I worry about you.*

"Well, thanks for that, and for all you do for me." She pointed out toward the detective. "I'd better get back to work."

But Chakrabarti knocked lightly and opened the door. "Need some info," he said, his phone tucked between his ear and shoulder while he wrote on his notepad.

Kayla full name and passport #.

"Max can find that in our system. I'll be outside."

Pranav passed her another note.

Don't go far.

Nicole felt conspicuous and out of sorts, appearing to dawdle outside the trailer when the whole rest of the team was noisily buzzing with activity. Pranav soon joined her, repeating Kayla's info over the phone. When it appeared he'd been put on hold, Nicole stepped toward him to whisper, but he raised a finger. "Al-'Ula? Thank you so much. You've been very kind."

"She's back at the hotel?" Nicole said.

Pranav shook his head. "Dropped off near another dig site."

"The one Qahtani is also visiting?"

"Your guess is as good as mine, Doctor," he said, working his phone.

"I doubt that."

He turned the screen to her.

"Hard to read a map that small," she said.

"Five miles from a U.S. Embassy consulate suboffice."

"So is she connecting with Qahtani or the U.S.?" Nicole said.

"Depends on who picked her up when she arrived."

CHAPTER 24

Servant Settlement, Shinar

The closer Terah drew to Mutuum's tent, the slower he walked. He prayed this terrible day would end, that his awful revelations would be over and he could set out after Belessunu and Abram. But he so dreaded confessing to Mutuum and his wife that he was tempted to pray that God would take him first—strike him down in this very village. He couldn't imagine having come this far back to his Lord and never seeing his wife and son again. But God had promised Abram would become an exalted father, so he could rest assured about his son's future whether he himself remained alive.

Yet God was not going to take him, he knew that. Terah would not have been assigned such a grim penance if the Lord planned only to discard him. The encounter with Wedum and his wife had proved a disaster—not that he expected otherwise. Terah had done as he was told, but they had not forgiven him and perhaps never would. In fact, he may have lost a longtime faithful servant. Still, what he had done to Mutuum and his wife was so much worse! What could he possibly expect here?

By now the sky was dark. Terah stood before Mutuum's tent where flames flickered through the fabric and low voices reached him. The aroma of dinner remained, but hearing no children, he assumed the family had finished its meal and the little ones were in bed. Not wanting to wake them, Terah quietly said, "Mutuum, are you home?"

The conversation inside immediately ceased and Mutuum peeked out. In the moonlight the man appeared to have aged even since Terah had seen him from across the market a few years before. "Who is it?"

"Terah."

"No!" Mutuum's wife whispered.

"Tiamat! Shh!" Mutuum reached for a lamp and held it toward Terah. "What do you want?"

"To speak to you and your wife, please."

"He is not welcome here," Tiamat said.

"It is too painful for her, Mast— Terah."

"I understand."

"You and I both know the pain of losing a child, so I must ask you—"

"No, we don't, Mutuum. That's what I want to talk with you about."

His former servant stepped out. "What are you saying? You know we lost our son at the same time you sacrificed yours to the king."

"Oh, no, yes, of course you lost a son. I'm trying to say that—"

"I can't hear this!" Tiamat called out.

"Please, I must ask you to leave, Terah."

"But I—"

"This is all history, sir. My wife and I have tried to cope with it, but even to this day it hurts merely to say your name, because we named—"

"I know. And I'm sorry…"

"You apologized that day. We've tried our best to forgive you, but to see you, to talk to you—"

"Please!" Tiamat whispered.

"You owe me nothing, Mutuum, but I'm begging you—"

The man stepped out. "If you must speak with me, let's walk."

"I'm afraid I must ask Tiamat to join us."

"No!" came from inside.

"Impossible," Mutuum said. "Don't you see—"

"I must obey God," Terah said. "He requires that I talk with you both."

Mutuum ducked back into the tent, where Tiamat whispered desperately that she would not leave the children, "and neither will I allow him inside."

"Let's all talk right here then," Terah said through the tent wall.

"Do I have to see you?" Tiamat said.

"I prefer to see you, dear lady."

Silence.

Finally, rustling from inside told Terah she might comply. Presently she appeared, wrapped in a shawl and holding her own lamp. And she too looked older than her years. "Say what you need to say and be gone," she said.

Terah fell to his knees before them.

"We've been through this before," Tiamat said. "We know your story, and enduring it again will not make it easier on us."

"Ma'am," Terah said, raising both hands to her. "I must ask that you let me speak. I have a most heinous confession, and then you may do to me or with me anything you wish."

She sighed and crossed her arms, cradling the lamp in her elbow.

"Thank you, ma'am. Let me start by saying that though I will not be able to stop weeping, I in no way claim this will be harder on me than on you and Mutuum. But my God has faced me with my sins, and I cannot go another day without revealing the ugly truth to you both."

Terah sobbed throughout the recitation, and his tears pooled on the ground. Mutuum reached for Tiamat's lamp when she staggered and had to grab his arm to stay upright. Terah forced himself to look at them both as he revealed the awful truth. Tiamat buried her face in her husband's shoulder.

Mutuum panted. "So your son is alive."

"He is."

"And your wife has not abandoned you," Tiamat said.

"Very nearly, but no."

"When the king learns of this," Mutuum said, "and you know he will—"

"I am a dead man."

Tiamat pulled away from Mutuum. "And rightfully so. You deserve worse, worse than what happened to our son."

"I do, I know. And I would not insult you by begging forgiveness, for I—"

"That's wise," she said.

"But if you would allow me, I long to in some way try to make some recompense—"

"What are you talking about?" Mutuum said. "You think you can repay our loss?"

"Oh, no, just that I want—"

"Everything you own would do nothing more than remind us of the most painful—"

"Everything I own was what I had in mind."

"What are you saying?" Tiamat said.

"As your husband says, soon the king will hear of this and require I pay with my life. So I must flee. And I must travel light. Anything I leave behind is yours, so your children will never have to want—"

"We want nothing from you!" Tiamat said. "Nothing you have ever even touched!"

"I understand."

"You understand nothing," she said.

"Now, Tiamat," Mutuum said, "at least the man has told us the truth. He didn't have to do that."

"And has it helped?" she said. "This makes things only worse—another memory I will never be able to forget."

"At least know that I am truly sorry," Terah said, sounding pathetic and inadequate even to him.

"Well, so am I," she said. "If this somehow absolves you before your god, good for you." She stepped back inside the tent.

"Thank you," Mutuum said softly. "I know how hard this had to be…"

"My pain is nothing compared to yours. I know."

"And Master, she's right. We do not want anything from you. Go."

"I do have a request, Mutuum."

"Please, just go."

"It's just that I still need to talk with the midwife and with Ikuppi's widow. If you could favor me by not speaking of this until I am on my way out of Ur—"

"I can't guarantee that, sir. Especially with Tiamat feeling as she does. Who else knows?"

"Only Wedum and his wife."

"Who's to say they haven't told others already? You'd better hurry on your way."

Terah rushed off to find Yadidatum, who also lived in the settlement. Ikuppi's wife lived closer to the palace of the king. God would have to protect Terah if he had a prayer of escaping after that. Especially on foot.

CHAPTER 25

Mada'in

"I so wanted to get in the ground today," Nicole told Pranav. "But Kayla is suddenly our top priority."

"Well, at least mine," he said. "Would you like my advice?"

"Always. You know that."

"I suggest you go about your business as usual. We're plainly being watched, monitored. I mean, I have found no bugs yet and hope Interpol was wrong about that, but until we're sure, be careful in the trailer and the car and the hotel. But our best chance to appear normal is you doing what you came here to do. Leave Kayla to me. Our mobiles, at least yours and mine and Kayla's, are securely encrypted."

"Which doesn't help if she's in touch with the Saudis."

"True, but I have an idea. I'm going to go through my diplomatic channels, NYPD, Interpol, and even see if I can get Detective Wojciechowski to prevail upon the DOJ. If Kayla's still in Al-'Ula, I need to see her, meet with her, talk to her."

"Is that even possible if she's being protected?"

"No idea, but I've got to get on it. This thing could quickly spin out of control. Imagine the ramifications."

"I don't want to think about it, but I can't think of anything else. And when Qahtani shows up here?"

"Be sure to let me talk to him. Meanwhile, do your work, and I'll keep you posted."

Do my work? A young woman Nicole wholly trusted might have had something to do with her mother's death, likely at the behest of those who opposed this very dig. Yet she knew Pranav was right.

Nicole headed to Square One and noticed the usual increase in activity as Suzie Benchford and the volunteers appeared to notice her. She descended the ladder and found Samir Waleed underground. "Didn't see you arrive, Doctor," she said. "Welcome."

He seemed to study her and pulled her aside. "Something's troubling you. What is it?"

"Sorry, I didn't want it to show. I may fill you in later, but for now bring me up to speed on how we're doing here."

"We're getting close to some very interesting finds."

"Oh, good."

"But…"

She cocked her head at him.

"Your overseer, Dr. Qahtani, has confided in me the opposition you're facing. A question I should have asked a long time ago is whether this is all going to be worth it, especially if you find what you hope to."

"You must know I was prepared for the pushback."

"But at the level Qahtani fears?"

"You both have me scared, if you must know."

"My intent is not to scare you, Dr. Berman. Just to caution you."

Nicole noticed other members edging closer. "Do you have a minute?" she said. "Let's talk up top."

He followed her out to the same awning-covered table she'd sat at with Nasim Qahtani and Pranav. "May I ask you to take notes—or at least pretend to—as if we're talking shop?" she said.

He smiled and pulled out a notepad. "Who are we trying to impress?"

"Maybe just the team. But I need your counsel on this as a Muslim. What the Saudis must understand is that if the Genesis record can be corroborated—in essence vindicated—that is not bad news for Arabs. We agree completely that Ishmael was Abraham's son and also received a blessing and a promise. The Genesis story affirms him and his role too. Ironically, those who oppose the biblical account and wish to thwart my efforts here draw only more attention to the issue."

Samir only doodled on his notepad. "My assessment may surprise you," he said. "Though naturally I worry what extremists might do about your findings, and of course what the government might do, but I don't see your excavation being as risky as some others might."

"Well, that's encouraging. I'm listening."

"This being a UNESCO World Heritage site and your having received your permit from the Department of Antiquities, it's not as if you're here secretly. And I know from experience that your father's foundation has influential friends in the Saudi government."

Nicole was tempted to ask who then was behind the attack on her mother—two attacks, in fact. But she dared not. "I can only hope all that works in our favor," she said. "So where are we—in the ground, I mean?"

"The deeper we go," Samir said, "the closer I believe we're coming to what you're hoping to find—more inscriptions on the flat, dressed surface of the cliff. You have a good, hardworking group—especially Ms. Benchford. Allah is smiling upon you."

The twinkle in his eye told her he intended the irony.

CHAPTER 26

Servant Settlement, Shinar

The years had proved worse for Yadidatum than anyone Terah had seen so far. She sat hunched before a small fire just outside her tiny dwelling, draped in a ratty shawl that appeared to weigh more than she did.

"Excuse me, ma'am," Terah said, making her look up with a start. "May I talk with you?"

"Never thought I'd see you again," she rasped. "Speak your piece."

"May I sit?"

"On the ground."

He settled across from her. "How is your son?"

"Married," she said. "Two little ones of his own now."

"That's good."

"Not for me. He ran south from this place as soon as he had the chance. I know only through gossip where he lives. Never met the wife or my grandchildren."

"I'm sorry."

"Oh, I'm certain you are, sir. Force me to join you in the most evil sacrificing of a child when you know my whole life was given to bringing babies into this world. Mutuum and his wife have not even looked at me since. And they warned everyone in this village against using me. All anyone knows is that the child was in my care when he was supposedly attacked and—"

"Mutuum and Tiamat know the truth now, ma'am."

She poked at the fire with a stick. "What are you saying? You wouldn't dare tell a soul...I certainly have never dared. And how I longed to! But though my son is lost to me, at least I know he's alive and has all his limbs. I owe you that much."

Terah grabbed a switch and tended his own side of the fire. "Yadidatum, you are right that I would not dare tell a soul the truth. But I have returned to the Lord my God, the one and only true Creator of the universe, and He has compelled me. I have already confessed my deceit to my servant and also to Mutuum and Tiamat."

"You have not!"

"I have just come from there."

"You fool!"

"I was compelled by my Lord—"

She struggled to her feet, so he rose too. "Do you not see the ramifications?" she said.

"Of course I do. I know this will soon get back to the palace, so I must flee. But—"

"I mean the ramifications for me! Of course *you* can flee! What am I to do? I barely subsist now, scraping by on the kindness of those I helped long ago. You made me lie to the king and then to my neighbors! What do you suppose the price will be for that?"

Terah was stricken. Indeed he had not thought this through. "Dear lady, it should become clear that I gave you no choice! No one can hold my deceit to your account."

"You think King Nimrod will care what prompted my lie?" she said. "The only servant to ever enter the court, and what I say causes him to murder an innocent child?"

"First, I'm pleading with you to forgive me for this awful thing I did to you, yet I do not expect you to bestow that upon me. I know I don't deserve it, especially in light of, as you say, what it means for you now."

"Terah, you ruined my life, and now you have sentenced me to death."

Desperately, silently praying, Terah found his mind crowded with conflicting messages. He had to get going, to confess to Ikuppi's wife and flee Ur at all cost, but he could not simply leave Yadidatum to her fate. Mutuum and Tiamat had rejected his offer of recompense, but maybe that was the answer now. What might the old midwife do with unlimited means?

"What if I were to help you get to your son and give you more money that you will ever need?"

"You owe me everything you own!"

"So let me do this."

"If my son wanted me with him, he would have sent for me by now."

"He's afraid, that's all!" Terah said. "He was very nearly tortured or worse, so who can blame him for fleeing?"

"But without me?"

"By now he must be longing for you. No more arguing about it. I will bring you the money—more than enough to buy you a ride to your son and also to provide for you and him and his wife and his children for the rest of your days."

"I would have to leave this very night."

"Wait here only long enough for me to return with the money."

"The gods know I have little to pack. And what becomes of me if my son rejects me?"

"He won't. He can't. But you will be able to afford protection."

Terah ran back to Wedum's place and offered him an exorbitant reward for going to Terah's home, locating his fortune, and delivering it to Yadidatum. "Find her transportation and ask her no questions."

"Very well, Master."

"And I will also be fleeing, so please take enough to care for yourself and your family for as long as you need to."

Wedum shook his head. "I will be able to find work, sir. But you must be on your way soon."

"You too."

"I will."

"I cannot thank you enough, Wedum."

"Seeing you try to put things right is thanks enough for me. Perhaps not for Tiamat, but for me."

Terah lit out for Ikuppi's widow's place, amazed and thankful afresh for the renewed strength the Lord had bestowed upon him with the squall at the cattle pen. He strode out of the village and past the guards, who ignored him almost as if they hadn't seen him. Was this how God would protect him on this most dangerous journey? He could only hope. Such a perilous journey lay ahead.

But what did he have to offer the widow he was about to see? He had committed the whole of his resources to Yadidatum and Wedum.

"Worry not," the Lord impressed upon him as he walked. "I, the God of your forefathers, will provide."

"But, Lord, I—"

"The Lord of hosts has sworn, and as I have thought, so it shall be. As I purpose, so shall it stand."

CHAPTER 27

Mada'in

Nicole took a call from Dr. Nasim Qahtani, who told her he would be arriving in time for the team's second breakfast. He sounded strange, perhaps distracted, but he seemed to do his best to affect his typically jovial air. "If there's enough watermelon—which happens to be my favorite—I thought it might calm nerves, get the team to see me as less of a threat, if I partook with you all."

"Fine," Nicole said, "but I do have a brief chat scheduled with a staff member then, if you can excuse me for a few minutes."

"Sure," Nasim said. "That will give me a chance to socialize a bit."

That's all we need, Nicole thought. *More women obsessed with you.* She was tempted to hit him head-on, to tell him she knew that he knew where Kayla was—and demand to know what was going on. But she mustn't. She had promised Detective Chakrabarti an audience with Qahtani. She'd leave him to the professional.

Qahtani arrived right at nine thirty, just as Samir Waleed was rounding up everyone for the late breakfast break. And here came Max from the trailer. He nodded toward Nasim's Jaguar. "Is he going to preclude our meeting?"

Nicole shook her head. "But we're going to have to keep it short. There's not much I can tell you anyway." In truth she had no idea what she could tell him, if anything. Who could she trust anymore?

"I'm working blind here," Max whispered. "All I know is that Pranav is worked up about something, worrying we're being bugged, and nobody knows where Kayla is. We both know you're not obligated to tell me anything, but if I've earned your trust…"

"Of course you have, Max. But frankly, I barely know you."

"You have to know I've grown fond of you, Nic— Dr. Berman."

"You've made that clear, yes. And I appreciate—"

"I'm not talking in any weird or romantic way. It's just that I admire what you're doing and how you've responded to the opposition."

You don't know the half of it, she thought. Or at least she hoped he didn't. But had he just used *weird* and *romantic* as synonyms? Nicole had to admit she might have been flattered if he felt more for her than mere professional respect. On the other hand, they had zero in common beyond archaeology.

"Max, I need to ask you something. If I'm unable to tell you everything that's going on—why Pranav is being cautious, what might be going on with Kayla, all of it—will that affect how you do your job?"

"Well, I'd feel a little neglected, but no, it shouldn't. But I do wish you could find it within yourself to trust me."

"I do, Max. I love your work ethic, and I'm well aware of your skills. Keep exhibiting all that, and I promise I'll tell you what I can when I can."

"Fair enough, but—here comes Pranav."

"Sorry, you'll have to excuse me."

Max seemed to hesitate but finally headed to the food tables.

Detective Chakrabarti pulled Nicole farther away. "Qahtani has the team eating out of his hand," he said with delight in his accent, despite the seriousness of the subject. "Look at them flock to him. As soon as the team goes back to work, let me speak with him. And I'll want you along."

"What's your plan?"

"I want to take him off guard. First, I suggest we meet in the trailer. Can you find something for Max to do so the three of us will have the place to ourselves?"

"Sure, but he's pretty exercised about not knowing what's going on."

"You've told him nothing, I hope."

"Of course, though I believe I could trust him—"

"Continue to hold off on that, please. I am studying all the applications for the slightest irregularity. We're concentrating on Ms. Mays, of course, but until I finish—"

"Got it. But tell me why we would meet in the trailer if you're worried about a bug in there."

"Simple. Qahtani can in no way worry we know anything about a bug, if there is one, if we're willing to speak to him there. Secondly, if the place is bugged, he's either behind it or knows about it, so it might affect what he says too."

"What tack will you take with him?"

"I play such things by ear, but my inclination is to start cordially and then drop a bomb on him."

"Such as?"

"First, let me ask you what you have planned to tell him about your findings so far? Surely he'll ask."

"Frankly, Pranav, we have some extremely revealing pieces that are most encouraging—at least from our standpoint."

"Which would prove troubling to the Saudis, I assume."

"Of course. But there's no way of hiding these things from them anyway. We're documenting and cataloguing everything, so before it's transported from here, they have to be aware of every detail."

Chakrabarti nodded. "And it would not serve you well if the Saudis discovered something you had not informed him about."

"Oh, that would be disastrous. In fact, he has to be as fully informed as Dr. Waleed. His reputation, his job, depends on ferreting out anything and everything the Saudis need to be aware of."

"Then let's start by your bringing him totally up to speed. If he has worried that you will try to slip something past him, this will put his mind at ease. By being entirely transparent with him, you'll force him to play right into my hands."

"Meaning?"

"I will move right from your total honesty to mine, and I will appeal to his sense of fairness. In essence, I will tell him that because you have been so forthcoming with information—even facts we might rather *not* share with his government—he owes us the same. I'll tell him we have a missing team member and that we know he knows where she is. And I want to meet and talk with her."

"Even if you're right, Pranav, he'll never allow that."

"He might, especially if I insist that he be present and assure him that he can take whatever precautions he wishes to protect her, especially if asylum is what she's after. It will be most revealing to see how such a bright mind responds to me if I take that straightforward an approach."

"'Bright mind' is right," Nicole said. "I can't imagine what he'll say."

"He may concoct any story he thinks will work," Pranav said. "But regardless, in the end he'll know that we know and that we are not to be trifled with. The Saudis will have to step very carefully not to incite an international incident. But I have an ulterior motive too, Dr. Berman."

"Something else?"

Chakrabarti nodded. "You remember this morning at the hotel, when Ms. Mays mentioned that she and her family were once Christians too and I said we would have to talk about that sometime?"

"Oh, yes, and I wondered what you would say to her."

"If Dr. Qahtani grants me an audience with her, I would eventually try to return to that conversation so it gives me a chance to explain my own journey of faith. Imagine, if Dr. Qahtani is there, plus we are monitored—which we surely will be—while I will be very careful not to appear to be proselytizing, I will fully explain my beliefs. And no matter what comes of all this, Saudi Muslims will hear the truth."

"I'd love to sit in on that," Nicole said.

"I will record every word on my phone."

Samir Waleed clapped for attention and asked volunteers to start clearing the area and get back to work. "I shouldn't have to remind you to stay hydrated and come back here for an extra bite or two any time you feel the need!"

Pranav said, "Now can you busy Max with something and introduce me to Dr. Qahtani?"

"I'll go get him. Wait for me in the trailer and tell Max I need him to talk with Dr. Waleed about how to best collect his documentation and start getting it archived into the system."

CHAPTER 28

Shinar, Ur

Terah worried that Ikuppi's widow, Zavian, might have already retired for the night by the time he arrived at her place, but lamps still burned in her spacious house. She came to the door with a wary look but quickly brightened. "So nice to see you after so long, sir! Come in!"

He asked after her three children, and she told him they were sleeping. "All have come of age and will soon look to marry. My husband and I will take each to the bridal auction when their schooling is complete."

"Husband?"

"I assumed you knew. Abilsin."

"King Nimrod's stable supervisor?"

"The very one."

"How did I not know this?"

"We all know you've been occupied with the tower for years. You know we can see it from here already."

"Oh, I'm sure. When it is finished it will be able to be seen for miles."

"What brings you to my home?"

"I have something very important to discuss with you, and you may want your husband to hear it."

"He should be home soon. He traveled half a day to a livestock trade where he hoped to reduce his inventory by a dozen horses."

Terah nodded. "Unfortunately, this cannot wait and I then must be on my way, but anything I say here you may feel free to share with Abilsin. It's likely to get back to the king long before he might tell him anyway."

Zavian furrowed her brow. "Back to the king?"

"You'll soon understand. Zavian, forgive me. I have been remiss in not checking in on you after Ikuppi's—"

"Oh, think nothing of it. I can never forget your kindness in arranging such a beautiful tribute to him. He loved you so and was so loyal to you."

"He was."

"And you saw to it that he was buried with honor."

Terah hung his head. Was he to tell this woman who knew only the best of her late husband, and who had somehow made a new life for herself, the truth about Ikuppi's death? Was that the truth he also knew would reach Nimrod? What might the king do to Zavian and her offspring if he learned Ikuppi had conspired in the lie? He would never accept that Terah had left Ikuppi no choice. The king would know only that one of his top aides had not kept him from murdering the wrong child.

Terah had so egregiously forced the man to abandon his principles that Ikuppi could not but blame himself for the death of Mutuum's child. He had done Terah's bidding—against his will—up to and through the dastardly deception, and then plainly fell on his own sword. "God," Terah prayed silently, "what value comes from her knowing this? Can she not retain an honorable memory of an honorable man?"

"Withhold from her the worst of it," the Lord seemed to impress upon him. "Confess only your own iniquity."

"What is it, Terah? You appear downcast."

He leaned forward and rested his elbows on his knees, head in his hands. "I must tell you the truth," he said.

"About what, sir?"

The story seemed to gush from him, as he forced himself to maintain eye contact with her. "It was all a lie," he concluded, "and I gave Ikuppi no choice but to go along with it."

"But he would not, could not, do such a thing."

"He fought me the entire way, ma'am. I threatened his life, his reputation, his role with the king. Everything."

She fell silent.

"I do not expect your forgiveness. But I simply had to reveal this to you." Terah would take to his grave that Ikuppi's own death was by suicide.

Zavian stood and turned her back to him. "I do not understand how you could have done such a thing."

"Nor can I, ma'am. What so compelled me at the time makes no sense to me today. I could not live with the guilt one more day."

A look of realization came over her. "Fate overtook Ikuppi before he could tell the king."

"Perhaps," Terah said. But he knew the truth. In all likelihood, Ikuppi had to fight with everything in him to keep from confessing to the king his role in the subterfuge. But Terah had threatened him and his family, so he took his own life to protect theirs. That Zavian could not, must not, be told.

She turned back to face him. "You say your god had promised your son—"

"—would become a father himself. An exalted one."

"What does that mean?"

"I don't know, but it sounds divine."

"And you believe it?" she said.

"I do."

"Yet you could not trust that same god to protect Abram?"

Terah shook his head. "I am of all men most depraved. But you must be rest assured, Ikuppi's part in this was wholly with you and his children in mind. He knew I had the authority and the power to ruin him."

She sat again. "Still, he lived by strong convictions, sir."

"I know he did."

"What you forced him to do is as bad as the murder you perpetrated."

"It haunts me every day. He was an upright servant of the king and the people of the kingdom."

Zavian slowly shook her head. "I will pray to the gods that the king will be so worried about your son that he will not exact vengeance on me for Ikuppi's part in this."

"We can hope King Nimrod will assume Ikuppi accepted my report and believed he was telling the truth."

"Oh, sir, have you forgotten? Ikuppi's story was that he was with you when the animal attack occurred. We can't claim he merely reported a faulty account from you."

It was true. Terah's guilt weighed more heavily on him than ever. Had he ruined both Yadidatum's and Zavian's lives as he had Mutuum's and his wife's? Why did this tangle of disaster have to grow?

"And now what will become of you?" Zavian said. "If the servant settlement knows of this…"

"It won't be long before the king decrees my capture and death."

"Do you want to hide out here? No one would think you came to see me."

"I told some my plans."

"Terah! Are you trying to get yourself killed, not to mention me?"

"No! I—"

"You must flee immediately! But you have no steed? No chariot?"

"Not of my own, no."

"Stay right here until Abilsin arrives. He'll know what to do, and he may be able to provide—"

"He can offer me nothing that doesn't belong to the king!"

"But he can, sir! We have our own horses and chariots. Surely he would lend you one of each—"

"But when would I ever be able to return it?"

"Worry about that later. Let us help you. You have obeyed the gods by telling me—"

"I have obeyed the one true God of my forefathers."

"Call it what you will, there is integrity in it."

"If nothing else…"

* * *

Terah waited two hours, trusting that Abilsin might indeed be the fulfillment of God's promise that He would provide. And when the man finally arrived—noisily moving several horses into his own stable behind the house—he expressed surprise at seeing Terah. Zavian quickly told him the whole story.

"I never liked you, Terah," Abilsin said. "But I didn't know why. Now I do."

"And I don't blame you. But I am in need."

"It's your lucky day. I was able to sell only eight horses today. Admittedly, they were the best of the lot, but the four I brought home are fine too. And I am free to do with them what I wish. Come, choose whichever you want and leave us. I don't ever want to see you again."

"Abilsin!" Zavian said.

"What? I'm already going to have to answer for this if the king's patrols overtake him. I'll deny I ever saw him and imply he must have stolen it from whoever I sold it to."

"You'll do nothing of the sort!" Zavian said.

"And what will become of you when the king makes an example of me—aiding an enemy of the court? With two husbands who have defied the king, you will be an anathema to the crown."

The truth of that seemed to appear on her face. "And do you have a chariot he could have too?"

"Yes, yes! But hurry."

"It must be one of ours," Zavian said. "One that can't be traced to the throne."

Abilsin appeared grim as he set about hitching to an old chariot the best horse of those remaining. Terah was nearly overcome by Zavian's offer to prepare a sack with foodstuffs for his journey, but he could not allow it. "My God has promised to supply all my needs."

"And you don't think he's using me as the way to do just that?" she said. "Because I don't believe in him?"

"It's not that at all, ma'am, and I am truly grateful—especially under the circumstances. I have put you in a most precarious position."

"Well, you pray *your* god will protect me, and I'll pray *my* gods will."

CHAPTER 29

Mada'in

In the trailer, Nicole introduced Nasim Qahtani to Detective Chakrabarti. "You watch out for her, do you?" Qahtani said.

"A privilege."

"Well, I assure you I pose no danger to such a lovely woman."

"Forgive me, sir," the detective said, "but I did not expect to hear that from an Arab. And I apologize if I'm coming across as culturally insensitive."

"Not at all, sir. I am simply a Saudi who sometimes says what all Arabs would like to."

"All right," Nicole said. "I'll take that as a compliment, uncomfortable as it makes me. I'd appreciate not being referred to as—"

"Oh, Dr. Berman, I sincerely apologize!" Qahtani said. Surprisingly, he appeared truly repentant. "I assumed you were used to such comments from Americans."

"Frankly, no. Most men know better even back home."

"Well, let me just say then that I pose no danger to someone like you—male *or* female—who exhibits such skill and knowledge."

"Thank you. Now just let me pull a file here so I can bring you up to speed on where we are..."

"And, forgive me, Detective," Qahtani said, "but you shouldn't feel obligated to stay—"

"Oh, I prefer that he does," Nicole said. "If only for the sake of protocol."

"Protocol?"

"Unless you have an objection?"

"Well, I can't imagine your personal security has anything to do with what we will be discussing."

"Let me worry about my own staff, please."

"No objection, but I hope you both know that Detective Chakrabarti's permission to carry a weapon in-country represents a significant exception—speaking of protocol."

"I was surprised myself," Nicole said. "And grateful."

"Your father has long been a friend of the Saudi government and the royal family itself. I daresay they would extend him every courtesy, including your dig permit."

So there it was again: the implication that Nicole was here on her father's coattails—not to mention her armed guard. She was not about to defend her credentials again. She opened a folder and spread pages before Qahtani. "Forgive me for relaying information you've known for years, but so far the majority of the remains we've uncovered date from the first century AD."

"The Nabatean kingdom," Qahtani said, "of course. It was the kingdom's southernmost and largest settlement after Petra. Have you found traces of Lihyanite occupation from before the Nabatean rule?"

"We have. And some evidence of the Romans after the Nabateans. But I know the Qur'an places the settlement of the area by the Thamudic between those of Noah and those of Abraham and Moses. I'm not as convinced of the veracity of that as you would be, because the Qur'an clearly deals with various subjects other than strictly chronologically. But we are finding evidence of why the Qur'an teaches that the Thamudis appeared to be punished by Allah for their practice of idol worship."

"Really?" Qahtani said. "You're going to corroborate *our* holy book now? Surely you haven't found evidence of the earthquake or the lightning blasts the Qur'an mentions."

"No, but some of our findings appear to support the idol worship idea. So that's something that corroborates the Qur'an." Nicole studied Nasim. "I thought that might please you, but it doesn't appear to."

"Ironically it's the reason this site is considered cursed—an image the government would like to overcome for the sake of tourism."

"I see. Well, if we find what I hope to, the Allah punishment angle will be a mere footnote."

Qahtani smiled. "Needless to say, I'm most curious about how that effort is going."

Nicole leafed through more pages. "Your colleague, Dr. Waleed, has outlined a bit of history here well-known to you, how—characteristic of Nabatean rock-cut architecture, as in Petra—the geology here provided the perfect medium for the carving of monuments and settlements with scripts inscribed on their façades. He writes about how the Nabatean kingdom flourished as the crossroad of commerce, monopolizing the trade of incense, myrrh, and spices. Situated on the overland caravan route and connected to the Red Sea, it reached its peak as the major staging post on the main north–south trade route."

"You're stalling, Doctor."

"I'm getting there."

"Finally," Qahtani said, glancing at Detective Chakrabarti, "I get to use one of the favorite phrases I learned during my stay in New York! Cut to the chase."

"All right," Nicole said. "You know many inscriptions unearthed in the early 1960s resulted in Mada'in being proclaimed an archaeological treasure within ten years. But few investigations have been conducted here since."

"Right," Qahtani said. "Not since the late '70s and mid-'80s. I'm sure you know the history of our prohibiting the veneration of artifacts, which really curtailed archaeological activities until this century, when we started inviting expeditions like yours as part of a push to promote cultural heritage protection and tourism. And you, dear dig leader, are still stalling."

"Guilty."

"Find something you'd rather I not know about? Because you know I'll get to the bottom of it anyway."

"Oh, believe me, I have no intention of trying to hide anything from you. I've been transparent from the beginning regarding what I hope to find here. And I'm finding it. We've uncovered many not easily deciphered inscriptions."

Dr. Qahtani seemed to perk up. "You know this is the twentieth anniversary of the opening of our museum in Riyadh. I'd love to update my Mada'in exhibit. Nothing has been added in years, and it didn't have a lot of pieces to begin with."

"Of course all this stuff ultimately belongs to Saudi Arabia anyway," Nicole said. "So in the end you'll have your choice."

"But you're not saying that's all you've found so far."

"No, I'm not."

"If I may interrupt," Pranav said. "Might we be able to visit your museum soon?"

For the first time since she'd met him, Nasim Qahtani proved less than glib. "Well, certainly," he said. "Yes, of course. But, ah, I would want some time to prepare for guests of your stature."

"You're not open to visitors daily?" Pranav said.

"Naturally, but we also have some renovation going on in more than one wing, and I would want the place to be in perfect shape before—"

"Don't go to any trouble on our account, Doctor," Nicole said. "Consider us friends."

"I do! I'll arrange an official invitation for you through the Saudi National Commission for Education, Culture, and Science. But meanwhile, tell me more. I need to get going soon."

Nicole found at the bottom of her stack of papers a computer-generated printout of a photo. "Let me show you something very special—and extremely rare."

CHAPTER 30

Shinar, Ur

Had Terah expected to feel a lightening of his burden of guilt after having fulfilled God's requirement of confessing to all those he'd so dreadfully ruined, he was mistaken. He wanted to embrace Zavian and Abilsin upon leaving, but he knew his very revelation had injured them anew—and perhaps for the worse. All he could do was hang his head, quietly thank them, and venture out. Terah found it impossible to push from his mind's eye Abilsin's scowl. He appreciated the man's honesty and was not surprised to know he had never liked him. Terah had sensed that but attributed it to the inherent jealousy among the king's inner circle.

Terah gingerly fingered the reins of the unfamiliar steed, realizing that the horse was not used to him either. But they quickly fell into rhythm and seemed to cover the two miles from Zavian's home to the servant settlement in no time. As Terah flew past there, Wedum came barreling out in Terah's government chariot behind Terah's old horse. Yadidatum sat in a back corner, wrapped in her shawl and wedged in by overflowing baskets.

Terah slowed and waved as they passed him going the other way, and shouted, "Godspeed and good luck!" But neither Wedum nor Yadidatum even glanced his way.

Terah was but a half mile from his house but sensed he was not to stop there. God seemed to impress upon him to get to the cave where Belessunu and Abram had lived for ten years. "What am I to find there, Lord?"

Silence.

Not this again! "Have I not done everything you required of me? I'm grateful for the renewed strength, but hunger has overtaken me."

Silence.

Thundering hooves behind him made Terah wrench around. And so it had begun. Illuminated by the moonlight came a king's brigade, six colossal purebred stallions, each pulling a two-man chariot. They would have been assigned a singular mission—to find him and drag him back to Nimrod. There he would be tortured until he revealed the whereabouts of his son, whom the king's own stargazers had prophesied would cost him his throne.

Terah resolved to remain silent, come what may, resting in God's promise that Abram was to become an exalted father. King Nimrod or Amraphel, or whatever he deigned to call himself these days, could put him to death for all Terah cared. But he would never give up his beloved son.

Outrunning this contingent representing the crown was futile, so Terah pulled the reins taut and leaned back with all his weight, tugging the horse to the side of the road to await his fate. He leaned against the rim of the chariot to face the dozen armed men. They blew past without so much as a glance in his direction. "Lord, what am I to do? Following them does not seem wise, but it's the only way to the cave..."

Silence.

"Please, God. I must know what You want me to do!"

"I have spoken."

With no choice but to obey, Terah felt grateful at least that he had heard from God again.

CHAPTER 31

Mada'in

The photo Nicole turned for Dr. Nasim Qahtani to see made him stand and bend close to it. Detective Pranav Chakrabarti had to rise to peek over the man's shoulder.

"This *is* a new inscription," Qahtani said. "Where did you find this?"

"It's all documented here. But this might show you why I'm less interested in the Nabatean era, which as you know dates from just a couple of centuries BC to a couple centuries AD and represents most of what we see aboveground. I mean, it's beautiful and fascinating, and you're right to invite the world to tour here and see it—it's so Petra-like. But I'm more interested in the much older, deeper layer that dates from the end of the third millennium BC to the beginning of the second."

"Abraham's time?" Detective Chakrabarti said.

Dr. Qahtani stiffened, but Nicole nodded. "Most biblical scholars date Abraham to about 2000 BC, give or take a century. I'm interested specifically in his descendants through both Isaac and Ishmael."

Dr. Qahtani and Detective Chakrabarti sat back down. "So you are open-minded enough to study both Abraham's Jewish *and* Arab descendants," Qahtani said.

"Of course."

"You link Abraham to this very site?" Pranav said.

She nodded. "Because of the inscription I just showed you. We found it here, but it corresponds to inscriptions on the Ebla Tablets."

"You *think* it does," Qahtani said. "Can you read Eblaite?"

"I'm lost," Chakrabarti said. "Define Eblaite."

Dr. Qahtani said, "It's just the modern name for the ancient Semitic language on the Ebla Tablets."

"Ebla is in Syria," Nicole said. "Tablets there date from about 2200 BC to 1200 BC. The text was pressed onto clay and then baked hard as stone—fortunate for us, because they survived in the ground for thousands of years."

"I knew you were brilliant, Dr. Berman," Qahtani said. "But I'd be really impressed if you know Eblaite."

"I'm not as proficient in it as I'd like to be, but I studied it."

"How many languages do you know?" Detective Chakrabarti said.

"Besides English and Eblaite, five. I wouldn't say I could carry on a conversation in all of them, but I can read and understand enough from them that it's helpful to my work. My main academic interests were archaeology and Semitic languages."

"Just curious," Dr. Qahtani said, "but what languages?"

"Ugaritic, Sumerian, Egyptian, Aramaic, and Hebrew."

"No idea what those first two even are," Pranav said.

"Don't feel bad," Nasim said. "This is my life and I'm not versed in most of those. Eblaite is particularly tough—most translations are just guesses. Jewish and Christian fundamentalists claim the Ebla Tablets prove everything their Bible says about Abraham and the patriarchs. Muslims believe that is overreaching. What do you say, Nic— Dr. Berman?"

Nicole fought a smile. "In other words, how much of a fundamentalist am I?"

"Maybe."

"I believe the Ebla Tablets, along with many other finds, prove that the Genesis record reflects an accurate picture of the world at that time. Our scriptures exhibit verisimilitude."

"Whoa!" Pranav said, throwing up his hands. "Verisi-what? Which language is that?"

"Just a fancy word that means something appears true or real."

"To some," Qahtani said.

"Fair enough," she said. "But you know what I believe. Archaeology and the ancient texts tell me the Bible's stories resemble the realities of the past. Of course I can't say the tablets alone prove the biblical accounts, but they show they're plausible. And of course Christians and Jews and Muslims agree at least that Abraham and the patriarchs were real."

"But back to this," Qahtani pointed to the photo on the table. "What do you make of it?"

"One of the Ebla Tablets seems to refer to Abraham in connection with the city of Dedan, which as far as we know was the name of Mada'in Saleh in the second millennium BC. Some think the name Ishmael is also found in the Ebla Tablets."

"You could be an American politician, Doctor," Qahtani said, "the way you evade straight questions. I want to know what you're showing me right here, right now."

"Another tablet actually refers to Ur of the Chaldees, the very location, according to the Bible, from which Abraham and Sarah emigrated."

"There you go again! Stop referring back to the Ebla Tablets and tell me what you've found here. You requested permission to dig in a specific location, and I want to know how you knew precisely where."

"Come on, Nasim. You've done enough homework on me to know that I'd dug here before. I spent weeks viewing every location, examining the monuments, the carvings, inscriptions, everything. You really want me to bore you with my dig strategy or why I find this inscription so important?"

"I think you know the answer to that. Tell me so I can be on my way."

Nicole sat back and sighed. "All right." She dug out her laptop.

"What are we looking at?" Qahtani said.

Nicole found the file and after a few mouse clicks swung the computer around so both Qahtani and Chakrabarti could see it. "This first shot is an aerial my techie took by drone. It gives you a feel for the layout of our whole site, especially in relation to the cliff along the north boundary. See the top of the cliff?" She paused the video on a close-up.

"A pedestal," Pranav said. "I'm no expert, but—"

"A large one," Dr. Qahtani said. "I've never seen a mention of that in reports from this site."

"Nor had I," Nicole said. "But this may be evidence of a statue that once stood atop that cliff."

Qahtani held up a finger. "What's your guess, Dr. Berman? Nabatean or earlier?"

"I don't want to guess, Nasim. I want evidence. And of course you know what I'm hoping for."

"That it's from the time of Abraham. Maybe even a statue of Abraham himself."

"Of course. Our priority now is to search for fragments of such a statue among the tumble we're clearing."

"Careful stratigraphy should help date the fragments," Qahtani said.

"Stra-what?" Pranav said.

Nicole said, "Stratigraphy. The study of the strata we uncover with each layer of earth as we dig. Each layer gives us an idea what period it's from."

The detective nodded. "So fragments that appear to be from that pedestal could tell you when it fell?"

Nicole nodded, but Qahtani broke in. "This is way more than I expected. Find enough pieces and you might be able to date it based on sculpture typology."

Pranav looked puzzled again.

"Sculpting was different in different eras," Nicole said. "As were forms of writing. That can tell us a lot."

"Okay," Qahtani said, "level with me. Have you found any of this alleged statue yet? A single piece?"

"Not a trace."

"So you're just dreaming, hoping, jumping to conclusions. That's so American of you."

"But here's what I believe, Nasim. We're going to find fragments deep. Very deep. And the deeper we find it, the older it's likely to be. Maybe even as old as the paleo-Aramaic inscriptions."

"Can't those ground-penetrating thingies your team uses help?" Pranav said.

Nicole nodded. "They have already. Ground-penetrating radar. We're getting GPR readings that tell us to keep digging."

"Well," Qahtani said, "that's something. Sometimes GPR shows just several feet of plain old dirt, and that's when you know you're done."

Nicole shut her laptop. "We're a long way from done."

CHAPTER 32

Ur

Though confident now in the Lord's protection, still Terah found it difficult to slow his heart. He had fully expected a horrid destiny at the hands of the king's men and the king himself—one he deserved, he knew, if anyone did. But God apparently had His own designs, and so Terah nudged the horse and chariot back onto the road. He remained famished and wondered if he had missed the providence of provision by declining Zavian's generosity. His priority now, however, was not his belly, but somehow overtaking Belessunu and Abram. How he missed them! How far ahead might they be? Why had he acquired for her such a young, healthy camel?

Terah slowed his own stallion to walk as he drew within sight of his home—his former home anyway. Any hint that God might have him stop for sustenance was dashed as the place appeared lit nearly as bright as during the day. The king's men must have lit every candle and lamp. He could hope only that Wedum and Yadidatum had found everything of value before this cadre arrived.

But was it suicide to dream of clip-clopping past, chariot rattling and wheels squeaking on the rocky soil? And when the king's men found nothing here, would they not light out in the very direction he was going? He'd have to traverse a half mile off the road to ensure he was not noticed, but he had grown weak from hunger and prayed God would allow him to rest when he reached the cave. Surely Belessunu would have left furs, blankets, something he could spread on the stone floor. Might she have left food-stuffs that would survive their long absence?

Guiding the horse to the right and through softer, sandier terrain sim-ply struck Terah as too much work. He stayed the course, holding his breath as he passed within feet of his front door, the horse ambling past the wide, empty chariots, beasts nickering in the night.

A hundred feet past his home, Terah clapped the right rein lightly on his horse's flank and went from walking to a gentle trot. This would get him to the cave in less than half an hour. If he stayed the night, he would have to push the horse all the harder in the morning. But a steed could not maintain a canter or faster trot without frequent stops. He hoped to catch Belessunu and Abram before they reached Shem, but camels trav-eled more efficiently than horses.

The refreshment of his soul and body that had come with the snow squall earlier in the day still energized Terah, though hunger gnawed. He was delighted at his ability to stand and pilot the horse—something he had been unable to do for so long in many years. Would God bless him with this renewed strength for his entire journey? He could only hope.

By the time Terah could make out the silhouette of the familiar cave on the horizon, he became aware of wild dogs gathering around him. He was immediately transported to the harrowing experience just before Abram's birth when such animals chased him while he was on foot in this very area and drove him into the cave for the first time. Cut and bruised and very nearly killed, he staggered all the way back home, though it took hours.

In all his trips back here, on foot or on horseback or pulling a cart of supplies, he had never again been accosted. But if these dogs spooked his horse, who knew what might become of it. All he needed now was for his steed to panic or kick at the barking dogs or race in a panic and pitch him out, destroying the chariot.

But the dogs merely ran along with him, four or five on each side. And while they yelped and yipped, he detected no ravenous growls or menacing sounds. The horse paid no attention, just staying at his task, head down and quickly moving. Terah directed him to the mouth of the cave and stopped him, and the dogs stopped too, immediately dropping onto their bellies, almost as if bored.

Still Terah was careful as he disembarked. No sense being careless. Was that light emanating from the cave? Who or what might await him?

CHAPTER 33

Mada'in

"I'll be back tomorrow," Dr. Nasim Qahtani said, standing. "I really must be off."

"Oh, begging your pardon, sir," Detective Chakrabarti said, "but I wondered if I could ask a question or two."

Nasim glanced at his watch and sat back down. "I can spare a minute, always, to educate the curious."

"I was hoping you would grant me a brief audience with Ms. Kayla Mays."

Nicole detected a blanch in Qahtani's visage, rare in a Saudi. "Sorry, who?" he said.

"We both know of whom I am speaking, Doctor," Chakrabarti said. "I am certain you want to avoid an international incident as much as we do…"

Qahtani sighed. "You're speaking of the attractive young Black woman who flirts with me here every time I visit?"

"She phoned you early this morning and you arranged to have her picked up near the other dig site."

The whites of Qahtani's eyes showed. "She told you that? Or have you traced—"

"You don't deny it, then?"

"I suppose that would be foolish," Nasim said. "And it shouldn't surprise me that you would have been able to track her phone. But if you have invaded my priv—"

"You may be rest assured we have not, sir. But I would like to know what justification she used with you to get you to—"

"She lied to me, if you must know."

"How so?"

"She told me Dr. Berman had asked her to do some research at the site. I should have checked with you, Nicole, but I had no reason to doubt her."

"You're not a good liar, Nasim," Nicole said. "Had I sent her, I would have informed you myself, and she would have gone directly there—not needing to rendezvous with you—or someone you designated—elsewhere."

"I did ask an aide to meet her and bring her to me."

"Why not just have the cab bring her there?"

"You Americans are insultingly direct, aren't you?"

"Just as you've been yourself…until now," Nicole said. "I thought you might appreciate that from us."

"Just remember who you're talking to and my role here."

"I'm well aware. But you still need to explain the rather clumsy attempt to hide where Kayla was going."

Nasim sighed. "I was trying to protect her. I couldn't imagine it would be difficult for you to determine where she was."

Detective Chakrabarti smiled. "You thought sending her close to the site but not directly to the site would throw us off her track?"

"It's just that I had an idea what she wanted and hoped to save her some embarrassment."

"Embarrassment is the least of her problems, but what was it you thought she wanted?"

"What she confessed to me."

"Confessed?" Chakrabarti said.

"Her feelings for me. She admitted she had lied about the research and merely wanted to express her desire to get to know me better. I was flattered, but—"

"Please stop this, Nasim," Nicole said. "You're clearly making this up as you go, and it makes no sense. As brilliant an archaeologist and geologist as you are, you're out of your depth in something like this. Just admit that she fled here this morning before dawn and took a cab to where you told her to go. And now you're hiding her from us."

"But why would I do that?"

Pranav said, "She's under suspicion by New York authorities for something that occurred there before she left the States. And we've also discovered that her volunteering for this dig came after two others had been blackmailed into canceling their trips."

"Blackmailed?"

"They and their families threatened."

"I have no idea what you're talking about."

"So you're sticking by your account? She's a star-crossed flirt who's imagined some potential relationship with a dashing Middle Easterner?"

"You find me dashing too, Detective?"

Pranav narrowed his eyes. "What you find humorous, sir, is soon going to spiral wildly out of control."

"The answer to your question is, 'Precisely.'"

"Then where is she? Why wouldn't you have disabused her of her folly and sent her straight back here?"

Nasim appeared to weigh his response. "She's homesick."

"We all are," Nicole said. "So, what, now she wants help getting back to the States?"

His eyes darted. "She's embarrassed, naturally. I was flattered, I told her, but that what she was hoping for was out of the question. Then she begged for help changing her return flight. Yes, she wants to fly back immediately."

"And did you accommodate her?" Pranav said.

"I asked a staffer to help her."

"Why am I not believing this?" the detective said.

"How dare you call me a li—"

"Because if there were a modicum of truth here, sir, you'd have let

Dr. Berman know of this as soon as Kayla revealed it to you. But no, you waited until you were asked and then pretended not to even recognize her name. You're harboring a fugitive, and I think you've known that from the beginning."

"I admit I was trying to protect her."

"To what end?"

"I was embarrassed for her. Clearly she's not happy here. And as I had to let her down easy, I thought it only kind to help her move on without further humiliation."

"And now that you know the truth?"

"I'll follow through with helping her."

"You don't see the political ramifications here?" Pranav said.

"More than you know."

"Then—"

"You said it yourself, Detective. You don't want an international incident any more than we do."

"'We'?"

"I'm anything but an independent agent here."

"Then if there is no solution to this mess, you won't mind telling me if you were aware of Ms. Mays before she left the States in the first place."

"Aware of her? Of course I was."

Detective Chakrabarti stole a glance at Nicole. "We'd still like to talk with her. In person."

CHAPTER 34

Ur

Nine wild dogs lounged near the entrance to the cave. Terah had never seen such beasts in repose. Was God showing him He would go before Terah and protect him all the way? Naturally he couldn't shake the trauma of the attack he had survived ten years before at this very spot. He had endured guttural growling, piercing barks, bared teeth, deep bites. The animals would have killed him had God not spared him. Yet at that time he credited himself and his own pantheon of gods. How insanely shortsighted!

Terah wished his new status before the Lord rendered him courageous. It did not. And his horse seemed no calmer than he. Its eyes showed wide in the light from the cave and the creature skittered in place. But the dogs remained still, lounging with their eyes closed, occasionally lazily opening one. Perhaps God had placed them here to ward off other threats. Myriad dangers lurked in the darkness of the desert.

Terah looked for somewhere to secure the reins. The last thing he needed was for this horse to bolt away with the chariot. Finding nothing, he used a trick he had learned once from his old friend Ikuppi. He tugged the animal until it was forced to turn back toward the chariot, then he wrapped the ends of the reins around the left axle. The horse would not know it had not been tethered to something stationary.

Still fearful of what he might find in the cave, Terah bent to heft a jagged rock. What he might do with it he had no idea, but it seemed better than nothing. The light from inside made no sense.

He crept in to find Belessunu's characteristic neatness—furs and blankets stacked neatly against the wall that led to the inner partitions where she and Abram slept and ate. But surely she would not have left lamps burning—and he didn't recall her having so many. Some were affixed to the wall, others lined the floor. As he moved through the alcove where she baked bread and conjured pottages that amazed him, considering her meager resources, again he found she had left everything in its place. What had he done, relegating his wife and his only son to such an existence?

His steps echoed, telling him it was unlikely anyone else was present. But if Belessunu had not left these lamps burning—and she couldn't have, for their oil would have been consumed long before—who had? Was someone already using this place, and would they soon return? What was he to do if they did?

Terah had supplied the eating area with a table and three chairs, just in case Belessunu ever invited him to join her and the boy for a meal—which she had done only twice in a decade. Usually his chair sat off to the side while Abram's and hers were placed at the meager table. Now he found the opposite. His was the only chair at the table, which bore a steaming pot. He found it too hot to touch. Next to it lay a cloth, a jug of wine, a loaf of bread, a plate, and a spoon.

Someone had to be nearby!

Terah tiptoed back to the mouth of the cave and peered out, listening for even the faintest footstep, an animal, anything.

"Return and eat," God said.

"This is from You?" Terah said.

"Those who seek the Lord lack no good thing. I satisfy you with good so your youth is renewed like the eagle's."

So that was what he felt in the cattle pen when the wind and snow had swept through, seeming to purify everything! His strength had been renewed. In fact, he had not felt such vigor for years.

Terah hurried to the table and bowed his head. "Blessed are You, Lord my God, king of the universe, Who brings forth bread from the earth and creates the fruit of the vine." He used the cloth to remove the lid from the pot, releasing the aroma of a stew so rich in vegetables and meat that he could barely contain himself. He scooped a huge portion onto his plate, poured himself a cup of wine, and tore a chunk of bread from the loaf. Given his hunger and knowing this was a feast provided by God Himself, Terah filled himself with a repast so perfectly blended and seasoned he was sure it could never be equaled, regardless how long he lived. And he hoped that would be long enough to see Abram grown to manhood. He delighted himself in the promise of God about his son. It might be ten more years before Abram became a father and he a grandfather, but who knew? Maybe even Terah himself would father more children.

"Now rest," God told him. "For tomorrow you sojourn."

Terah spread furs and a blanket on Belessunu's cot, doused the lamps, removed his sandals, and lay on his back. Somehow the chill from outside did not reach him. He rolled onto his side, as exhausted as he could remember. He pulled the blanket and a thick fur to his neck, closed his eyes, and within seconds slept the sleep of the dead.

CHAPTER 35

Mada'in

"I'll check with my superiors," Dr. Nasim Qahtani said. "But I can assure you, if we grant you an audience with Ms. Mays, she will have the complete support of the Saudi government."

"Meaning?" Nicole said.

"Meaning I would be present, along with an attorney for her. You would have no physical contact with her, and everything would be recorded."

Pranav shrugged. "So you're determined to make this as difficult as possible for both governments?"

"No, only for yours."

"I'm no independent agent either, Dr. Qahtani," Pranav said. "I have to check in with my superiors too, and you know the NYPD will be seeking the counsel of the U.S. Department of Justice's Office of International Affairs."

Qahtani snorted. "You might as well save their time and trouble. Any extradition request will be denied."

"So in truth you have no one helping Kayla arrange a flight back to the States…"

"Knowing what awaits her there? No."

"Tell me," Nicole said. "Is Samir aware of all this?"

"What would be your guess?" Qahtani shook his head. "You don't really think we'd keep him in the dark on something like this..."

Oh, no. "All right," she said, clearing her throat. "It appears all the cards are on the table. You've been more than forthright with me from the beginning about what I can expect from your government here. I did not, however, anticipate subversion from my own codirector. I can't say it surprises me that he'd share your views about the impact of my finds upon Islam. So what would your counsel be? Do I keep him on, remain transparent with him as I have been with you? Dare I trust him with my research?"

Qahtani's smirk rattled Nicole.

"I have to tell you, Nasim, that you find this humorous astounds me. I feel like we're playing a very reckless, dangerous game here with potentially explosive consequences."

"Forgive me, Nicole. I don't discount that in any way. But yes, I have to say I find laughable the suggestion that your findings here might have some impact on Islam, a religion only a few hundred years younger than your own. And I'm saying this—as I've made clear to you—as very nearly an outsider. But I don't need to be a rabid devotee to believe that even if you were to find evidence that would undermine Muslim leverage over Israel or even strengthen Jewish claims to a so-called Promised Land, you will never be more than a footnote in the vast history of opponents to Islam."

"So you don't even want to know the truth."

"Oh, I do. But even a *ghair-muqallid* like me cannot deny that Islam is the fastest-growing religion in the world, destined to easily usurp Christianity as the largest within forty years. Judeo-Christians, as you like to refer to yourselves, are on the decline."

"That may be," Nicole said. "But even to an unaffiliated Sunni, facts are facts and truth is truth. Back to my question. What am I to do with Samir Waleed?"

"Interesting you should ask. Few here could believe you chose him over your own father. We know it was a political move you believed would help your application, but…"

"Ironically, Samir was my father's idea. We agreed his name would look better on my prospectus because I was already facing charges of nepotism. How would it have looked to list my father as codirector?"

"Your father is revered here. It would have been a testament to his character."

"Maybe it's not too late for me to replace Dr. Waleed with him."

"Frankly, I think that would be wise. When the Saudi government discredits your findings, I'm sure they'd just as soon not besmirch the reputation of the renowned Dr. Waleed—one of their own."

"So much for their reverence for Dad."

"That's his risk, yes. And the almost certain result."

Pranav stood, staring at his phone. He looked stricken.

"Problem?" Nicole said.

"Well, ah—I'd better take this. Pardon me." He turned to Dr. Qahtani. "If you must leave before I return, just know that Dr. Berman and I want to speak with Ms. Mays as soon as it can be arranged."

"I'll see what I can do," Qahtani said. "If it happens, it will come with many conditions."

Nicole had not seen Pranav so exercised and could hardly wait to find out what was going on. She found it disconcerting to suddenly be alone with Nasim Qahtani, especially with the way he looked at her. If she didn't know better, it appeared he was leering. She began stacking and packing her materials.

"And here I thought we might actually become friends," he said.

"Did you?"

"Didn't you?"

"Cordial acquaintances, maybe," she said. "But we're worlds apart. And knowing what I know now…"

"And what is that?"

"Come now, Dr. Qahtani. You have lied to my face, claiming you didn't even know Kayla by name, when it turns out you knew of her before she even arrived here."

"I just didn't want to embarrass her."

"Oh, stop with that. You were involved in getting her over here, and then you both pretended zero prior knowledge of each other."

He chuckled. "You can't just chalk that up to a little diplomatic game playing? Aren't both you and I looking for an edge on each other?"

"Frankly, no. I have not deceived you an iota, and that's still my plan. I have nothing to hide and assumed you didn't either. You're good, I'll give you that. The tone you set from the get-go completely took me in. I thought I'd found a Middle Easterner with a dose of American candidness. I bought whatever you were selling."

"That doesn't sound like a compliment."

"It's not. I've found so many of your countrymen to admire, even if we're diametrically opposed when it comes to worldview, politics, religion, you name it. I so hoped you'd prove to be one of those."

"So no chance for us to even be friends?"

Nicole stood with her stuff in her arms. "My faith teaches me not to repay evil for evil and that, if it's possible, to live peaceably with all. But tell me, Nasim, could you call a friend someone who lies to you?"

He seemed to study her. "You must know that I am also versed in your scriptures. The same passage you're quoting tells you not to avenge yourself because vengeance belongs to God."

"You need not worry about vengeance from me," Nicole said. "But no, I don't believe we're destined to be friends."

CHAPTER 36

Ur

Had Terah entertained even a sliver of doubt that the previous night's feast was from God Himself, it vanished in the morning. Just before dawn he ventured out to relieve himself and bathe in a brook. The frigid water refreshed him, and on his way back in he noticed flecks of straw around his horse's mouth. Squinting in the darkness he found a mound of vegetation right where the animal could reach it. The nine wild dogs still lay where they had the night before, eyes closed. Their breathing rhythmic and deep.

Back inside, an aroma from the eating chamber drew him to the table. There sat the pot, re-covered and steaming anew. He lifted the lid to discover a bubbling broth of cheese and fish—a combination he had never tried. Terah eagerly sat, thanked the Lord, and found the meal succulent. As soon as he was satisfied he felt an urging from God to get underway. He folded the fur from his bed, knowing it would serve him well on his long journey, but as he carried it out to the chariot, he found something he had not noticed earlier. Lined neatly on either side of the exit of the cave sat leathern bags stuffed with edibles. He dragged each into the growing light where he found heaping supplies of grain—wheat, barley, beans, chickpeas—and every variety of vegetable grown in the area. The Euphrates-enriched soil had long produced abundant crops of leeks, melons, onions, garlic, lettuce, and cucumbers. In other bags lay stores of fragrant fruits—dates, pomegranates, apricots, plums, figs, apples, grapes, and pears. In others he found pistachios and other nuts, plus herbs and spices.

Terah could lug only one bag at a time to the chariot, where he arranged them just so to keep things from spilling. Were he to run into bandits or marauders, they could be made rich off his supplies alone. But he knew the God who had so richly provided would also shield him from danger.

The question now was how to pace his horse. The animal would pull much more weight than it had the night before, and they had hundreds and hundreds of miles to traverse. It appeared young and healthy, but who knew? Perhaps the Lord had imbued it also with strength beyond its years? Still it seemed prudent to start slow and steady. He laced the reins between his fingers and lightly steered the chariot onto a path that led to the smoother, more evenly packed soil of the trade route. The horse ambled deliberately as the sun rose behind them, prompting Terah to raise his hood to protect his head and neck. He would have to carefully monitor the horse's sweat as the heat grew so he could rest and water him.

But as soon as the chariot settled onto the main route—with not another soul or beast in sight—the horse broke into a trot with no prodding. Alarmed, Terah wondered if it had been spooked, seen a snake, smelled a threat. He spoke to it as soothingly as he could manage and gently pulled back on the reins, but to no avail. So he shouted and yanked, but still the horse clipped steadily along.

No matter what Terah tried, he could not slow the beast. What was he to do? This was no good! It would surely exhaust itself soon and he would be forced to rest it, find it water, losing whatever time he might have otherwise gained on his wife and young son. Terah was no expert equestrian, but anyone knew this was no way to pace a long journey. What would he have to do—apply the brake at this speed and risk upsetting the chariot, drag a foot, yank so hard on the reins that it might hurt the horse?

Something had to be done before this animal spent itself before they had barely gotten underway. Terah pressed his sandals to the front of the chariot, wrapped the ends of the reins around his wrists, held them tight to his chest, and leaned straight back with all his weight. That forced the horse's head back, its nose high, but it slowed not a bit. Terah somehow turned himself all the way around and bent far toward the bountiful food-stuffs he had laded in.

But nothing slowed this horse.

Finally the Lord impressed upon him, "Trust Me."

"This is of You, God? You want us at this speed?"

"Fear not, for I am with you. Do not be dismayed. Others may grow weak and hungry, but those who seek me lack nothing. Behold, I will keep you and will bring you back. I will not leave you until I have done what I have promised."

"Thank You, Lord."

"I alone am God. There is no other Savior."

Terah spread his feet and turned back to face the horse, untangling the reins from his wrists and feathering them with his hands. And as he rocked gently with the swift chariot, he relaxed, neither steering, whipping, nor really even guiding. He let the horse have its way as it trotted north toward the horizon, the great Euphrates to their right.

A couple of hours later, despite a now high and unyielding sun, the wind generated by their speed kept Terah cool and refreshed. It had been ages since he'd been on his feet this long, yet he felt no fatigue, no weakness, no hunger. The horse should have been frothing, his coat drenched with foam, but it too seemed as invigorated as when they had begun.

By midday, the sun bore down harshly and Terah's skin glistened. But he was not profusely sweating as he would usually on a day like this in the cloudless desert. An oasis in the distance would normally have made him eager to stop and drink and eat, to rest in the shade of the rare date palm trees. He felt no such urge, but he was quickly reminded that he was not in charge of this expedition. As the oasis drew near, the horse finally slowed and pulled the chariot under a tree unlike Terah had ever seen. It rose at least a hundred feet, despite that it appeared rooted not next to running water but a small spring.

He had quit wondering how such things could be, knowing this had to be of God. Terah stepped out and bent to drink, finding the water cool enough in the shade to more than satisfy. The horse stepped to the edge of the spring and drank long and deep.

Terah would ordinarily be weak with hunger by this time of day, and the plentiful supplies in the chariot would have drawn him. But he had remained satiated since his bountiful breakfast. He would wait until hunger gnawed, but shouldn't he rest the horse? He'd never seen an animal trot that long or that far in the heat of the desert. Yet it still looked as fresh as it had at dawn. And it appeared eager to continue.

He stepped back into the chariot, and without prompting, the horse sauntered back toward the route and quickly resumed its former pace. How much faster might they be going than Belessunu and Abram and their camel? Or had God bestowed upon Terah's family miraculous speed as well? Terah felt confident it was not his concern.

For weeks, Terah's days repeated themselves. Every night he spread his fur far enough from the trade route so he could remain hidden, and he slept under the stars. The sounds of the desert and relative coolness of the night lulled him to a deep slumber under his blanket. In the morning he bathed in the Euphrates or a nearby spring, cooked his plentiful breakfast, fed and watered his horse, and drove—more precisely rode—the chariot at a trot for twelve hours—stopping only for meals and sleep. Along the way he had come upon and overtaken many other travelers—individuals who walked, groups who pulled carts and wagons, clusters of camel riders, donkeys, other horses. Invariably they shouted at him, some in languages he could not understand. But those who spoke his language pleaded with him to slow his horse, warning him he would run it to death here. And they covered their faces against the dust as he flew by.

Strangely, sojourners coming from the north did not do this. It was as if God had blinded their eyes to him. They neither looked nor covered themselves nor acknowledged him in any way. This was true also of the jackals and wild dogs. He'd seen others attacked and having to fight off the creatures with sticks, swords, knives, arrows, rocks—whatever it took. But the creatures never so much as glanced at him.

As his chariot shambled along, never needing repair, Terah found unimaginable a horse with such stamina. Yet he himself enjoyed the same. Even a half day's trip like this would have exhausted him before his encounter with God in the cattle pen. Now he had the sense he was fast gaining on his wife and son and delighted in believing he would overtake them before they even arrived at the dwelling of Shem.

After having opposed Belessunu's plan to take Abram to see his ancient ancestor, Terah now recognized her wisdom. He himself was ninth in the long generational line from Noah—who had died just two years prior. Shem would by now be 460 years old, despite that much of his more recent progeny were living only about half that long. Terah had never met Noah or Shem and only vaguely recalled his own grandfather and great-grandfather. His father, Nahor, had died a little more than ten years before Abram was born.

He had been told, of course, of his ancestors' devotion to the one true God of creation, but after having long abandoned that idea, Terah had never been interested in traveling to meet them. Until now. Now he was eager to meet a son of Noah, a man who had been on the ark, a man who had for centuries worshiped the Lord God of heaven.

Within a day's journey to his destination, especially at the speed he had been traveling, Terah found a secluded spot for the night and woke at dawn knowing this would be the day—he would either reunite with Belessunu and Abram on the road or he would find them at Shem's home. Wouldn't it be just like God to harmonize the reunion he so longed for?

He hurried through his morning routine, noticing that he had consumed about half the stores of food the Lord had provided so many weeks before. What could this mean? A return trip? He had not considered even that possibility, with King Nimrod lying in wait.

CHAPTER 37

Mada'in

Nasim Qahtani roared off in his Jaguar behind a huge plume of dust.

Her bag stuffed with files, loose sheets, and her laptop, Dr. Nicole Berman headed for Square One to find Samir Waleed three meters into the hole. "Walk with me, Doctor," she said.

The older man followed her up the ladder and to the canopied folding table. Naturally, she was dying to know what had made Detective Pranav Chakrabarti blanch and leave the trailer. And in the distance, there he sat behind the wheel of the Range Rover. Heat waves shimmered off the hood, telling Nicole he had the engine running for the air-conditioning. He was on the phone, and she hoped he wouldn't drive off before telling her what was going on. The dig alone was complicated enough.

As she and Waleed sat at the nondescript white tabletop supported by spindly metal legs and outfitted with cheap, wobbly chairs, she couldn't help but think how strange it was that this had already been the meeting place of so many monumental discussions. But here she was again, an awkward confrontation looming.

"I have an idea what this is about," Dr. Waleed said.

"Do you?"

"From your look and tone and the fact that my colleague Nasim has just come and gone."

"I don't fault you for your loyalties, Salim," she said. "I might have hoped our history—yours and mine—afforded me a little consideration. You couldn't tell me what was going on with Kayla, one of my most trusted people?"

He sighed. "I was not at liberty—"

"Friends are always at liberty," Nicole said. "I would have confided in you if the shoe were on the other foot."

"Perhaps you would have," he said. "And you're right. I should have. I suppose no more harm would have been done."

"Tell me this, Samir. Did you too know Ms. Mays's true role here before we even arrived?"

He shook his head. "I was informed only a few days ago. I hope this doesn't mean I'm to be replaced here."

"What else can it mean? Would I not be a fool to have my codirector conspiring against me? Especially if I could replace you with my own father? You know he has as much experience as you do."

Dr. Waleed turned away and stared. "You could do no better than Dr. Berman," he whispered. "But I would be sad."

"Sad? Surely, you can't feel any differently than Dr. Qahtani does about what I'm after here."

He turned back. "Of course the decision is yours, and I will understand either way—truly I will. But I beg of you to hear me out. You have already proven to be a brilliant archaeologist. Naturally I knew that from past digs. But your assessment of the drone evidence and your prescience about what the magnetometers are revealing has been incisive—nothing short of genius. I would hate to lose the opportunity to continue working with you and learning from you."

"I have nothing to teach you, Samir, though I appreciate the sentiment."

"You have already taught me much, Dr. Nicole! Now let me make you a pledge. I want you to know that, should you find your way clear to keep me on, I will hide nothing more from you and will represent everything we find in the most honorable way possible, come what may. I cannot deny that it may not be what our government, or any Saudi Muslim, wants revealed. And neither will I pretend it convinces me of anything that violates my own beliefs. But I will treat it with the dignity that any honest, scholarly pursuit deserves."

Nicole was impressed, moved by his openness. It was the kind of candor she'd hoped for from Nasim Qahtani—and thought she'd seen until he initially denied even recognizing Kayla Mays's name. "You must have uncovered something, Samir."

"You see? Brilliant."

"You're most persuasive," Nicole said. "Tell me everything and I pledge to keep an open mind."

"About keeping me on?"

She hesitated. "Yes."

He pulled a pen from his pocket. "Lend me a blank sheet?" She dug one out and he immediately set to work, sketching the layers they had uncovered already. "Just this morning, not long before you fetched me, the magnetometer was giving us readings all over the map. We had already started processing the last three inches or so—and I have to say Suzie and your Square One volunteers are delightful! While moving the stuff that survived the dry sifting operation to the wet sifting area, they were teasing about all the souvenirs they planned to take with them. But of course they know better. I reminded them, 'Jewels, coins, gold, whatnot all belongs to the antiquities authority. No finders-keepers.' They assured me they know that you will photograph all these items, catalogue them, document them, write about them, but that's all."

"We've been finding and processing that kind of stuff for several days now, Samir. What has you so excited today?"

He smiled. "What most excites any archaeologist—gets talked about, written about it, causes theories to be challenged, new interpretations proposed?"

"You're not saying…"

"I am. Text. Find an interesting inscription and people talk about it for decades, maybe longer."

"Enough teasing," Nicole said. "What have you uncovered?"

"I'm sure you know," he said, "that in the later Islamic period this place was known as Al-Ḥijr."

"Or Hegra?" Nicole said. "Stony Place?"

"Exactly," he said, showing her photos on his phone. "My hope is that in removing the debris and tumble, we will find much better protected and therefore much more legible writing from the face of the cliff. Do you see those curious designs near the bottom?"

She squinted. "Barely visible. Remains of paleo-Aramaic writing?"

"Everything I'm seeing suggests typology dating to about 2000 BC."

Nicole could barely find her voice. "Could we be near a temple or a mausoleum? Imagine the artifacts!"

"Priceless," Samir said. "If there was trade between Ebla and Dedan, there might have been treaties too. Names of important people. Names of gods."

Nicole had dreamed of finding something here dating to the Abrahamic period. "Have you been able to decipher any of the text?"

"Look here. I made out a few letters here and there, but only two complete words."

bny mwt

Nicole reeled back in her chair. "'Stones of death'?"

Dr. Waleed nodded. "Could refer to a tomb, probably right below the inscription itself."

"I'm about to hyperventilate," Nicole said. "Could this site be a royal necropolis?"

"Radar should confirm it. If ruins lie beneath the tumble, imagine what we should be able to see. But there's more. A paleo-Aramaic inscription."

"You're not serious!"

"I am. And I have cleared enough debris to the right of the find to be sure we are at the beginning of the inscription."

"Show me!" she said, standing.

"I was about to when you made me follow you here."

As they hurried back to Square One Nicole waved at Pranav in the Rover. He didn't appear to see her, so she texted him.

camera to sq 1 asap

CHAPTER 38

Outside Salem, Canaan

For several days, Terah had squinted and leaned forward at any dot on the horizon, any hint of another band of travelers upon which he might gain. Would it be, could it be, Belessunu and Abram and their camel? He stared intently, hoping to bring into view a tall, sturdy woman, a boy a little more than half her height, and a beast of burden. Might one or both be riding the camel? Surely they had to occasionally to conserve their strength that way.

How foolish Terah felt for letting them go without him! He should have known he would fret over them and pray for them, seemingly every minute. He missed them so, worried for their safety. He hated the man he had been for so many years. What would they think of him now? It would all gush from him, the whole story, and he could only dream his wife might hear and understand—and forgive.

And what of the boy? Terah knew him well enough by now—despite their estrangement—to know the lad had a keen mind and a deep devotion to God. Or at least devotion to his mother, whose faith had never wavered. Terah could not fathom returning Abram to anywhere near the evil Nimrod, who now insisted he be referred to as King Amraphel and considered himself equal to any of the gods in the vast panoply of deities his subjects were expected—no, commanded—to worship. What lunacy!

The once valiant and legendary warrior manifested no more divinity than the blind, deaf, and speechless chunks of wood and stone Terah had wasted so much of his life fashioning into idols.

But if the one true and living God of heaven guided Terah and his family back to Ur at the end of all this, who was Terah to argue? The Lord had proven Himself over and over—on this trip alone—leaving Terah no defense to remain such an undeserving excuse for a man. God had forgiven him, that was clear from His protection and all the provisions. The One who had promised a decade before that Terah's firstborn would become an exalted father could surely be trusted to shield him—and his parents—from a wicked king.

Terah began passing more and more travelers from both directions as he drew nearer to Canaan, but he was disappointed each time to find they were all strangers. When the sun reached directly overhead, his horse slowed to a steady walk and an oasis came into view. Though Terah was eager to keep going, wanting not even one more delay, he had learned to trust God. Unfortunately, as the horse strode toward a small cluster of palms near a spring, Terah realized he would not have the place to himself as usual. Four other groups had spread out, feeding, watering, and resting their animals and themselves.

Terah took his turn doing the same with his horse and then sat to eat with his back pressed against one of the trees. He looked up with a start when small dirty toes in worn sandals appeared before him. "Father?"

He leapt to his feet, dropping his food. "Abram! Abram!" He embraced the boy. "How I've missed you!"

"I've missed you too, but I almost didn't recognize you. You look so—different." Abram leaned back from the embrace, seeming to assess Terah. "You look younger! And you have come all this way…"

"I'll tell you all about it," Terah said, "but first—"

He scanned the area for Belessunu and found her with her back to him, on hands and knees, drinking from the spring. Terah held a finger to his lips and winked at Abram, slipping behind her. He affected a strange, low voice. "Pardon me, madam, but that water may not be good."

Belessunu responded without turning. "Animals do not drink bad water, sir. If it's good enough for them—but thank you."

"Mother! Look who it is!"

She turned and paled. "Terah?" she whispered. "Is it really you? What are you doing here?"

"Belessunu," he said, with more affection than he had felt in years.

"I don't understand," she said. "You look—"

"I know!" Abram said. "Doesn't he?"

"What's happened to you?" she rasped.

"Come, come," he said, leading them to the other side of the spring where they could be alone. "Sit and I'll tell you the whole story."

For more than an hour, Terah spoke, leaving out nothing. He told them of the murders Nimrod orchestrated on the tower, how the Lord had spoken to him, urging him to call out the king and flee before having to worship the dastardly man. He recounted the depth of his guilt, his shame, and all the Lord had required of him. The miracle at the cattle pen clearly most fascinated Abram and made Belessunu weep. "I—we, we've prayed for this for so long, Terah!"

Eventually he told her he had given away all his possessions but that he felt God might be leading them back to Ur. "That may make no sense to us now, but—"

"But God will provide, Terah. I know he will. And there is much I must tell you, but not in front of the boy. And I want to get to your ancestor Shem."

Terah asked if Abram had learned to ride the camel.

"Of course!"

"Then let's let your mother ride with me so we can talk, and you lead the way."

The camel proved not to have been imbued with speed as had the horse, but now the horse only ambled along behind it anyway.

"I need to tell you that as overwhelmed as I am by all this," Belessunu said, "I cannot say it is a total surprise."

"What do you mean?"

"Oh, I did not expect to see you on this trip and I had no idea what to expect if we were to make our way back to the cave. But I knew I was supposed to return. And I knew something would happen to you."

"How?"

"I have not told Abram this, but the Lord spoke to me."

"He always has. And not just to you, but also through you."

"Perhaps He won't need to do that again, since He is now speaking directly to you. But you need to know what He told me."

"Pray tell."

"That we are to have two more sons."

"Oh, surely not!" Terah blurted. More offspring at their ages? Impossible! Their having a son a decade before was just short of miraculous.

Belessunu looked sharply at him. "Be careful about opposing the will of the Almighty. He's never wrong."

"But we are both much older. Didn't you find this hard to believe?"

"I was overwhelmed. Was I in wonder? Of course I was! Yet I have learned that God does what God says."

"But two more sons *and* we are to return to Ur? Do you think the Lord will slay King Nimrod before we get back?"

"I don't pretend to know His plans, Terah. But I trust Him, for He has told me He is with me and will keep me wherever I go. He said, 'I will not leave you.'"

CHAPTER 39

Mada'in

Nicole could barely contain herself as she followed Samir Waleed down into Square One.

"We'd found a few Nabatean-era coins and pieces of iron," he said, "but nothing older than that. Until now."

She squinted in the artificial light, running her fingers along a lengthy block of porous brick. "Dressed stone?"

Dr. Waleed squatted. "It is. And what do you make of these?"

"Collapsed walls. And what? At least two chambers?"

"I'm guessing three," he said. "Now I need your opinion on this—and naturally we have a lot of analysis ahead of us, but the typology suggests vaults."

"Burial vaults?"

"We don't want to get ahead of ourselves, Dr. Nicole. But they very well could be."

"And of course you're taking soil samples."

"Already submitted for analysis."

"Astounding, Dr. Waleed. But you mentioned text."

He pointed his light just beyond the collapsed walls to a well-protected, north-oriented portion. "An inscription. Enough there to translate."

Nicole leaned in but turned at someone descending the ladder. "Pranav, good! We need a shot of this."

"I must talk with you privately," he said.

"This first, please. And perform whatever magic you need to give me high contrast. Readability is everything until we can get this out of here."

The detective shot from several angles, changing his settings each time. He turned the back of the camera to Nicole and Samir and scrolled through the results. "Tell me when to stop," he said.

"Right there!" Nicole said. "Just what I need." He handed her the camera. "May I borrow your shoulder?" she said, and steadied the camera body on him, peering intently at the image. She handed the camera back to Pranav and studied the actual inscription again. "Samir, are you reading what I'm reading?"

"I'm not as astute with the language as you are, but I think so."

"Is it possible this is actually a blessing from Abraham to his sons?"

"It's certainly a father's blessing, Dr. Nicole, but we had better be very sure what we're talking about if we're going to attribute it to Abraham."

"Oh, I know. Pranav, get that image to me and secure it on your device at all costs. Dr. Waleed, needless to say, you and I will be right here working on this until we know exactly what we have."

He nodded. "And what do you supposed caused the collapsed walls?"

"The statue?" she said.

"We'll soon find out."

Pranav headed for the ladder. "I can tell that whatever you've found here is monumental—"

"Potentially," Nicole said. "Keep it between us for now."

"Of course, but as soon as you're able—"

"I'll be right up."

It was back to the rickety plastic table for Nicole where she could speak privately with Pranav. Every fiber of her being longed to get back down into Square One to determine if she really had anything or was kidding herself. But when an archaeologist with the pedigree of Dr. Samir Waleed—with every reason in the world to keep from her such a find—agrees they might be onto something, well…

Pranav pulled out a chair for her.

"I prefer to stand, Detective. Just tell me."

"You'll want to sit, Nicole."

That he referred to her by only her first name alarmed her, it was so unlike him. Still, she stood. "Please, Pranav. I have so much on my plate."

"And I hate to add more, but you must tread very cautiously."

"I've been tiptoeing since I arrived in-country. What now?"

"Among all the other things I've been tracking down and trying to arrange, you know I was double-checking all the volunteer applications, just to make sure Ms. Mays is the only suspicious—"

"Right."

"You're not going to want to hear this."

"Oh, no. Who?"

"I'm afraid Max is not who he claims to be."

"I know that, Pranav. His real name is Rith Sang. He just goes by Max to make it easier for westerners to—"

"It's more than that, Nicole. He's not Rith Sang either."

Nicole dropped into a chair. "Don't tell me that."

"I'm not claiming any ill motive, but he's here under false pretenses. At least under a false name."

"So who is he?"

"We don't know yet. But we do know that no Rith Sang from Cambodia earned a master's degree from International University in Phnom Phen when he says he did. The home address he listed does not exist. There are Cambodian Rith Sangs, but he's not one of them."

CHAPTER 40

Canaan

Terah had heard that Shem's wife was still alive too, well over three hundred years since the great flood. He imagined her wrapped in a blanket before a cozy fire or reclining somewhere. So he was amazed when the handsome woman strode out from her home barefoot and greeted him and Belessunu and Abram and introduced herself as Naam. "That's my husband's pet name for me, as my real name is too long and needn't be bothered with. Come in, let me wash your feet. Tell me who you are, where're from, and what has brought you to us today."

She led them into the entryway of a spacious house where Terah introduced himself and his wife and son and explained that they were descendants of Shem and Naam. That caused her to throw her head back and laugh. "There once were just eight of us," she said. "Everyone alive is a descendant of one of us!"

"He means directly from your husband's line," Belessunu said. She told Naam their story and why she'd brought Abram to meet Shem.

"He'll be so pleased to meet you, Abram," Naam said. "He's tending the garden, but he'll be in soon. And you've come all the way from Ur of the Chaldees! What a journey it must have been."

Terah sat amazed at the vigor and presence of such an old woman, and he sensed in her both compassion and wisdom. He had planned to tell Shem, if he had the opportunity, the story of his abandoning the faith of his youth and having only recently returned to it. Now it seemed prudent to tell Naam first. As she sat staring into his eyes, he told her all he had told Belessunu. He finished with the story of the horse that seemed never to tire.

Naam shook her head. "The Lord God has surely performed a deep work in you. You are most fortunate that He forgave you and has reconciled you to Himself. We suffered nearly bottomless grief over friends and loved ones who never repented of their sins and were found unworthy to join us on the ark. Shem's own great-grandfather, Methuselah, perished when the rains came, yet Methuselah's father, Enoch, was known widely as a man of God. Had he still been here, he surely would have been found righteous." She turned at the commotion at the back of the house. "Here's Shem now."

Like his wife, Shem proved remarkably spry for a man nearly five hundred years old. The couple's hospitality seemed limitless, especially once Shem had heard the little family's story. Naam fed them and poured them wine and insisted she and Shem had plenty of room for guests for a few days. "We've done this almost daily for years," she said. "You can't imagine the number of people who want to hear of our time on the ark."

"My father was five hundred years old when I was born," Shem said. "Even older when my brothers, Ham and Japheth, were born."

"How old were you when the flood came?" Abram said.

"Nearly a hundred. But don't look so surprised. That was young in those days."

"Mother has told me all she has heard about the great flood and that your father somehow knew it was coming."

"God told him, Abram!" Shem said. "He even told him He had lost patience with His creation and would soon limit human life spans to a hundred and twenty years. My brothers and I were blessed to have a godly father and mother, but the Lord told Him he regretted creating people and was so grieved in His heart that He had decided to destroy everything

He had created—people, animals, and even birds. But He was gracious to my father, whom He called a just man. One thing was certain, our father loved God."

"And God must have loved him!" Abram said.

"Enough to save him and his whole family," Shem said. "He told Father exactly how to construct the ark, what kind of wood to use, how to divide the massive craft into rooms and decks, even how to cover it with tar to make it waterproof. He told him how long and high and wide to make it and even where to put the window and door. He said He would send water to cover the earth and destroy everything. But He established a covenant with Father and told him to go into the ark with our mother, his three sons, and our three wives."

"And animals!" Abram said.

"And birds!" Shem said. "Of all kinds, male and female."

"Two of every sort," Abram said.

"Actually, that's not entirely true. A week before the rains were to come, God also instructed Father to have us take seven each of every clean animal, but two each of animals that were unclean and also seven each of the birds."

"Why seven?"

"Abram, I don't know. Father said the Lord said it was to keep the species alive."

"How did you feed them all?"

"We had to gather and store enough food. For the creatures and for us. That's a lot of mouths to feed."

"Did you know how long you'd be on the ark?"

Shem nodded. "Father told us that God told him He would cause it to rain forty days and forty nights. But we were on board a lot longer than that. And all those animals, bleating, mooing, baaing, chattering, tweeting, roaring, and trumpeting—imagine the noise!"

"What about the smell?"

"Abram!" Belessunu said.

"It's all right," Shem said. "There was that too, and plenty of it. That's when my brothers and I realized why we had been included. Can you envision the work it took to keep up with that? And the worst part was, I began to lose faith."

"Lose faith? Why? God had been speaking to your Father for how long, telling him how to build the ark?"

"Over a hundred years! But the actual building started after my brothers and I were old enough to help. And Father certainly had the faith to keep going. But some days even Ham and Japheth and I wondered if it could really be true and that a flood would eventually come." Shem shook his head and looked away, falling silent. Finally he said, "All the work on that huge ship for all those years, and then the loading of the creatures…" He turned back to face them. "Once we four men and our wives herded in the last of the animals and we were also safe inside, God Himself shut the door."

"How?"

"I do not know the mind of God or how He acts. All I know is that my brothers and I were about to tell Father what kinds of rope we would need to pull the gigantic entrance shut, and it simply closed."

"And it couldn't have been the wind, the storm?"

"No, Abram, that's just it. Clouds had barely begun to form, and they were anything but dark. The wind was calm, and it would have taken a hurricane to even budge a huge door like that. It simply rose and settled into place, slamming shut. It could have been heard for miles."

"That certainly would have been enough for me," Abram said. "What could make you lose faith after that?"

"The smell, the noise, our new home, and hours and hours of feeding animals and mucking out their stalls."

"Didn't you know that would be part of it?"

"Of course, but we also expected the flood, and at first there was no sign of it. I knew what rain clouds looked like, and I always enjoyed a good storm. When I was younger, my mother had to pull me inside the tent and force me to just watch from an opening. So I was looking forward to what I knew was going to be the biggest rain I had ever seen, and for forty days. For one thing, it would prove my father had been right all along. But by evening, already exhausted, yes, I started to wonder. I kept telling myself, *God closed the door! It has to be true.* I was tempted to ask Father what he thought, whether he was worried. But I could tell from his expression, and Mother's too, that they were expectant and resolute. And then the rain began, and I mean rain."

"A big storm," Abram said.

"That doesn't begin to describe it, son," Naam said, clearing bowls and mugs. Belessunu rose to help her, but Naam insisted she stay put. "Let Shem tell you."

"When the sky drew dark, I claimed the spot at the bottom of the window as we all crowded around to watch. Clouds rolled in and covered the entire horizon for as far as we could see. Great winds arose from all directions, seeming to battle each other and make trees bend to the ground. The sky turned black, and my brothers and their wives eventually wandered away from the window. It grew cold and the wind whipped our garments and our hair, and the others complained of not being able to see anything anymore anyway."

"I almost did the same," Naam said. "I'm so glad Shem urged me to stay. I would have missed God's handiwork."

"Yes," Shem said. "The lightning lit our entire field of view every few seconds, so we could see trees and bushes uprooted and flying about. The rain that had started slowly soon became a torrent, sheets pouring from the sky. Already it was the most magnificent storm I had ever seen, and to think it was to continue for forty days and nights thrilled me. But that was not all, not nearly all."

Naam said, "Tell them of the—"

"Just getting to that," Shem said. "The ground opened!"

"The ground?" Abram said.

"Springs gushed forth everywhere, and it seemed more flooding came from below the earth than from above. At least an equal amount. When

God had promised Father He would flood the entire earth, He meant it. And this was how He accomplished it. It was as if all the fountains of the deep rose up and the windows of heaven opened."

"How long did it take for the water to lift the ark?" Abram said.

"Not long! So much water rushed from the ground that the whole ship began to tilt and rock. But just think how heavy the craft must have been with all those animals, not to mention all the lumber that went into building it. The vessel creaked and groaned, but it held fast. We knew we had been freed from the ground when it began to drift, but at first we kept bumping into little knolls and mounds and humps in the earth. We were tossed from one side of the deck to the other, and the animals protested with deafening cries.

"Finally we floated free and saw only hills and mountains on the horizon. Within just a few hours we rose high and the ark glided about. Soon all the high hills under the whole heaven were covered. The sky was so dark for so long, we could not tell day from night and assumed much more time had passed than really had."

"How did you know?"

"We kept guessing when the rain would stop and the water would stop rising. Tonight? Tomorrow? A day from now? Father estimated the waters rose fifteen cubits above the hills, and soon even the mountaintops were covered."

"I would have been sad," Abram said.

"Aah," Naam said. "Sensitive boy. And we were sad. We missed so many friends and relatives and wished they had found grace in the eyes of the Lord. Everything that moved on the earth was killed. Only we in the ark remained."

"What was it like when the rain stopped?" Abram said.

"God brought a mighty wind," Shem said. "The waters began to subside. Father said the fountains of the deep and the windows of heaven also stopped. So he sent out a raven and a dove, which he knew would return unless it found somewhere to land. The dove came back to the ark, so Father reached out and drew her back in. Seven days later he sent her out again, and this time she returned with an olive leaf in her mouth. How we rejoiced! We knew the waters had receded, especially when he sent it out yet another seven days later and it did not return. That told us everything.

"On the one hundred ninetieth day since the rains began, Father found the surface was dry. We had settled on Mount Ararat, and Father told us the Lord had spoken to him yet again, saying, 'Go out and bring with you every living thing so that they may abound and be fruitful and multiply.'

"The first thing we did was to build a huge altar and offer burnt sacrifices to the Lord. It was the most flavorful aroma I had ever enjoyed, so we hoped God was pleased with it too. He must have been, because He impressed upon Father that He would never again curse the ground because of man's sin, even though men's hearts are evil. He would never again destroy every living thing. He also promised that seedtime and harvest, cold and heat, winter and summer, and day and night would never cease."

"You must have been lonely," Abram said, "just you four men and four women."

"We were!" Naam said. "But God blessed us. He told us to be fruitful and multiply, and repopulate the earth. He said that every creature that moves on the earth and all the fish of the sea were given to us and shall be food for us."

"It was wonderful," Shem said. "And we felt a great responsibility to be the new fathers and mothers of everyone who was to come. But God also warned us. We were not to eat the flesh of any animal with its life's blood still in it. And He told us that whoever sheds man's blood, by man shall his blood also be shed, because He had made man in His own image. Then Father raised his face to the sky and beseeched, 'Lord speak to us.' And he did!"

"What did He say?" Abram whispered, eyes wide.

"He set a rainbow in the clouds and said it was a sign of His everlasting covenant with us and with our descendants about never again destroying the earth with a flood."

"What happened next?" Abram said.

"We needed food, so we began farming. Father planted a vineyard, which produced bounties of grapes and wine. But that conjures a painful memory."

"I want to hear it!"

"I'm sure you do. But it's sad."

"I won't tell anyone!"

Shem shook his head and chuckled. "You wouldn't need to. Its consequences are known to this day."

CHAPTER 41

Mada'in

The last thing Nicole wanted was to face Max. Naturally she couldn't say a thing about what Pranav had told her about him, but would her angst show? For what possible reason would he have joined the dig team under an assumed name? Was he somehow in concert with the Saudis?

Nicole forced herself to march directly into the air-conditioned trailer. She had to be able to be around him without arousing suspicion, and if she put this off, she might never accomplish that. Max greeted her warmly, as always, and she fought with everything in her to seem normal, casual. "Just need a spot to camp out and analyze some stuff away from the heat and the others. You know how it is."

"Make yourself at home, Chief," he said. "Making progress?"

"Not as much as I'd like, but yes—slowly but surely."

Nicole immediately felt guilty about deceiving him, then chastised herself. Why should she feel obligated to tell the truth to an interloper, potentially one with an ulterior motive—though she hated even suspecting that. There had to be some reasonable explanation for his ruse, but what? She had grown to care for Max, yet she couldn't allow herself to naïvely dismiss such a threat.

On the other hand, it would prove impossible to keep the discovery of the inscription under wraps for long. Max was sure to hear of it soon, and he'd rightly demand to know why she had misled him, especially after his having made so much noise about hoping Nicole would trust him. And even if Max was working for the other side, until he was exposed and Nicole learned what was going on with him, she had to continue to treat him like one of her inner circle.

Some judge of character I am, she thought. The only remaining member of the team she could trust was Pranav.

"Just teasing!" she blurted as she laid out her papers on the desktop across from Max.

He smiled. "How so?"

"We might be onto something big."

"Do tell," he said. "Isn't this the whole reason you came to this site?"

She nodded and handed him her phone. "Dr. Waleed and the Square One team uncovered that."

He enlarged the image. "Languages are not my thing, you know. Have you been able to make out what it says?"

She took the phone back and studied it. "I need to get down there again and really examine it, but from what I can decipher, it looks like, '—*ham our father blessed his sons and said: "Hear the words of your father, hear them and obey them. May Yah, the Lord God, judge between the two of you…"*'"

Max narrowed his eyes and shook his head. "That's more than huge! It starts with 'ham,' as in 'Abraham'?"

"Well, it certainly could, but I agree with Dr. Waleed that we don't want to jump to conclusions."

"Are you kidding? I'd be breaking out the champagne and shouting this from the rooftops!"

"Well, you need to understand that I'm only guessing at the vowels, so in that first word or word fragment, all we really have are the two consonants, *h* and *m*. So it might have originally been pronounced 'him' or 'hem.'"

"Or even 'hom' or 'hum'?" Max said.

"Less likely, because those would more likely require a third consonant."

"So, bottom line, Dr. Nic—how likely is it that this could be an actual quote from Abraham?"

"You mean more than my wishful thinking? Of course I want it to be what it appears to be, but I'm trying to temper my expectations. Yet I *can* tell you what's really intrigued me, encouraged me. The name of the deity mentioned is *Yah*, the primitive form of *Yahweh*."

"The Hebrew name of God," Max said.

"The God of Abraham, Isaac, and Jacob."

"That sure suggests the first word is 'Abraham,' right?" he said.

"I'd like to believe that," Nicole said. "But to play *advocatus diaboli*, the name *Yah* is also found in non-Jewish Ancient Near Eastern texts."

"You're playing devil's advocate against your own find?"

"I'm just saying that the inclusion of *Yah* is suggestive, not conclusive. *Abraham* is a reasonable inference, but I need confirmation. Get that wrong, and my entire reputation—"

"Is there more to this inscription?" Max said. "Or is that it?"

"I hope there's more, and Samir is convinced there is."

"Can't believe you're in here when you should be down there digging. How can you not be?"

"Oh, I will be soon. There could be even more treasure. If it turns out this inscription was on the base of a statue we think might have tumbled down there, we'll need all hands on deck to uncover one of the greatest finds of all time."

"I'm ready to get out of this office, you know," Max said.

"Meaning?"

"I assume you're getting the metal detectors in there."

"Of course, but we've got a guy for that."

"I know, and I wouldn't have a clue how to use those two-handed thingies and the pistol-type gadget. But I've got all the equipment you need for me to be your surveyor. Satellite connections, GPS, all of it. And you know by now I'm nerdy enough to want to measure everything to the inch."

"Max, you know we've been surveying everything since we broke ground."

"Yeah, but with this discovery and what you hope comes next, you need someone to take that work to the next level."

"And that's you?"

"That's me."

Well, Nicole thought, if it's true that one should keep her friends close and her enemies closer, this was one way to keep an eye on Max. She hated all the more the idea that he could be an opponent. Nothing had made her even suspect that until the news came from Pranav. Max was so helpful, charming, and, she dared concede, attractive. Which was irrelevant to what she was considering, of course. How she hoped his using a pseudonym would prove somehow reasonable, explainable. It simply had to be.

Until she knew why Max was using a phony name or was ready to confront him, Nicole had to treat him as she always had. And that meant taking him up on this offer. Starting tomorrow, she'd maneuver him into the role of surveyor for Square One. Pranav would think she had lost her mind, and maybe she had. But for now, she would still need to trust her gut. It wasn't that Max was incapable of betraying her—but if that were his intention, she wanted him in plain sight.

CHAPTER 42

Canaan

"Still, Shem," Naam said, "you should tell the boy the tale. It could be an important life lesson."

"Very well," Shem said with a sigh. "The water had, as God had told my father it would, destroyed everything on the face of the earth. If we were to survive and start an entirely new generation, we would need food. So Father planted a vineyard and began to farm. It wasn't long before we began to harvest the richest, healthiest grapes any of us had ever seen. The flood had cleansed and enriched the soil, and countless brilliant, cloudless days bathed our crop in sunshine until the grapes were plump and delicious. We ate many as we picked from dawn to dusk, the juice running down our chins! Still we filled storehouses with the fruit.

"We built a wine press and produced gallons and gallons of juice Father stored in a cool grotto for weeks. One morning he called us into the cave so we could sample the first of the fermented wine. Young Abram, let me tell you, it was as if God Himself had been our vintner!"

"As good as the wine you just served us, Naam?" Belessunu said.

"You cannot imagine," the older woman said.

"Japheth compared it to nectar!" Shem said. "And he was right! It tasted like the most fragrant flowers smelled on a summer breeze. We each sampled a small portion and could hardly speak. Father filled a half-gallon jug and Ham cackled, 'That much will render you useless in the fields for the rest of the day!'

"Father laughed and said, 'This is for a feast we and our wives will enjoy tonight. Keep working and I will get them started on baking the bread and roasting the meat. Then I will again join you.'"

"That must have been some feast," Abram said.

"Sadly, it had to wait a few days. My brothers and I returned to the vineyard and split up, reaping more and more of our lush crop until I heard Japheth call out for Ham and me. 'Has Father not returned?' he said. 'I've not seen him.'

"Ham and I looked at each other and shook our heads. 'Perhaps the wives put him to work,' I said. 'I'm sure he'll be along.'

"Ham said, 'I'll go check on him.'

"He soon returned, unable to control his giggling. 'Come, brothers! Come! You must see!'

"I imagined Father in an apron, having been pressed into duty helping the wives, but no. The women were busy at the ovens several yards from Father and Mother's tent. Ham led us to the opening, pressing a finger to his lips. 'Ready?' he said.

"'What?' Japheth said.

"Ham pulled back the flap with a flourish, and as soon as I saw Father's bare legs and the upended wine jar, I knew what had happened. 'Naked!' Ham chortled. 'Passed out! Blind drunk!'

"I elbowed Ham aside and yanked the tent flap closed again. 'Ham!' I cried. 'Do you not fear the Lord your God! We must not see our father's nakedness!'

"Ham doubled over, he laughed so hard. Japheth grabbed a clean garment Mother had draped over the top of the tent to dry, and we laid it over both our shoulders and backed in to cover Father."

"That would have been evil, seeing him, wouldn't it?" Abram said.

"Looking upon another man's nakedness had long been considered most wicked, let alone the nakedness of one's own father," Shem said.

176 | JERRY B. JENKINS

"Father stirred when we pulled the garment up to his neck, and he rose up on his elbows.

"'What happened?' he said. By now Ham was trying to stifle his laughter outside. 'Ham!' Father bellowed. 'Show yourself!'

"Ham entered sheepishly, now looking grave. 'Sorry, Father,' he whispered, 'I—'

"But Father interrupted him and cried, 'Cursed be you and your progeny Canaan! You shall be a servant of servants to your brothers.'

"'Oh, Father, no!' Ham said. 'Please!'

"But Father said, 'Blessed be the Lord God of Shem, and may Ham and your descendants be his servants. And may God increase the fortunes of Japheth so that he may dwell in the prosperous tents of Shem. And may you and your offspring be his servants.'"

"Your brother was cursed by his own father?" Abram said.

"He was, young man. And ever since that day, he has paid the consequences. While Japheth and I have been blessed by the Lord and prospered, Ham and Canaan have greatly suffered. As you mentioned, your own King Nimrod is descended from Ham. And for some reason, despite Father's curse on him, God saw fit to bless Nimrod early on. Perhaps to show him what might have been, God allowed him to become known far and wide as a brave hunter before the Lord. Little surprise he became a king."

"Yet he considers himself divine," Naam said. "Dares to refer to himself as Amraphel and commands worship?"

Belessunu nodded. "And he crows that the tower to the heavens he is building—with Terah as the foreman—not even God could cover it with another flood."

"A dangerous claim," Shem said. "The Lord is likely to strike him dead before he accomplishes such a thing. And you say he is unaware of your opposition to him, Terah? Has no idea?"

"He is unaware, and I need your counsel about what to do. Returning would mean suicide, given what he believes about Abram's threat to the throne."

"And what do you believe about that, Terah? Did not God Himself promise He would build a nation from Abram's loins."

"Yes, but—"

"Then what do you fear? Do you place the cursed Nimrod's threat above the promise of the true and living God?"

Terah hung his head.

"Return, Terah. Face the king. Defy him. God will be with you."

CHAPTER 43

Mada'in, the next day

To Nicole, Detective Pranav Chakrabarti looked more than dubious about Nicole's decision to make Max surveyor of Square One. Pranav appeared stricken. "I told you," he said, "the man is not who he app—"

"I know what you told me, Pranav. But what was I to do? For all I know he would've heard about the find by now, and how would that look?"

"But if he's working for the Saudis, he'll go straight to them and—"

"Pranav! Dr. Waleed is the one who informed me of the discovery! Who do you think he reports to?"

Chakrabarti shrugged. "I'm just finding this hard to manage. My plan was to negotiate a trade—Kayla in exchange for details of what you've found. We want her extradited to face charges, not only for cooperating with the Saudis but, you know—your mother's…"

"But surely they're already aware of what we've found—I mean, Samir uncovered it, after all."

He nodded. "We have a problem, though."

"I'm listening."

"The Saudis don't want you talking with Ms. Mays."

"Why not? She's here under my auspices and—"

"You know better than that, Nicole. She's under asylum with the government here now. They call the shots. My guess is that she's desperate to talk with you too, to deny any involvement in your mother's death. And as for her involvement with Dr. Qahtani, I can't imagine she's a veteran, some kind of double agent."

"Of course she's not."

"I'm sure they fear you might have some power of persuasion over her."

"They're right, Pranav! Why else would I want to talk with her? I want her to come to her senses and extricate herself from this mess before—"

"She's already in pretty deep, ma'am. Who knows what she's revealed to a foreign power? If anything at all, she's in deep trouble with the U.S. government."

"So, what's next? They'll let you speak with her?"

"They will, but with all kinds of conditions—through glass, their presence, all that. They even have an attorney for her."

"Then shouldn't we have one?"

"The U.S. is assigning me one from the embassy. The question is how much you want my counsel to know about all that's going on here."

"Not much, naturally," Nicole said. "But it wouldn't surprise me if the word is already out. I mean, this is a huge find already, and if we can uncover more tomorrow morning…I know how quickly these things can get out of hand. Pranav, is there no sense in appealing this and seeing if I can come along?"

"None. Done deal. Anyway, I know you. You're going to want to be down in Square One anyway."

"I am. It's going to be hard to concentrate though, I'll tell you that."

"I can only imagine. Somehow you must maintain ownership of this find and not let the Saudis claim credit for it."

"I wouldn't even dream of trying to take it out of the country. It belongs to them and it should. But the discovery? Yes, that's all ours. It's the whole reason we're here."

"And do you have enough security here?" Chakrabarti said.

"Now that a priceless treasure is just several feet from the surface? I trust you, Pranav. And you know I have two locals here from the time we leave each day until the UN gate guards arrive before dawn."

"You trust them?"

"The locals, yes. They go way back with Dad. I mean, they are Muslim, of course, but—"

"What about the UN guys? I've never even seen them leave their shack except to board a bus."

"Yeah, they ignore this site like they couldn't care less."

"Your locals keep any records?" Pranav said.

"They do. I check their log book occasionally. Basically it just tells where each of them was each hour during the night and whether there was any suspicious activity."

"And?"

"They've shooed away some animals now and again—hyraxes, dormice, bats. Can't imagine what they're foraging for here. Our food is all locked away in the refrigerators or freezers."

"But no trespassers?"

She shook her head. "Should I check their log again?"

"Wouldn't hurt," the detective said. "I'm going to bounce off the Department of Justice and the State Department my own caveats for meeting with Ms. Mays."

"Such as?"

"Primarily the freedom to record every word."

"For my sake, if no one else's," Nicole said.

At the end of the day, with Pranav on his errands with the Land Rover, Nicole told the shuttle bus driver to take the rest of the team back to the hotel and that she would find her own way back. She met the local security guys at the gate and strolled with them toward the trailer. "Just checking in," she said. "Anything new?"

"Nothing out of the ordinary," the older one said. He handed her the log book. "You'll see I documented that your tech guy was down in Square One when we arrived here yesterday afternoon."

"Sorry?"

"Assumed that was okay. I put his name in there, right from his badge. He said you and he had discussed his work there. Surveying?"

"Yes, but…"

"A problem?"

"No, I just thought he was on the bus back to the hotel."

"Doesn't the guard make sure that everyone who's checked in in the morning also gets checked out at the end of the day?"

"He does. Thank you."

Nicole headed back up to the UN guard at the gate. "Are you not to inform me when the return manifest differs from the arriving one?"

"I am, ma'am, but your boy said he wanted to surprise you. Said he was getting a head start on a new assignment and wanted to be ready to hit the ground running."

"Did he happen to pay you for this little favor?"

The guard looked away. "Not much."

Nicole phoned Detective Chakrabarti and asked him to come and pick her up.

"Problem?" he said.

"Not on the phone."

She debriefed him on the way back to the hotel.

"We need to be very careful about this," Pranav said. "I'm trained not to jump to conclusions, but—"

"This is kind of a no-brainer…"

"No kidding. Part of me wants to arrest and detain him immediately. But we must find out how deeply he's tied in here."

Nicole sighed. "So I guess confronting him in his room as soon as we get back is out of the question."

"I'm afraid so. For now, just text him and say tomorrow morning's inner circle meeting is off, with Kayla away and me busy and needing the Rover, so you'll see him on the bus."

"But aren't I gonna look like a dunce, pretending not to know he was down in Square One without my permission?"

"Oh, you can confront him about that once you're both on-site. Just don't accuse him of anything. Give him a chance to make up a story. Or, who knows, maybe he *did* have a legitimate reason."

"Fat chance."

CHAPTER 44

Ur of the Chaldees, two months later

Terah led Belessunu and Abram all the way back toward home, despite that he had ceded the entirety of his land, house, property, and money to the former midwife, Yadidatum, and his former servant, Wedum. "You realize what we face," he told his wife as the three of them traded places on the backs of the camel and the horse throughout the long journey.

"Indeed," Belessunu said. "The wrath of King Nimrod and a certain death sentence for all three of us."

"Yet you have not questioned my wisdom."

She smiled. "It has been a long time, husband, since I have thought of you and wisdom at the same time. But I trust in the true and living God and His solemn promises. How can the king harm us when the Lord has vowed to make Abram a father of nations? You have gone from worshiping other gods to believing that Yahweh will perform all He has said."

"That may mean that Abram will be the only one of us to survive," Terah said. "I know not how God will protect us, or even where we will live, how I will provide, or how I will be viewed by others in Shinar."

"I have reason to believe we will all survive, Terah," she said. "Has the Lord not spoken to you?"

"Not specifically. He has just imbued me with peace and confidence. As He has purposed, so shall it stand."

"He has spoken to me," Belessunu said.

"Pray tell."

"He said to 'return to your home and'—"

"But it is no longer ours, love. I bequeathed it to—"

"Hear me, Terah. I said He has spoken to me. Will you believe the Lord your God or will you—?"

"I cannot ask Yadidatum or Wedum to—"

"You shall not have to. God referred to 'your home,' which should tell you something. Either Yadidatum or Wedum chose not to accept what you offered, or they took only what they needed."

"I just cannot imagine—"

"Do not let your faith waver now, love," Belessunu said. "Besides, you know I believe God has promised me more offspring."

"But having Abram at seventy was a miracle in itself. I hate to seem faithless after all the Lord has done, but more offspring after eighty?"

"And not just one."

"You are still saying that, woman?"

"It's not what *I* am saying. It's what the Lord has impressed upon me. You don't think I find it astounding? Or that I look forward to mothering more children now? Frankly, it makes me grateful that you have concubines. But if this is of God, we both know He will provide."

When the little family finally drew within sight of their home, Terah stopped and stared. The place lay encircled by palace chariots. "They will not even let us see whether we can move back in," he said.

Belessunu kept walking, pulling the camel, as Terah walked and Abram rode the ambling steed. "They'll see you!" Terah said.

"Let them," she said. "God has proven Himself to you long before this. I'm eager to see what He does."

"Lord, give me the faith of my wife," Terah whispered.

About a quarter mile from home, a dust plume rose in the distance and a single chariot came racing toward them. A tall young man skidded to a stop. "You are wanted at the palace!" he shouted. "Follow me."

"Do you think I don't recognize you, Iva?" Terah said. "I don't report to you. You report to me."

"You'd be wise to do as you're told, Terah. You report to the king. It was his scouts who discovered your return trip days ago."

"I answer only to God."

"Your king is your god!"

"Not today. We are moving back into our home, and I will meet with the king when I am ready."

"You'll meet with him when *he's* ready," Iva said. "And that's today. Now."

"I trust you will inform him of my response."

"I'm to bring you to him."

"And I'm telling you that is not to be."

Terah noticed hesitation on the young man's part for the first time. "I am under assignment, sir. And the king is not well. The sad truth is that he may not be up to seeing you tomorrow."

"Is that so?"

Iva nodded. "He's being attended to as we speak."

"By azu or ashipu?"

"Ashipu. King Amraphel wants nothing to do with conventional herbal treatments. He insists a deity must be treated by religious medical practitioners."

"What ails him?" Belessunu said.

"I'm not at liberty to—"

"Out with it, man!" Terah said. "Is it serious?"

Iva looked away and spoke softly. "His aides believe an insect has invaded his ear. The buzzing has him in torment."

"That should not be serious and can no doubt be easily remedied."

"He's suffered with it for weeks. They have been unable to extract it. I tell you, he's in agony."

Terah knew the polite response was to say he was sorry to hear that, but he couldn't force himself to. Perhaps this was the judgment of God on the man, and he was grateful such had not been visited on Terah himself when he was at enmity with his Creator. He deserved nothing less.

"Tell the ailing king I will appear at court tomorrow morning with both my wife and my son."

"Terah, sir, have mercy on me. Who knows what the king might do if I fail to complete my assignment? Especially in the state he finds himself."

"I'll put in a good word for you with him in the morning."

"He could execute me tonight!"

"Surely not. But if you're convinced of that, you'll have to take me in chains."

"I'm not going to bind an old man—"

"Then tell him you did everything short of that. If he threatens your life, tell him you'll come for me, and I will go. For now, remove your troops from our home."

CHAPTER 45

Mada'in

Nicole fought to maintain her composure when Max joined her at breakfast in the hotel. While the other team members were mostly subdued, apparently still trying to wake up, he was his usual gregarious self. "Big day for you, eh?" he said.

"Could be. Eager to get in the ground. What do you have going today, Max?"

"Just archiving some documentation—yours and Dr. Waleed's. And of course standing by for when you need me to survey Square One."

An hour later she found him in the trailer.

"Uh-oh," he said. "I can tell from your look, Chief. I've been busted."

"Enough with the 'Chief' stuff, Max. What's going on?"

"Sorry."

"For what?" she said.

"I just wanted to be ready for when you let me down there."

"Great, so now that you've been nosing around, you're ready?"

"Yeah, I think so. I confess I hardly know what I'm looking for, but it seems you and Samir have—"

"It should have seemed like the find of a lifetime, not somewhere you should feel free to go without my permission, let alone without my knowledge."

"Sorry, Nicole, really I am. I didn't mean to upset you. I sincerely thought it would help me get an idea—"

"I haven't been clear about who reports to whom here?"

"I thought you trusted me."

"I thought I could."

"My apologies. Seriously. It won't happen again."

"See that it doesn't."

"May I ask you something else?" he said.

"Depends. What?"

"I understand what I did was wrong, and like I said, I'm sorry. But I have to say this seems like an overreaction. Was it really that egregious? You've allowed me full access to everything else so far."

Nicole caught herself. Would she have been this upset if she hadn't been informed of Max's pseudonym? "Maybe not," she said. "It's just that I'm under a lot of stress, and there'll be no keeping the lid on this discovery."

"I'll do everything I can to help," he said. "You know that. I've proved that. I hope you won't change your mind about having me—"

"No more clandestine forays."

"Deal," he said. "You'll find me nothing but open and cooperative from now on. Promise."

"When it comes to Square One, do what I ask when I ask."

"Got it. You'll let me know when to—"

Nicole's glare stopped him. "You think I'll forget surveying anything and everything we happen to find?"

He raised his hands. "Ignore me," he said.

Suzie Benchford busied the Square One team sifting debris and poring over buckets of finds, and she told Nicole that Dr. Waleed had instructed her to allow only himself and Nicole down into the dig until further notice. "He's waiting for you."

Nicole stored her phone and notepad in her multipocketed vest and strapped on her headlamp and tool belt. But before she reached the ladder, she took a call from Pranav Chakrabarti. She mouthed to Suzie to let Dr. Waleed know she'd be a minute.

"We're all set," Pranav said. "There'll be five of us meeting at a Saudi government building here in Al-'Ula, not far from the hotel: Qahtani, Kayla, her Saudi attorney, my counsel, and me."

He did it. We can get to Kayla. "And you can record?"

"Every word. In fact, my attorney is bringing a recorder so I don't have to rely on my phone—which I may use as backup anyway. Have to say, though, this embassy lawyer seems a little snotty."

"How so?"

"Made some crack about this being his first time in such a high-level diplomatic session and he'd be working with an NYPD cop. Like I don't have a clue."

"He'll learn differently soon enough, Pranav. Keep me posted and wish me luck. I'll be in the ground in a minute."

"Luck? Are you serious?"

"Well, then pray for me."

"You've got it."

Three meters underground, Nicole found Dr. Samir Waleed, feet spread, hand to his chin, his headlamp scanning the partially collapsed walls next to the inscription. "Glad you're here," he said quietly.

"What's got your attention, Doctor?"

"Someone's been here since you and I last were. I hope it was you."

She quickly explained.

"Your IT guy? And he's a surveyor too?"

"Probably more qualified for that than what I have him doing. But he's most capable."

"Dr. Berman, he did more than look around and familiarize himself with our progress. Look at this."

Samir knelt under the inscription and ran his fingers lightly over the ground. "There's fresh tumble here."

"Could it be this area is just less stable than we thought?"

"Maybe, but—"

Oh, Rith. What were you up to here? "But the soil under the inscription felt solid, didn't it?" she said.

"It did. This is not just shifting soil. I can't believe he would have used a tool down here. We can't have amateurs playing in the dirt when—"

"Well, Max is no amateur, Samir, but you're right. He had no business—"

"It doesn't appear he's done any damage, but for the sake of documentation and just how I know you like to do things, I wish he hadn't poked around."

"I'll deal with him. Meanwhile, can we uncover more of the inscription?"

"Certainly. And I'm hoping we can see if we're right about any chambers that may be beneath here."

They both began working, meticulously scraping and brushing until more of the inscription was revealed.

CHAPTER 46

Ur

Terah slept fitfully, imagining every hoofbeat past his home might be Iva, coming for him under an edict from King Nimrod.

Belessunu slumbered peacefully, if her deep, rhythmic breathing was any indication. And when Terah found himself unable to shut his eyes, he peeked through the drape separating their bedroom from the living area where he had fashioned a bed for Abram. The boy was sleeping at home for the first time. The glowing embers in the fireplace seemed to agree with him.

By dawn Terah had slept only a few hours but was eager to get to the palace in Shinar. Having spent years preparing his own meals, he busied himself unloading the remaining foodstuffs from their journey. He built a fire in the stove and began baking bread. While he waited for that, he prepared a mash of vegetables and lentils with a cornucopia of spices and oil, creating a thick sauce to accompany the bread. The aroma of the bread apparently woke Belessunu and Abram, and they padded to the table.

"I had no idea you could cook, Father!" Abram said, digging in after Terah had offered a prayer of thanks.

"I had no choice."

"I'm speechless," Belessunu said, then proved that untrue. "I assumed you found the easiest way to feed yourself all these years. So you haven't been merely consuming raw fruits and vegetables from the marketplace?"

"I have not. I missed your savory meals and began experimenting. I confess I neglected meat for too long, but eventually I taught myself how to butcher and prepare flesh from the cows and pigs and lambs."

Abram had appeared to eat hungrily at first, but soon he slowed and pushed his food around on his plate as if something were on his mind. "Are we sure it's wise that I come with you to court?"

Belessunu shot Terah a glance. "God's ways are beyond our wisdom," she said. "How strong is your faith?"

"I don't know," the boy said. "How will I know until I face true danger? I've never even seen the king who considers me a threat."

"We have not hidden from you the Lord's promises concerning you," Terah said. "You are to become—"

"Forgive me, Father, I know. But He has not spoken to me yet. Will He not speak directly to me if I am to become what you say?"

"You are but a child! He speaks to you through us."

"I might be braver if I heard from Him myself."

"You shall be a better man than I," Terah said. "Many times God spoke to me when I had turned my back on Him, but it made me no more courageous. I became more and more at enmity with Him. To my shame."

"I cannot imagine," Abram said. "You knew it was God and still decided to disobey Him?"

"I didn't want to believe it, but yes, I knew. I wanted my own way. I didn't want anyone else determining my fate."

"You thought you were wiser than God?"

"I thought more of myself than I did of Him. Let me just say I did not dwell on Whom I was dealing with. I was consumed with myself—what I wanted. I have had to repent of that almost as much as anything. And, as you know, I was responsible for the deaths of others—innocents."

Belessunu began picking up the dishes. "That the Lord forgave him and restored him in spite of that speaks to His great love toward His creation. And, Abram, that gives me a confidence I could not find within myself alone to face God's enemy. Without the Lord, I too would be petrified to stand before the king."

"But he sees *me* as a menace to his throne."

"And you may be," she said. "But not now. Not as a child. Whether the Lord will put you on the throne, any throne, is known only to Him. But one thing we know for certain is that your life is not in danger. I don't care what King Nimrod thinks or plans, he cannot interfere with the plans of Almighty God."

"Why don't I feel that courage?"

"I daresay it'll be there when you need it," Belessunu said. "What's the worst he can do to you?"

"Kill me, of course!"

"No, he cannot. You rest under the protection of God most high, because He has promised—decreed—what your future holds. The very fact that we appear before the king with confidence is sure to rattle Nimrod to his core."

To Terah, Abram still appeared ashen as they slowly sojourned into town, he and Abram afoot and Belessunu on horseback. Terah was mostly quiet and at times appeared to shudder. "You won't bolt on me, will you, boy?" he said. "How you conduct yourself today determines a whole new season of life for you."

The lad seemed to force a chuckle. He shook his head. "It won't be easy to face the king, but I fear Mother even more."

Their entrance through the Shinar city gate was met with stares from everyone they passed. Had the entire populace heard what was happening? That only made sense to Terah because of the position he had held for so long. Word had to have spread far and wide—not to mention quickly—from the servants' settlement after Terah had made his rounds of confession. Yadidatum, Wedum, Mutuum, their wives—anyone could have spread this news.

"The family of death!" someone called out, and others whooped and whistled.

So it may seem, Terah thought. *May our experience before the king bring glory only to God Himself.*

CHAPTER 47

Mada'in

Nicole fought to keep from trembling as she worked alongside Dr. Samir Waleed, painstakingly scraping with her trowel and pick, brushing debris from the most monumental find of her life. So far the inscription had read:

> —*ham our father blessed his sons and said: "Hear the words of your father, hear them and obey them. May Yah, the Lord God, judge between the two of you…*

They cleared away two more lines as legible as the first. "Samir, let me shoot this and take a minute to try to decipher it."

The old man holstered his tools and blew the last of the dusty residue off the lettering. Nicole photographed it with her phone and squatted to study it. She recited slowly, just loud enough for Dr. Waleed to hear:

> *…and may he bless me in my old age. May he bless you and multiply you in your days and may your days be long; may you have many sons and daughters;*

"Amazing," Samir said. "Clearly an admonition of some sort. And doesn't it sound like some sort of a deathbed pronouncement?"

Nicole nodded. "A covenant, maybe? I can't wait to see what the father wants the sons to hear and obey."

"But who are they?"

"You know who they are, Samir. I hardly want to voice it before we confirm, but I so want it to be Abraham speaking to his sons."

He smiled. "And you want the sons to be—"

"Don't say their names yet, please. Let's just stay at it."

Nicole found herself even more slow and meticulous this time, and Dr. Waleed seemed to follow suit without another word. More than an hour passed before they had exposed enough more of the inscription that she signaled another break to shoot a picture and peruse the lettering carefully enough to translate it.

…and may you live in this land that he has given to me and you forever. May your land blossom with fruit, may it flow…

"Of course there has to be more," Nicole said.

"I know you don't want to hear this, Dr. Berman, but we reached a jagged edge just before we stopped. I don't believe there is any more, at least here."

Nicole stood and let her headlamp bathe the edge of the inscription. "The rest of it has to be here somewhere." She felt the slightest movement beneath her. Had her boot rolled off a pebble? "Did you feel that, Samir?"

"Feel what?"

"Just felt unstable there for a second."

He shook his head. "You want to bring in some equipment, make sure we're safe?"

"No. We're okay. Can we keep going?"

"I don't know," he said. "If you're right about the statue having plunged here—and I suspect you are—any more of the inscription will be deeper. And if there *are* burial chambers below, we could be talking twice as deep as we are already—maybe more."

"That'll take more people and bigger tools," she said. "But I hate the idea of volunteers hacking away in here. Let's at least see what's beyond the end of what we found. That should give us an idea of what awaits us."

"We won't get much farther with just handpicks," Samir said. "Do you have your walkie-talkie with you?"

"I do. What do we need?"

"Have them lower us a mattock and a tape measure."

"A mattock? Are you sure? I'd hate to—"

"I'm as determined as you are to keep this site pristine, Dr. Berman. You know I'll be careful."

Nicole radioed Suzie while also patting her pockets. "…and I left my tape measure in the trailer. Max will know where it is."

A few minutes later her radio squawked and Suzie told her, "Mattock on its way down. Couldn't find Max and didn't want to poke around in there without permission. I shoulda thought to just send my tape down anyway. On its way too."

Nicole moved to the ladder to watch for the lowering of the black plastic bucket and found herself in a better cell coverage area. Her phone lit with a text from Detective Pranav Chakrabarti:

mtg about to begin; confiscating my phone, but atty
recording; back to you in a few hrs

The bucket proved a bit small for the mattock, but she was able to reach it and guide it to the ground. Nicole pocketed the tape measure and took the digging tool to Samir. If she wasn't mistaken, the ground under where they had been working felt different somehow. Angled perhaps?

"You're braver than I am, Samir. Wielding that thing down here."

"No worries," he said. "I won't be swinging it. I just want to poke through between the bottom of the inscription and the crumbled dressed wall. If I can get a light in there, we'll know whether it's worth seriously digging deeper."

"That's where my surveyor was messing around, isn't it?"

Samir nodded. "Almost makes you wonder if he knew what he was looking for."

"Just be cautious."

"Believe me, I will."

CHAPTER 48

The King's Court, Shinar

Terah suddenly felt his age as he led his little family to the entrance, fingers trembling and knees weak. At his core he had decided to wholly trust God, and he must not show fear before little Abram. He held Belessunu's arm and detected not an iota of hesitation on her part. She seemed eager to get on with this. Oh, for an ounce of her courage!

The lanky, youthful Iva—who had been one of the king's top aides for the past four years—met the three of them. "I have been assigned to escort you in."

Terah was struck that Iva came arrayed in his finest dress uniform, the type reserved for parades and victory pageants. "Big day for you, eh, son?" Terah said. "Expecting a lot of spectators?"

"You'll see."

"And why do we need an escort? I've worked alongside the king since long before you were born. I need not be introduced, and I know every inch of this palace, let alone this court."

"Unlike you," Iva said, "I know to follow orders and not question my superiors—especially King Amraphel."

Terah couldn't stifle a mocking grunt.

"I need not tell you," Iva said, "the etiquette protocol for greeting your king. Your wife and son are to bow and wait at the bottom of the steps to the throne. Then you alone will ascend and—"

"I thought you said you need not tell me," Terah said, smirking.

"—you alone will ascend and kneel at the king's feet. If his feet are exposed, you are to kiss them—"

"We will neither be bowing or kneeling, and I will most certainly not kiss the man's feet."

"You would be advised to address him as 'King Nimrod' or 'King Amraphel.' He prefers the latter."

"I know his preferences, Iva."

"You realize you risk your life by flouting convention here."

"The Lord God of my forefathers goes before me."

"Suit yourself."

As commoners were not officially allowed in court, Belessunu had never even been there, though before Abram was born she had interacted with the king elsewhere at dinners and ceremonial functions. In fact, the last—and only—commoner invited in was the midwife Yadidatum ten years before, when Terah had included her in the brazen deception of the king, offering Mutuum's son as a gift to the king.

So now Terah was stunned to find the court packed with hundreds of people—employees of the throne dressed, like Iva, in their finest—standing stock-still behind the rows of pillars on either side of the gleaming edifice. He recognized most of them. They seemed to stare with pity—as well as eager anticipation—at him and his wife and son. Did they expect them to be executed in their very presence? Upon the dais forty feet from the entrance, five men stood on one side of two thrones and five stood on the other. The ones to the right were Nimrod's stargazers, those on the left his chief advisers.

On the throne to the left sat Nimrod's wife, Ninlia, ten years younger than the king and—Terah had to admit—eye-catching in her robes and crown. Despite that Nimrod refused to refer to her as the queen or even royal by blood, the populace treated her as such.

Iva waited until the two-story doors thundered closed behind him and borrowed a spear from one of the guards. He held it vertically and pounded the other end to the floor three times, the sound reverberating and causing every eye to turn to the back of the hall. "The king's servant, Terah!" he bellowed. "His wife Belessunu! And his son—"

Ninlia leapt to her feet, banging her scepter on the floor. "Silence, man!" she screeched. "Do you not see that the divine King Amraphel's throne is empty? Nothing happens until he is present! Await him with reverence!"

Iva appeared sheepish as he returned the spear to the guard. "Apologies, my lady! Forgive—"

"Silence!" she yelled. "Reverence!"

Iva bowed.

The wait might have been only two minutes or so, but Terah found it interminable. Clearly something was expected to happen here. How could he avoid it? How could he protect his family?

When a side door behind the dais opened, Terah was astonished to see the king, supported on either side by brawny soldiers, slowly make his way through, both hands on his scepter. Wearing his gaudiest crown and magnificently embroidered robe, he hunched over from the waist and, even at that distance, appeared to have aged twenty years since Terah had last seen him.

Ninlia dropped to her knees, and the men on either side of her did the same. Soon all spectators were on their knees, including Iva and the guards. Abram looked to his father, who remained standing and offered his son a slight shake of his head.

"Bow to your king, you fool!" Iva whispered urgently.

"I bow only to God."

"King Amraphel *is* god!"

The big men situated Nimrod on his throne and left the way they'd come. The king leaned over to his wife and rasped something Terah could not make out. She stood. "Iva! Now is the time to do your job!"

He quickly rose. "Apologies, my king!" And he announced the three who had been summoned to court.

Again Nimrod leaned to his wife. "Approach!" she called out.

Iva nudged them forward, but Ninlia hollered, "Not you, soldier!" and he stopped.

Strangely, Terah felt his confidence build as they advanced toward the throne. He sneaked a glance at Abram, who seemed hesitant.

They waited at the bottom of the steps to the dais, and from that close, Terah could tell the king was worse than he had imagined. His face was lined, his eyes liquid and baggy. Pale and frail, he appeared out of breath. One eye closed and he seemed to study Terah with the other.

Ninlia spoke softly. "They have not yet showed you deference, my king."

"How dare you?" Nimrod managed.

CHAPTER 49

Al-'Ula

Pranav was nowhere near as optimistic as the Saudi lawyer appeared. The detective had spent an hour with his American counsel at a U.S. Embassy consulate substation some nine miles away—where he left the Land Rover and rode with his lawyer to the meeting. Beauregard Judd, who insisted Pranav call him Bo, was thin and well-dressed, in his late thirties. Bo had advised Pranav to mostly listen at the meeting. Pranav was having none of that. "This will be my meeting, sir. We asked, all but demanded, an audience with Ms. Mays because she came here under our auspices. I want the right to ask her what's going on."

"Let me tell you something, Detective. My role will be to keep you, and Ms. Mays, alive."

"What are you talking about? Neither of us has been accused of anything by the Saudis. You and I both know Ms. Mays is wanted in the U.S., but—"

"I forbid you to breathe a word of that at this meeting," Bo said.

"You forbid me?"

"Look, we're both representatives of the U.S.—you I'm dead certain for the first time in your life…"

"True, but—"

"I am a designate of the embassy, and we'd better get straight who calls the shots here. Ms. Mays is officially in the diplomatic custody of the

Saudi government. That means she's under asylum. What you and I are allowed to say to her or ask her will be entirely up to them. Anything you say or do in this meeting will have far-reaching implications for us, and I cannot allow you to jeopardize our relations with Saudi Arabia."

"Forgive me, Mr. Judd, but don't assume I just got off the boat. I became an American citizen as a child and earned my rank and title in the NYPD by working my way—"

"Well, forgive *me*, Detective, but you must know *you* sound like you just got off the boat. Talking to you is like talking to customer service at my internet service provider."

Pranav was stunned. How was it possible for a man so demeaning, so lacking in social grace, to be assigned a diplomatic role in—of all places— Saudi Arabia? Were the detective the type to file a formal complaint, he knew he could have Beauregard Judd on the next plane to Washington.

"Tell me," Pranav said when he finally found his voice, "how does your xenophobia play here in Riyadh?"

"I merely speak the truth, Detective."

"So do you tell the *Saudis* what you think of their accents?"

"And their titles and clothes and customs, yes."

"Why do I find that hard to believe?"

"Believe what you want," Judd said. "You'll see how it goes in the meeting. Believe me, a little personal insult will seem like nothing compared to what these people mete out on people they *really* don't like."

"The way you feel about Asian Indians?"

"Come now, Chakrabarti. If you've been an American as long as you say you have, you should be able to tell when a compatriot is joshing you, testing you a little, seeing how you'll stand up to real prejudice."

"Now I'm your compatriot? And that's what this was—a test? You discount my title and station to relegate me to the cliché of a foreign customer service representative?"

"Ooh, did I hurt your feelings, friend?"

"You deeply insulted me, test or not. So don't compound it by referring to me as a compatriot or friend. I may be diametrically opposed to the religion and worldview I encounter in this country, but as a representative of my people and my adopted home country, I will not disrespect my hosts."

"And do you expect the same courtesies from them?"

"I do not know what to expect, sir, but I will not tolerate your speaking to them the way you have spoken to me."

"You won't tolerate it? Do you know what the punishments are for crimes here?" Bo Judd held up four fingers. "Lashing, stoning, amputation, and beheading."

"As I said, I may be opposed to their worldview, but, number one, I am a guest here, seeking a favor. And two, I am neither on trial nor suspected of a crime."

"Just watch yourself in there, Detective. That's all I'm saying."

"Well, that's not all you're saying, but I would urge you to follow your own advice."

He recognized Dr. Nasim Qahtani's Jaguar in the parking lot and wasn't surprised to find him in a customary natty suit. Kayla avoided eye contact but said hello when Pranav greeted her. She wore long pants and an Islamic head covering, neither of which he had seen her wear at the dig site.

No surprise to Detective Pranav Chakrabarti, the Saudi attorney—a heavyset man with a neatly trimmed black beard and wearing horn-rimmed tortoiseshell glasses—brought his own recording device to the meeting. What did surprise the detective was how jovial the man seemed—almost giddy. He looked resplendent in a white robe and introduced himself as Mr. Fares Harb.

The four men shook hands all around, and the lawyer Harb said something to Dr. Qahtani in Arabic.

"Whoa, whoa!" Bo Judd said. "English only, please!"

Here we go, Pranav thought, but Harb quickly said, "Oh, good! That's all I was asking about, whether we needed an interpreter."

"All those details were already ironed out," Judd said, "which of course you know. And we all speak English."

"Perfectly acceptable," Harb said. "Shall we sit?

"As you know," Harb said with a smile, "we have agreed to allow your counsel to record this meeting, but I will confiscate your camera, Detective, and all cell phones for the duration." Kayla had already apparently surrendered hers, but the four men all produced theirs, switched them to vibrate only, and Harb carefully placed them in a wicker basket at the edge of the table.

As they settled in, both lawyers set their recorders in the middle of the table and turned them on. Harb began, "Let the record show—"

But Judd held up a hand. "Your thobe is not black, Mr. Harb. Making a statement?"

"As a matter of fact, I am, sir. I believe lawyers in black could be mistaken for women, as if we were wearing the abaya."

"Well, black or white," Judd said, "your robe is flattering. Especially if one is hiding a weight problem."

Pranav detected a freeze from Harb, but the man smiled again and said, "If I were trying to hide my weight, I would have to cover my face as well."

"Oh, I wasn't aiming that comment at you, honorable friend."

"Of course you were, but I can take it. Now, may we begin?"

CHAPTER 50

The Palace Court, Shinar

To Nimrod's command that his family bow and he kiss the king's feet, Terah wanted to say, "I shall do no such thing," but the Lord God stopped him and impressed upon him to remain silent. In his peripheral vision both Belessunu and Abram stole glances at him.

The king slowly leaned forward, as if in great turmoil. He groaned. "Do you not hear me, man?"

Terah merely stared into Nimrod's one open eye.

"Are you begging the divine Amraphel to slay you where you stand?" Ninlia said. "Because he will…"

"Hush, woman!" Nimrod said. "I admire that the great Terah knows his own mind and also the consequences. Let's see what he has to say for himself before I send him out to be beheaded."

"I have little to say for myself, sir," Terah said. "I acknowledge that I deceived you ten years ago when our son Abram here was born. I was right to fear for his life, for I knew you saw him as a threat to your reign and meant to kill him. The blood of the son of my own servant is on my hands, and I have had to repent of that sin before Almighty God Himself. To my shame I involved others in my deceit and am responsible for all manner of iniquity, which only the Lord Himself could forgive."

King Nimrod appeared to listen with alarm, but when Terah fell silent, the man tilted his head and rested his ear in his palm.

"Are you all right, my lord?" Ninlia said.

"I am in agony," the king whispered, just loudly enough for Terah to hear. He pressed his hand hard against his ear and rubbed. Suddenly he rallied and tried to straighten on his throne, forcing both eyes open now. "You leave me little choice, Terah, my trusted confidant for so many years. Your wife had been complicit in this grand lie that forced my hand to shed innocent blood. But I give not a whit about the loss of a lowly servant's son, any more than I shall regret wiping the three of you off the face of the earth. This lad before me appears but a wisp and not a threat to anyone's throne, but I shall follow the counsel of my soothsayers and ensure he never…"

King Nimrod's voice trailed off and he lowered his chin to his chest, panting. Terah had never seen him so pale, in so much obvious distress.

"What is it, my love?" Ninlia said, reaching for him.

"Don't touch me!" he rasped. "It feels as if this monster is deep in my head, eating me alive."

"Then get this over with so you can go and be attended to. You need not torture yourself any longer."

"Have Iva approach," he managed.

"Iva!" she called out, but when the guard did not respond, she stood. "Iva! Your king beckons you!"

Hearing no footsteps, Terah turned to see what was going on. Whispering broke out among the crowd.

"You dare turn your back on your sovereign, Terah?" King Nimrod said, his voice raw, shoulders heaving.

"I serve only one Sovereign," Terah said, but was interrupted by the huge doors at the back being forced open. A small contingent of guards jabbered at Iva, who desperately tried to shush them.

The king sat with his head in his hands as if on the verge of exploding. Ninlia shouted, "What is going on back there, Iva? Answer me now!"

"Apologies, dear lady and my king! These men were among those I assigned to the tower!"

"What do they want? Is there some news?"

"I don't know! I cannot understand a word they are saying!"

The soldiers remonstrated, gesturing, yelling, eyes wide. They pointed to their mouths and then to their ears.

King Nimrod pressed his feet to the ground and lifted himself off his robe so he could raise it to cover his head. "Make them stop!" he whined.

"Get them out of here, Iva!" Ninlia said. "And send someone to the tower to find out what's going on!"

Iva shooed the prattling guards out and barked instructions to others. "Shall I go too?" he asked Ninlia.

"Yes, yes! Go! And hurry back!"

At this, King Nimrod leaned forward until his head lay between his knees. He turned and slowly rolled off his throne, his wasted frame loudly slamming the floor. Ninlia screamed and rushed to him. "Summon his physicians! And assign guards to drag out and kill this blasphemous family!"

"No!" came faintly from the fallen king. "Wait for news from the tower. Just take them to the dungeon."

Ninlia looked to the men on the dais, but none moved. "Someone do something! Your king has commanded!"

Still no one moved, and Terah was left dumbfounded. He had never seen anyone else defy King Nimrod.

Finally the king's physicians arrived, making Terah wonder what took so long. Surely they would have been close by, with him so obviously ailing. As they bent over him, one called for help to carry him off the dais. When Ninlia followed them, no one seemed to know what to do. The stargazers and advisers stood in place, appearing to glance nervously at one another, while the hundreds of spectators murmured. Finally the chief stargazer stepped forward and the place fell silent. "In deference to and with respect for our divine king, please vacate the court in an orderly fashion. And I beseech you to pray to the sun god Utu for your king. We shall await a report from the tower and announce any news."

The guards busied themselves herding the people out, leaving Terah and his wife and son standing below the dais. He raised his eyebrows first to the stargazers, then to the advisers, but none maintained eye contact with him. Terah turned to Belessunu and Abram. "Let's go," he whispered.

"What?" she said.

"Father—" Abram began.

"Now," Terah said and turned to leave. They followed the crowd, including the guards, and no one appeared to pay them mind.

"They will never let us reach the road," Belessunu said as they untied the steed. "I feel like walking, husband. You ride."

"Are you sure?"

"Absolutely. You look exhausted, and I'm fine, at least for now."

Terah wearily pulled himself up onto the horse and immediately felt conspicuous, leaving his aged wife on foot. "Don't wait for me," he said. "Abram, take your mother and go straight home."

"No!" she said. "What am I to do if you never arrive? Why don't you ride on ahead and we'll follow?"

"Let's just all stay together then," Terah said, sighing. "Abram is the vulnerable one here."

Terah felt as if all eyes had to be on him and his family, but when he peeked from his perch he realized how wrong he was. It was as if God had blinded the people or somehow made him and Belessunu and Abram invisible. He clicked his tongue, and the mount began to saunter away from the palace through the crowd and toward the road.

The people continued to mill about, as if more interested in waiting for news of whatever was happening at the tower than in the fate of this doomed family who had been summoned before the king. With Belessunu on one side and Abram on the other, Terah gently led the horse through the crowd, the city gate, and toward the road. As he reached the straightaway, those ahead of him scurried to either side as a cloud of dust and the roar of hoofbeats approached. Terah guided the horse out of the way as half a dozen two-man chariots thundered past. All twelve soldiers waved people aside and hollered, but not one word made any sense to Terah.

CHAPTER 51

Al-'Ula

"As long as we're on the record, Mr. Harb," Bo Judd said, "let me reiterate what I told you on the phone. This meeting should have been held on neutral ground. We're talking about an American citizen here who—"

"Fine," the Arab lawyer said pleasantly. "Let the record show that before we have even established the participants, U.S. counsel Beauregard Judd has registered his protest over the location of the meeting. Of course, the U.S. Embassy consulate would not have been neutral either, so we might otherwise have had to meet at sea."

Pranav was impressed that Harb appeared unable to be rattled.

"Now if counsel is finished with the typical American tactic to misdirect, let the record show the participants of this meeting include National Museum director Dr. Nasim Qahtani, American citizen under Saudi asylum Ms. Kayla Mays, New York Police Department detective Pranav Chakrabarti, and the aforementioned Mr. Judd. Dr. Qahtani has requested permission to offer a brief opening statement. Is that acceptable to our honored guests?"

The detective nodded, then remembered he had to give oral approval for the recording and added, "Yes."

But Judd said, "And what if it isn't acceptable? Can we stop him?"

"No."

"Just making sure. And may I ask, is this room bugged?"

Fares Harb narrowed his eyes at Judd but again seemed not to take the bait. Judd had to be trying to get a rise out of the man, but Pranav could not make it compute. He couldn't fathom an endgame to these insults, especially when Judd had warned him about what to say or not say here.

"Well, of course it is," Harb said. "You would expect no less, the same as we would expect at your facility. But as both sides here are recording every word anyway, does it matter?"

"Just determining how transparent you plan to be."

"As transparent as you, Mr. Judd. Now may we get on with this, or shall we plan on this wasting the entire day?"

"I don't have time for that!" Judd said, chuckling.

"That's a relief, because neither do we. Dr. Qahtani?"

Nasim surprised Pranav by standing. It seemed a quaint gesture, especially with the other four seated fairly close together in a small conference room. He wondered if he would be expected to stand when he spoke.

"Thank you," Qahtani said, "and let me again welcome our guests. My hope is that this would be other than an acrimonious meeting. I just want to stipulate that Ms. Mays here came to me, seeking asylum. You may rest assured that we have never met or interacted before I was introduced to her at the dig site. I took her initial friendliness as a form of the harmless flirting I found common among American women when I studied in New York years ago, and I was surprised when she asked to meet with me. She will affirm that I did not encourage her flirtation. I confess I was surprised when she asked to see me privately and sought asylum rather than just attention."

"She will be able to speak for herself," Judd said. "Will she not?"

"Of course," lawyer Harb said. "In due time."

"The time is now," Judd said.

"The time will be when I say it is," Harb said, still with that disconcerting pleasant look.

"Excuse me," Judd said, "but this meeting was requested by Detective Chakrabarti for the purpose of asking Ms. Mays some qu—"

"In due time," Harb said evenly. "Do either of you gentlemen have questions for Dr. Qahtani?"

Qahtani sat, and Judd said, "I do. Sir, you said you and Ms. Mays had no knowledge of each other until you met her in country at the dig site."

"Correct."

"I've been informed that she was a late addition to the list of volunteers, due to the surprising cancellations of two others."

"I would know nothing about that."

"If I told you that the two dropouts both felt threatened and had been warned against joining this dig team, would that change your recollection?"

"No."

"Does that not sound like the work of the World Islamic Network, ensuring that their own volunteer is planted on the team?"

"The World Isl—"

"Don't play ignorant, Dr. Qahtani! You're highly enough placed in the Saudi government to be aware of the clandestine organization's ties to the major Muslim nations. Would that not include Saudi—"

"Of course I've *heard* of the WIN, but even the implication that I would somehow play a role in it—"

"Offends your sensibilities, does it?"

"Yes, it does." Qahtani didn't appear to even pretend he was rolling with the punches the way Fares Harb was.

Pranav himself was well aware of the World Islamic Network, but he had not expected Bo Judd to raise this. "Could I have a moment with my counsel?" Pranav said, standing and moving toward the door.

"Certainly!" Harb said.

"And where can we go to ensure we won't be heard or recorded?" the American attorney said.

"I would tell you the hallway is safe, but I wouldn't expect you to believe me. Feel free to go outside."

* * *

"What do you want?" Judd said, as soon as they were in the parking lot. "We had a little momentum going in there, and it doesn't make sense to look like we might not be on the same page."

"I'm not sure we are."

"That's our business, but why, what now?"

"Do you really think this Dr. Qahtani is affiliated with the World Islamic Network? I mean—"

"I don't know, but why not? He'd be perfect for it. Listen, people who don't want peace between Israel and her neighbors want war. Why do you suppose that is?"

"Because war requires arms?"

"Bingo! Maybe you *are* smarter than you sound, Detective. Arms sales equals profit. Big profit. What's the oldest cliché in geopolitical circles?"

"Follow the money."

"There you go. Now what else? Can we get back in there?"

"Just one thing, Bo. How much of a threat to the Saudis is the discovery Dr. Berman believes she's on to? I'm not a theologian or anything close to an archaeologist, but she and her number two—"

"Let me just say this, Chakrabarti: if whatever she's finding threatens Muslim leverage over Israel…"

"What if it strengthens Jewish claims to their land?"

"I think you know the answer to that. Now let's get back in there. You must know that the news about this dig and what the Berman Foundation is after has been known for months. Long before she arrived, the embassy had fretted over what might come of all this. I mean, I'm way outside my lane when it comes to all this archaeological and historical stuff. But if she's finding what she hoped to find, she may be lighting the fuse to a powder keg none of us wants to even think about."

CHAPTER 52

Ur

"I have a deep sense of peace," Belessunu told Terah when they arrived home. "And yet I am also overwhelmed with curiosity. Aren't you?"

"*I* sure am," Abram said. "Will not the king, or his wife, send troops to kill us? Or at least throw us in the dungeon, as she threatened?"

"The Lord God apparently has other plans," Terah said. "But curious? Yes, more than ever. I'm tempted to go to Babel."

"Oh, no, husband! Why test fate?"

"If we were to be apprehended, it would have happened by now. The king had us right where he wanted us and I brazenly disobeyed him, all but mocked him. It's not like I will be more conspicuous at the tower. I supervised that site for years, so everyone there knows me. But if we slipped away from the very throne unharmed, who could touch us?"

"You want us all to go?"

"Yes!" Abram shouted.

"I'm going," Terah said. "That's all I know. God has imbued with me courage from on high. Either of you are free to come with me or stay here, alone or together. I have no doubt God will protect us all. But, woman, if either your time or mine has come, so be it. The Lord will protect His chosen, promised one. Abram will be fine whether he goes or stays."

"I want to go!" Abram said.

"That is your choice," Terah said.

Belessunu shook her head, but apparently more in resignation than disapproval. "I don't know about giving a ten-year-old such a choice," she said. "But as I told you, God has given me peace. I do not need to go. I will stay and prepare a feast. And I will pray the Lord will send you both back to me."

"Abram," Terah said, "hitch the cart to the horse."

From nearly a mile away Terah smelled the bubbling tar that served as mortar for the hundreds of thousands of baked bricks that comprised the great tower. Nearly eighty different clans—all, of course, descendants of Noah—had labored for years on the edifice that at just over the halfway point already reached three quarters of a mile high and could be seen for miles.

Terah had kept a steady pace with Abram hanging on to the sides, bouncing around in the bed of the cart over the rocky roadway. As he gently pulled back on the reins and feathered the horse between the great ovens that tempered the bricks and massive pots boiling the pitch, workers streamed toward him. He stopped the steed and had Abram stand holding the reins as he climbed down. More than a dozen workers surrounded him, wearing only sandals and loincloths, their hairy chests pouring sweat in the merciless sun.

Such attention was nothing new to Terah. During his years at the helm of the sweeping project, his every appearance at the site triggered supervisors rushing him with requests, informing him of issues, underlings who needed to be dealt with. But this was something entirely different. Grimy faces wide-eyed, these men all talked at once, earnestly, gesturing madly, clearly trying to tell him of some problem he must remedy immediately. But they all seemed to be speaking gibberish! He understood not one word, and worse, they didn't seem to understand one another either.

"What are you saying?" he said, over and over.

They pointed to their mouths and their ears and shouted at each other, clearly arguing but accomplishing nothing. Then a few who seemed to understand only each other talked excitedly, appearing to commiserate.

Terah leapt back aboard his cart and stood over the cacophony. He lifted his hands for silence and put a finger to his lips. When they quieted, he shouted, "Does anyone here understand me?"

A man near the back of the crowd waved. "I do!" he said. "Praise Utu!"

"I do too!" shouted another, who hurried to join the first.

"You two come to me!" Terah said. "And anyone else who understands!"

Five men approached, but the others must have assumed Terah had summoned them too, so they followed. Terah separated the five from the others and stepped down into their midst. "What is going on here? What has happened?"

They all began speaking at once until one Terah recognized as a supervisor took over. "All of a sudden, no one can understand what others are saying! You've heard the prattle!" He pointed. "I told that man, right there, that the tar in that pot was about to boil over, and he responded with words I'd never heard before! I demanded to know what he was saying, and he only said the same thing louder. My guess is that he was saying that cauldron was not his responsibility, but how would I know? I ordered him to lower the fire or have men lift the pot off it, but he looked at me as if *I* were the crazy one. It's been this way for hours! Nothing is getting done. Bricks are baked too long or sit too long without being cured. And tar pots are boiling over everywhere. Men above are shouting down, probably for more supplies, but no one down here has any idea what they're asking for. If you don't figure this out, don't fix it, the tower is doomed."

Terah found himself as confused as anyone else at the discord that had swept the tower site. As he tried to reason with the few who could understand him, fights seemed to break out all over. Soon marauding workers began spilling pots of bubbling tar and throwing bricks at one another. Terah knew he had to get young Abram out of there and so began plotting his escape. He drew the boy near and spoke into his ear. "Bring the reins back into the cart and be prepared to whip the horse as soon as I sit."

All around, workers retrieved their clothes and put them on, packing whatever they'd brought with them into coarse cloth bags, and abandoning the site. King's guards, in chariots or high on horseback, tried to stop them, shouting for them to get back to work. But the workers just hollered back in unintelligible tongues and ran.

As hundreds streamed from the place, Terah slowly backed toward the cart while still trying to converse with the men. Finally, he clambered up and in, and as soon as his backside hit the seat, Abram snapped the reins and yelled, "Yah!" and the horse fled at full gallop.

CHAPTER 53

Square One, the Mada'in dig

"Curious and excited as I am," Nicole told Samir Waleed, "I'm skittish about the integrity of this foundation."

Dr. Waleed appeared to study her in the light from his headlamp. "I'm not feeling whatever it is you are, but I'm all about safety. If you want to delay until we get more tools, shore up the walls—"

"No. If you're okay, I'm okay."

"Could it be you're afraid what we find will confirm everything you've dreamed of, and you're not sure you're ready for what follows? You could win awards, be on the covers of magazines, go viral, as the kids say. Are you reluctant to become Newsmaker of the Year? I can say I knew you when…"

Nicole waved him off. "All that stuff means nothing compared to the find itself, Samir. No, I'm not happy about all the visibility that could come from it, and I have no illusions about the opposition I'll get from the Muslim world. But even you wouldn't argue with the facts, if they prove to be facts, wouldn't you?"

The old man chuckled. "It would put me in a precarious position, that's certain. I must remain true to my country, to my faith—"

"But also to your profession, no?" she said. "The whole point of what we do is discovery, isn't it?"

"Yes!" he said. "But put yourself in my shoes. What if what we uncover shows *you* to be entirely wrong and corroborates *our* view of religious history? Would you admit that publicly, at the risk of your own—"

"I hope I would, Samir."

He laughed aloud. "I very much admire that sentiment, but you should hear the tone of your own voice. I must say, you're not terribly convincing. You're so sure of what we're finding that you can afford to be magnanimous and claim you would concede if things went the other way."

"Okay," Nicole said. "Guilty. Now let's see what's under this mess."

* * *

Al-'Ula

"May I take notes?" Kayla Mays said. To Pranav she sounded timid. That was so unlike her. Up till her fleeing the dig site, he had enjoyed her personality and what he could deduce of her character. Besides her beautiful countenance and gleaming smile, she had proved quick and witty. Also forthright. Her asking permission rather than just saying what she wanted to do jarred Pranav.

"Certainly!" Fares Harb said, digging in his briefcase for a pad of paper and a pen. "Though of course you know you will have full access to this recording and the transcript that comes from it."

She nodded, but her eyes darted.

"May I ask Kayla a few questions?" Pranav said.

"After she gives her opening statement, Detective," Harb said. "The floor is yours, Ms. Mays."

Kayla seemed unnerved by this and glanced first at Dr. Qahtani and then at Harb. "That can wait," she said. "I'll talk to Pranav."

"Now just a minute," Qahtani said. "Ms. Mays and her counsel worked together to prepare a statement that—"

Harb held up a hand. "It's all right, Doctor, I'm not opposed to the detective asking her questions before she makes her statement. I do, of course, reserve the right to advise her on her answers or help her decide *which* questions to answer."

Bo Judd shook his head. "Is it your aim to make this as complicated as possible? This is not a trial! Let the two converse."

"That's exactly what I'm doing, counsel. But I shall not cede the right to look out for the best interests of my client."

"Just let us get on with this," Judd said. "Go ahead, Detective."

Pranav moved his chair directly across from Kayla. She was clearly uncomfortable and avoided eye contact. "Kayla, dear…" he began.

"I'm sorry," Harb broke in. "I clearly understand the differences between our views of the treatment of women in our respective countries. But is it not considered offensive in your culture for a man to patronize a woman by using a pet name for her?"

"Yes, it is," Bo Judd said. "Detective, you know better than that."

"But I'm nearly twice her age, and we're friends, aren't we, Kayla?" She nodded.

"Still," Judd said, "knock off the familiarity."

"I will if she prefers," Pranav said. "I'll call you anything you wish, Kayla, but you need not fear me. You know that, don't you?"

"I'm not offended by anything you call me," she said quietly.

"I would like you to look at me, however," he said.

She met his eyes. "Sorry."

"Kayla, as a friend, not as a detective or representing the United States, I just want to know what's happened. Until you bolted, we considered you a valuable member of our team. Dr. Berman in particular was fond of you and trusted you. Naturally, she's deeply concerned that we may have offended you. What can you tell me?"

Kayla looked stricken. She appeared to want to say something. Finally she whispered, "I choose not to respond."

"But, Kayla—"

"Do not badger, sir," Harb said. "You heard her."

Pranav sighed and looked to Bo Judd, who shrugged. Pranav tried again. "Kayla, let me ask you this: Do you recall a conversation not so long ago in which you asked Dr. Berman about her silent prayer before breakfast?"

"You don't have to answer that," Harb said. "This is the last place where we want to get into religion. Ms. Mays is under asylum to a Muslim country—"

"Actually," Kayla said, "I want to talk about this. Is it okay if I answer?"

Harb raised both hands. "That's entirely up to you. Just be careful."

"I do remember that, Pranav. Nicole said she prayed some kind of Jewish prayer even though she's a Christian."

"Great," Bo Judd said. "Thanks, Detective, for introducing the two most offensive religions on the planet to these people."

"We're just talking personally. I mean no offense to anyone."

Judd shook his head. "Then, by all means, continue! I don't see this ending well."

"You might be surprised, Beauregard," Pranav said. "Do you remember what you asked me, Kayla?"

She nodded. "Whether you were Hindu."

"And what did I say?"

"That you were Christian."

"Not to put too fine a point on it, but I would say *a* Christian, not just Christian."

"That *is* putting too fine a line on it, sir," Harb said. "I will likely regret asking and expending more time than I want to on this, but what in the world is the difference between being Christian and being *a* Christian?"

Pranav could not believe his good fortune. He had hoped and prayed he could say what he wanted to at this meeting, on the record before Saudis and Americans, but he did not expect the question to come from the Muslim counsel! "I'll keep this brief," he said. "But just as your country is known as a Muslim country, America is known as a Christian country. Less so now than ever, of course, and we are constitutionally bound to respect all faiths. But being *Christian* could mean something as innocuous as not being of another faith. Or acting like one thinks Christians should.

"But when I refer to being *a Christian*, that means I have identified with Jesus Christ, received Him as my Savior. I worship Him, study about Him, pray to Him."

"Yes, yes," Harb said. "We get it. Our citizens are not just Muslim but are also practicing Muslims. I don't say only that I am *Muslim*, but also that I am *a Muslim*. So thanks for clarifying. Now move on."

"I would like to, if I may, explain to Ms. Mays my own faith, my spiritual journey."

"To what end?" Harb said.

Finally, it seemed Bo Judd took Pranav's side. "You may limit dissent among your own citizens, Counselor, but I must defend my client's freedom to say what he wants to say. I sense nothing coming that should in any way threaten you or your country or your government or your god. Am I right, Detective?"

"Of course. If I may?"

Harb shrugged as if to surrender. "I don't know about you, but this is not my only meeting today. Can you get to your point so we can make some progress?"

CHAPTER 54

INTERLUDE

Ur of the Chaldees

For the next several months, the talk of the entire region, from Shinar to Babel and beyond, became the ruin left of the tower. The structure led to nowhere but the clouds, and the area sat strewn with half-baked bricks and enormous pools of tar that nearly solidified overnight, only to be rendered goopy and sticky again in the next day's sun.

The confusing languages caused disharmony among all the clans, who banded together in groups who understood each other and scattered to the ends of the earth.

Meanwhile, news of the king's demise also swept what was left of the kingdom. Nimrod, depending on who spread the tale, either lingered at death's door or had gone mad. Rare sightings of the man started new rumors that he had lost half his body weight, including the prodigious muscles that had made him a hunting and military legend. Word came that Ninlia had taken over the throne, and though many Nimrod loyalists denied this, no one else stepped forward to lead.

Whatever dictum that should have come from the king's court relating to Terah, his wife, or his son, somehow faded into oblivion. Terah had, of course, lost his role as supervisor of the construction of the so-called Tower to the Heavens, and he needed not be told he was unwelcome at the palace. So he merely taught his son the business of raising livestock, brought back his old servant Wedum, and even suggested to Mutuum that he was invited back too. Mutuum understandably declined.

Around this time, through a concubine, Terah bore a daughter he named Sarai, sending her off to be raised by a wealthy tradesman and his wife.

Over the next few years, as God had promised, Belessunu bore Terah two more sons—whom he named Nahor (after his own father) and Haran. Terah hired more and more servants as God blessed his business, and he became one of the wealthiest landowners and animal producers in Ur. Occasional visits to the family raising his daughter revealed Sarai as a most beautiful child who grew into a striking teenager.

Belessunu soon fell ill, her age having ironically caught up with her—despite Terah remaining healthy in his dotage. He and their three sons nursed her faithfully every day, and he prayed for her constantly. "What will I do without her, Lord? It was really her, after all, who steered me back to You. She has been a rock when I was shifting sand."

The day finally arrived when she called him to her bedside. "I believe God is calling me," she rasped.

"No!" he cried. "I need you!"

"Let me go, love."

"Oh, Belessunu, have you forgiven all? I have tried to assuage my guilt, but I was so wrong for so long, and to you especially."

"Has not the Lord forgiven you, Terah?"

"I believe He has, and you have not thrown in my face all the ways I so horribly treated you for so many years."

"That is your answer. If God forgave you, who would I be to not do the same? Know that I die loving you and having forgiven you."

Terah bitterly grieved her death, only to suffer again months later when their son Haran—who had married and begat children, including a son named Lot—contracted a mysterious ailment that took him much too young.

When Abram was twenty-nine years old, Terah arranged for him to marry his half sister Sarai, by then nineteen. They and Abram's brother Nahor and his wife, Milcah—also a daughter of Haran—helped raise Lot.

As the decades passed, Abram began to doubt the promises he had been told by his parents. God had not spoken directly to him, and as the eye-catching Sarai had thus far been unable to bear him a child, let alone a son, he despaired of the idea of becoming a father at all.

Somehow King Nimrod managed to survive, though from all reports, it was clear he was but a shell of the man he had once been. He still declared war on neighboring tribes and responded vigorously to threats against his realm. But he was mostly invisible, sending instruction to and through his aides and letting Ninlia serve as the face of the throne.

But with the dwindling population, Shinar lost its status a trade center, and Terah began noticing an erosion into his produce and profits. He conferred with his sons and their wives, and they agreed it was time to move on. Terah felt led to take what was left of his family and trek toward Canaan. By now Abram was seventy, the age Terah had been when Abram was born. He and his father and brother enjoyed possessions and wealth beyond their dreams, but he had abandoned any hope of becoming a father.

On the long journey with the family, many servants, and thousands of head of livestock, Terah found himself drawn to a settlement named Haran. Had God provided this oasis that happened to share the name of his beloved late son, to encourage him to rest ahead of the remainder of the trip?

What Terah intended as a brief stop to fortify himself grew to five years, and by the time he was ready to get back on the road to Canaan, he was too old and feeble to travel. When he knew his time was coming to an end, he took to his bed and called his beloved Abram close. "My son," he said, "I have never truly forgiven myself for straying from our God, though He and your mother forgave me."

"But Father, she and you taught me that His grace and mercy endures forever. What's past is past."

"Abram, you are to be the fulfillment of God's promises, so always remember that following Him is the only thing that matters."

"Father, I bless you for all you've done to add such blessings to our lives."

"It was not I, but the Lord above who provided. Promise me you will stay strong in Him, my son."

Abram embraced his father, then sat holding his hand. "Leave me your blessing that I may have the faith you and Mother instilled in me."

"May God bless you and hold you to the truth of all He has promised, whenever it shall come to pass."

Not long later, Terah died in his sleep in the city that bore his late son's name.

CHAPTER 55

Mada'in

Nicole stood behind Dr. Samir Waleed as the old man appeared to carefully wield the mattock. Its head consisted of a cutler blade on one side and a three-pronged claw on the other. She took off her headlamp and aimed it where he gently scraped with one of the outside claws between where they had found the inscription and the edge of what they had determined was a dressed but crumbling wall.

When Samir had opened a cavity approximately four inches high and eight inches wide, he stood and faced Nicole. "My, my, my," he said.

"Tell me," she said.

He handed her the mattock. "All I will say is that you are going to like what you see, and I think you should take the lead from here."

Nicole strapped her lamp back on and traded places with him. She peered through the opening, tilting her head so her light illuminated a vast opening to what appeared to be at least two chambers, maybe three. She was eager to get to them and see if they were indeed burial vaults and anything else that might be there. One massive column was curved, looking like it could be the leg or arm of the statue she suspected had plunged into this area. The question was whether the rest of the inscription would be discoverable.

She turned the cutter blade head of the mattock and reminded herself to stay calm and move only at a safe pace. Priceless treasure was at stake, not to mention a revolutionary view of history with the potential to change the world.

"Slowly, slowly," Dr. Waleed whispered. "We need just enough room to get through and see what we have. If it takes an hour, don't rush."

* * *

Al-'Ula

Pranav felt a rush deep in his gut, that rare sensation when you know you're at a pivotal moment in your life with a chance to speak for God. He prayed silently, "Use me."

The detective leaned forward and tried with everything in him to communicate to Kayla with his eyes. What was it he detected in her? Regret? Fear? Plainly she was in over her head, but what could he do to help?

"Kayla, dear," he began, and for once no one objected, "to the best of my recollection you were surprised to discover I was a Christian. You said you used to be, though you didn't go to church and your mother was the one who prayed, if anyone did."

Kayla nodded. Her eyes looked red and dry.

"Are you all right?" Pranav said.

"I'm okay," she said, and leaned back to apply eyedrops.

"May I tell you my own story?" he said.

"I guess."

"As you can tell from my accent, I grew up in India. I belonged to an ancient tribe that adhered to animism. Do you know what that is?"

"Not really." Kayla jotted some notes and folded the sheet of paper.

"It's a belief that everything, even inanimate objects, has a soul. But I went further than that. I was what you'd call a monist. To me, any and every kind of religion was okay. I worshiped all the Hindu gods and Buddha and Jesus. As I got older, I grew uneasy with that kind of belief system, somehow knowing intuitively that not all religions could be valid. I did worry about what might happen to me if I died. I like the idea of heaven and wanted to know I was going there and not to hell. I was surprised when a friend told me he believed Jesus was the only way to God.

"That appealed to me, but many where I lived thought Christianity was a threat to our culture. When I chose to believe in Jesus's death on the cross for my sins, and His burial and resurrection, I received Him as my Savior and became the first Christian in my family. I told no one of my new faith, especially my parents. I couldn't keep it from them for long, though, because my college friends were all Christian believers, and when they visited my home, they made no secret of their faith. Sadly, my parents turned me out and disowned me, but nothing could make me reject my faith. Shortly after they died, I immigrated to the U.S. and deepened my devotion to Jesus. My wife and children are also believers. And now I want to tell everyone about Him."

Pranav fell silent, certain he had stumbled in his effort, especially considering where he found himself. He worried he had not made a walk with Christ sound interesting, let alone vital.

Kayla sat in tears. "That's beautiful," she said finally, and she slid the folded sheet to Pranav.

"What is that?" Harb said, reaching for it, but the detective quickly slipped it into his pocket. "She is not to be communicating with you without our knowledge."

"So," Bo Judd said, "she's not under your protection. She's your prisoner?"

"I didn't say that."

"She is not allowed to confide in us?"

"You can't be trading secrets."

"Why not?"

"Because she's under our jurisdiction."

"That doesn't sound like protection to me, Mr. Harb. It sounds like detainment."

CHAPTER 56

Ancient Haran

Abram and his extended family greatly mourned his father. Yet almost immediately following the burial and the traditional season of lament, Abram felt in his heart a deep sense of anticipation. If God were ever to speak to him, ever to explain what his parents believed had been a promise, now was the time.

He spent several nights tossing in bed next to his aging wife, who retained her stunning beauty. When he left their sleep chamber to wander the plains, upon his return Sarai was awake and asked what was troubling him. "I don't know," he said. "I believe the Lord God of my ancestors wants to tell me something, but I don't know what it is."

"Just continue listening," she said. "Try to be prepared for whatever it is He has for you. I will stand with you, no matter what."

"How can I prepare when I am in the dark, Sarai?"

"Well, be willing then, to do whatever He tells you."

"Of course I'm willing. But in times past He spoke to me mostly through my mother, only more recently through Father. I'm not sure what I would think if He spoke directly to me."

"I know what I would do," she said.

"And—?"

"I would fall prostrate in fear!"

"It is wise to fear God," Abram said.

"I don't feel wise. But I also think this is something I do not have to worry about. Your mother is the only woman I've ever heard of whom God has spoken through. I trust He will reveal Himself to you alone."

Abram lay next to her in the night, finding her breathing rhythmic and deep. Moonlight through the window highlighted her remarkable beauty, dark hair cascading down her neck, framing dramatic features that never ceased to thrill him.

He interlaced his fingers behind his head and sighed, remembering the man his father had become in his old age. Terah had gone from a worshiper of idols—indeed a crafter and seller of them—to first a murderer estranged from his wife and child—then finally to a fully repentant believer in the one true God. What a legacy! But what of his and Abram's mother's assurances that the Lord had revealed to them that their firstborn would one day become an exalted father? The time had long since passed when that would have been even possible, hadn't it? Sarai often smiled and told him the gray in his hair only added to his charm. He did not mind growing older. It simply made him wonder how, or if, God could accomplish what He had promised.

Abram rose quietly and slipped out into the night. "God of the universe," he whispered, "what would you have me do? I am willing to do whatever it is You desire of me, for You have blessed me beyond measure. But is this the place I too am to grow old and die with the bride of my youth?"

"No."

Abram froze where he stood. Had that been an answer? What else could it have been? "Speak, Lord."

"Go to a land I will reveal to you and I will make of you a vast nation. Your name will be known far and wide for generations. You shall bless many."

"But where? When?"

"Walk by faith from Haran to Canaan."

Canaan? For him alone, let alone his household, that would mean a month's travel of five hundred miles into who knew what kind of danger? Whom should he take with him? Only Sarai? What of all the others?

"Take also your nephew and his people and all that you both own. I will go before you and prepare the way."

Abram nearly regretted having longed for God to speak directly to him. And yet when he told Sarai what had happened, she urged him to obey. Soon the couple, and Lot and his people, grew eager to get underway. With all the livestock God had blessed them with, they set out for Shechem, where they would rest and fortify themselves for the rest of the incredibly long journey.

While there, God spoke to Abram again, telling him He would give his offspring "this land." Abram dared not ask the Lord what He meant by "this land." How much land would he need? Still, Abram constructed an altar there so he and Sarai and the rest of the clan could acknowledge that God was with them.

From there Abram headed south and camped in the hills between Bethel and Ai. There he dedicated another altar to the Lord before moving on toward the Negev. Perhaps in the desert he would be able to find what he was looking for.

When they finally arrived in Canaan, the land had been ravaged by famine. Abram and Lot determined the family would only starve to death there, so they remained on a southern course toward Egypt. As they neared the border, Sarai said, "My husband, what troubles you? I cannot believe the Lord God of the Universe would lead you astray. Do you no longer believe this is the best course?"

"It's not that," he said. "It's just that we will be foreigners here. I fear that as soon as the Egyptians see you and assume you are much younger than your years because of your beauty, they will want to kill your husband so they can have you."

"Oh, no, Abram. Surely not."

"Tell them you're my sister! That's not entirely untrue, and it's the only way to keep them from killing me."

Shortly after they arrived, word came from the palace that Pharaoh had heard of Sarai. He sent male and female servants to Abram as gifts, along with dozens of head of livestock—bulls and cows, goats, donkeys, camels, sheep, and goats. "We are yours," one of the servants told him, "in exchange for your sister as a gift to Pharoah."

Terrified for his own life, Abram sent Sarai to the palace.

Not long later, a messenger arrived at the settlement where Abram and Lot and Lot's wife and progeny camped. By now Abram's household had grown vast with hundreds of workers and servants, yet he was not happy. He missed Sarai terribly and hated himself for what he had subjected her to. And beyond all that, he remained childless. How could God bless him as He had promised without even an heir to his name?

The messenger told Abram, "Pharoah summons you immediately."

CHAPTER 57

The dig site, Mada'in

Nicole felt only vaguely aware of more shifting beneath her as she scraped and brushed at a glacial pace.

"Is that more of the inscription?" Dr. Waleed said, leaning close. "This is incredible!"

"I can only hope," Nicole said. "Can you get more light on it?" She didn't want to jinx this by being too eager.

Samir knelt and pointed his lamp into the enlarging cavity. "Tell me it is," he said. "I can hardly believe this."

"I need to make enough room to get my head in there," she said.

"Careful, Dr. Berman."

Care was the last thing on Nicole's mind now. Half an hour later, she angled her head and tried to wedge through. Her headlamp stopped her. She removed it and handed it to Samir. "Once I'm in up to my neck, shine both lights right there. See it?"

He nodded and she gingerly led with her chin, turning her face this way and that until her ears cleared.

"You've left no room for either lamp," he said.

"Dig a little more, Samir."

He began carefully picking at the soil surrounding her head with the mattock. "I don't want to risk nicking you."

"I'm fine. Keep going. I have to see this. The area is bigger than we thought, and the air is cooler."

"I can feel it," he said.

"I'm breathing it," she said.

Finally he cleared enough away that she could move her head side to side about four inches. He pressed the lamps together and pointed them. "Let's both try to remember what I translate here," she said. "Once we get fully in there, we should have enough room to take notes—though it does look like we'll have to squat."

Once again Dr. Waleed illuminated the area. "The last bit of the inscription," he said, "to the best of my recollection, was '*May your land blossom with fruit, may it flow…*' Is that what you remember?"

"Sounds right to me."

"What's next?"

"I wish I could get a brush in there. But what I can make out so far, is, ah, this, I think. Ready?"

"Affirmative."

She recited slowly as she deciphered each word of the ancient text:

…with milk and honey, may your sheep and your cattle multiply.

"Oh, Samir! Isn't that sounding more and more like—"

"—like exactly what you hoped it would say."

"Is this possible? Am I dreaming?"

"Can you make out any more?"

"I see a lot more lettering, but I don't have the angle. We have to get in there, Doctor. I can hardly believe this is real."

She carefully extricated herself and again took over the mattock work. Much as Nicole tried to stay calm, she couldn't slow herself. "I just want to be sure I have the best look at it. Don't let me ruin anything."

"I was about to say…Just stay steady. I'm as excited as you are."

"It has to be just big enough for us to wriggle through," she said. "Once in there we can sit on our heels and get a close look at it."

"But, Nicole, if we're right about what all is below us, that area and the bulk of the statue, if that's what it is, could be weighing on the ceiling of the first chamber. If it is a burial vault, we must be extremely cautious, not just for our own sakes, but for the integrity of all we might find there."

"Believe me, I know," she said. "But if anything were ever worth the risk, this would have to be it, wouldn't it?"

"That's not the archaeologist in you talking," Dr. Waleed said. "You know this site and whatever priceless cache may be here is thousands of years old and will still be here tomorrow."

"Tomorrow?" she said laughing. "You may be willing to wait, but I'm not!"

Her walkie-talkie crackled. "Nicole? Dr. Waleed?" Suzie said. "You still okay down there?"

"Roger," Samir said.

"Need anything?"

"Negative for now, thanks."

"Finding more?"

Nicole shook her head and pressed a finger to her lips. Samir said, "Nothing to speak of yet."

"Ten-four."

An hour later, Nicole and Samir had opened a clearing large enough to crawl through single file. The old man was shorter than she but slightly broader in the shoulders, and he was able to just barely squeeze through behind her. "I'm not wild about this," he said. "My students and protégés would never believe I'm breaking every rule I've known and taught for years."

"Something tells me you'll get over it when you see what I see," Nicole said. "I think we *are* on the ceiling of a burial vault."

"How can you tell?"

"I can just feel it."

"Again, Dr. Berman, that's not a professional speaking."

"If you're not comfortable, Samir…"

"Oh, I'm not," he said, "but if you think I'm going anywhere, you don't know me at all."

She chuckled. "Is that the archaeologist in *you* speaking? Or is that your inner Indiana Jones?"

"Don't blaspheme," he said.

Nicole crawled to where she could position herself directly over what appeared to be the rest of the inscription. "Oh, Samir," she said. "We're going to remember this day for the rest of our lives. Listen to this." And again she began quoting what she could make out, one agonizingly slow word at a time, determined to get each exactly right. How could this be anything other than what she thought it was, believed it was, needed it to be?

> *I admonish you, my sons, that you live in peace, that you love one another, that you never raise your hand against the other, that the sword is never taken up. If you heed my words, my sons, you will be blessed and you will live in peace forever in this rich land that Yah has given me and you.*

"That looks like the end of it, Dr. Waleed."

"There should be a bit more that identifies who is quoted. Don't tell me we have all that but no—"

"There's more." She leaned close to the end of the lettering and squinted. "'*The wo*—' could be '*word*,' but that's faded to nothing. More empty space, so maybe '*The words*,' but I couldn't swear to it. More completely faded space, then '*bra*…' Could that be '*of Abraham*,' Samir?"

"Don't get ahead of yourself."

"I'm trying not to, but I can hardly breathe."

"I'm shuddering," he said. "So many in our circle—outside my faith or yours, of course—are not convinced Abraham ever really existed."

"I know, but he and Sarah had to be more than just symbols."

"That's something Muslims, Jews, and Christians agree on, Nicole. If Abraham didn't exist, neither Ishmael nor Isaac existed either. We revere Ibrahim, as we call him, as a saint who never wavered from his faith in Allah, who promised Ibrahim would lead all the nations. Our scriptures show him as the very ideal of obedience."

"The next few words are clear, Samir. '...*friend of God, to...*'"

"To whom?" he said.

"Blank faded spaces, then '...*son,*' blank, '...*mael and Isa...*' and blank. Oh, Samir, let me add this to what I stored on my phone. It has to be 'The words of Abraham, friend of God, to his sons, Ishmael and Isaac,' doesn't it?"

"It very well could be, Nicole. Think of it. Soon enough, every archaeologist in the world will want to weigh in on this."

"And not all will agree, will they?"

"Many won't dare, even if they are convinced the find is not a fraud. Imagine the ramifications."

"How about you?"

"Don't ask," he said. "People lie. Facts don't."

She keyed in her translations as fast as she could and held the screen out before them both.

—ham our father blessed his sons and said: "Hear the words of your father, hear them and obey them. May Yah, the Lord God, judge between the two of you and may he bless me in my old age. May he bless you and multiply you in your days and may your days be long; may you have many sons and daughters; and may you live in this land that he has given to me and you forever. May your land blossom with fruit, may it flow with milk and honey, may your sheep and your cattle multiply. I admonish you, my sons, that you live in peace, that you love one another, that you never raise your hand against the other, that the sword is never taken up. If you heed my words, my sons, you will be blessed and you will live in peace forever in this rich land that Yah has given me and you.

> *The wo[———]bra[—], friend of God, to [—] son[———]mael and Isa[—].*

She took several pictures of the portion of the inscription she had uncovered here, planning, of course, to piece it together with what she had found before.

Samir said, "We both need to document this and make sure every detail is absolutely, exactly—"

"But we also need to see what's below here, don't we?" Nicole said. "I mean, if it is what we think it is…"

"Well, of course, but until we can get more tools—"

"The roof seems solid enough that we could at least poke through, don't you think? Enough for a peek anyway."

"Oh, that's not wise, Nicole. You've already pushed your luck further than it should have ever been pushed today."

"But your government is going to want to take over this site as soon as they hear of this! Don't you want to know what's down there before that?"

"Naturally," he said. "But everything we've done today could be ruined if we aren't careful."

Nicole pressed her back against the cold wall next to the inscription and slid her seat to the floor. "I know you're right. But I just want to take this in."

"I'd feel a lot safer out where we started," he said.

"I know. Me too. Go ahead. I'll be right behind you."

He handed her her headlamp and took both her hands in his. "This is a remarkable achievement, Nicole. What a privilege! When I retired I never dreamed I would get an opportunity like this."

"You'll have to come out of retirement now, won't you, Samir? You'll become a media darling, especially here."

"Or a pariah. Let me just say, it will be very interesting what the Saudi press does with this."

"No kidding," she said.

"Don't stay in here too long, Nicole."

"Don't worry. Right behind you."

He grabbed the mattock, crawled the few feet back to the opening, tossed it through the hole, and headed in, alternating his shoulders until he had cleared up to his chest. As he started to inch his way, Nicole heard a grunt and wheeze as the soil above him gave way and locked him in place.

"Samir!"

She strapped on her headlamp and scrambled toward his feet, which quivered and jerked. Could she extricate him just by pulling him by his boots? Maybe if he wasn't buried by moist, heavy earth.

Just before she reached him, the ceiling beneath her gave way and swallowed her. She plunged what felt like at least three more meters, bouncing off a massive leg of the statue. Her light tore from her head and she slammed onto a new floor.

CHAPTER 58

Egypt

Before Pharoah in the palace court, Abram stood stock-still, staring straight ahead. What could this possibly be about?

"Do you know why I have required your presence, sir?" the Pharoah said.

"I do not, honorable ruler."

"You have treated me with contempt, Abram. Why did you not tell me that Sarai was your wife? Why did I have to learn this from God and the terrible curses He has rained on my house?"

"Forgive me, Pharoah. I—"

"For whatever reason did you tell me she was your sister and allow me to take her? Because I had not yet taken her to my bed was the only reason God spared me. Now take her and leave this land—you and your entire household and possessions!"

Greatly relieved, Abram traveled north into the desert with Sarai and Lot's family and their great stores of animals and precious metals. They continued toward Bethel and camped between there and Ai, where Abram had built an altar and urged his entire household to worship God there again.

Lot had also amassed huge flocks of sheep and goats, countless head of cattle, and numerous tents. He and Abram found the land they had come to could not accommodate their flocks and herds together, and discord arose between their herdsmen.

Finally Abram went to Lot. "Let's not let this come between us. As you are my brother's son, allow me to offer you the entire countryside. You choose any land you want and I will take what's left."

Lot chose the plains of the Jordan Valley with its rich stores of water near Sodom. Abram settled in Canaan. Once they were established in their respective areas, God spoke to Abram and told him that He was giving all the land he could see in every direction "to you and your progeny forever. And I will bless you with so many descendants that they will not be able to be counted!"

So Abram remained in Hebron near an oak grove, where he constructed yet another altar to God.

CHAPTER 59

Riyadh

Fares Harb's assistant entered, excused himself for interrupting, and whispered in the Saudi attorney's ear.

"Yes," Harb said quietly. "Just text him back that I'm in a meeting and will get back to him. My phone's in the basket there."

The assistant started picking through the basket, but at a scowl from Harb just took the whole thing into the hall. When he returned a few minutes later, he carried both the wicker basket and a metal briefcase about a foot square that appeared heavy. He set it next to the recording devices, replaced the wicker basket, and left, taking the briefcase with him.

"I've changed my mind," Kayla Mays blurted.

"I beg your pardon?" Harb said.

"I don't want asylum. I want to return with Detective Chakrabarti and explain myself to Dr. Berman. I'm sorry to have caused any inconv—"

"Sorry, but that's not how this works, Ms. Mays. We have gone to considerable trouble to harbor you and to accommodate the detective's wish to speak with you. But we cannot allow—"

"Excuse me," Beauregard Judd said. "Don't forget, Counselor, that we too are recording this meeting. I just heard as clearly as you did the wishes of a United States citizen that she be returned to her American chaperones. Unless you have reason to detain her, I'm going to have to insist—"

"Do not force our hand in this, Mr. Judd."

"Meaning?"

"You know full well that she is wanted in the United States, so—"

"I'm what?" Kayla said.

"That has nothing to do with this meeting," Judd said.

"It does now!" Harb said.

"Wanted for what?" Kayla said, pulling off her head covering and plopping it onto the table.

"You see what your stubbornness has accomplished, Judd?" Harb said. "You've forced us to reveal information none of us wanted disclosed yet— particularly your side. I cannot fathom that you would want this—"

Kayla's eyes filled and her voice sounded quavery. "I demand to know what you're talking ab—"

"Ms. Mays!" Harb shouted. "We're not accustomed to women demanding anything. You disrespect us and our culture by removing your head covering? Now you will—"

"Just tell me what's going on!" she said.

"Well, Mr. Harb," Judd said, "since you let the cat out of the bag, you might as well go ahead and tell her."

"I assumed we would get to this point," Harb said. "This is going to evolve into a significant trade, isn't it? Ms. Mays for a complete report of everything Dr. Berman has found at the site."

"It's going to do nothing of the sort," Judd said. "I formally request an end to this meeting and an immediate return of Ms. Mays to the custody of the United States, per her clear wishes and request."

"Does she know what that will mean?" Harb said.

"What *does* it mean?" Kayla said.

Harb squinted at her and appeared to steal a glance at Bo Judd. "Only that you will immediately be extradited to the U.S. to face charges for the murder of Dr. Nicole Berman's mother."

Kayla leapt to her feet. "What? Impossible! I loved her! I would never—"

"You'll have your day in court, Ms. Mays," Judd said. "And you know you have a right to counsel and a fair trial."

"Do I have to go?"

"Of course you don't," Harb said. "You can remain here under asylum with the Saudi government."

Pranav Chakrabarti reached for her hands. "What status do you think you'll have here? A non-Muslim American female..."

She appeared apoplectic and sat back down. "I don't know what to do, Pranav."

"Sure you do. You're in a very difficult predicament, but back home you have an entire support system and a culture you know and understand. You'll never be really free here. If I were you, I'd face the music under the auspices of the U.S. Embassy."

"But I'm not guilty! I didn't—"

"Say nothing, please," Pranav said. "When you're arrested you'll be awarded the privilege of remaining silent, and I suggest you exercise it. This is hardly the time or place to say anything about what you may be charged with."

Kayla gave a slight nod and plainly stared at the pocket where Detective Chakrabarti had slipped her note. He retrieved it.

Pranav, whatever happens, investigate Doctor Qahtani. Please!

"This meeting is over, gentlemen," Bo Judd said, standing. "Based on Ms. Mays's clear statement of her wishes, we will take her to the U.S. Embassy for disposition."

"I guess that's what I want," Kayla said.

"You guess?" attorney Harb said.

"If I can't get assurances from Dr. Qahtani that nothing will hap—"

"Leave me out of this," Nasim said. "I'm warning you."

Kayla stood again, tears streaming. "Pranav!" she wailed. "You must protect me! Please!"

"Of course, dear," the detective said. "What's going on? Protect you from whom?"

"From him!" she said, pointing at Qahtani. "I'll confess! I'll tell you everything! But don't make me stay here!"

"You'll confess nothing!" Qahtani said. "Turn those recorders off if she's going to concoct some sort of a story. You can't believe a young wo—"

"I'm listening!" Bo Judd said. "Are you, Mr. Harb?"

"This is highly irregular," Harb said. "You *want* all this on the record?"

"I don't!" Qahtani said. "At least not until we know what she plans to say."

"How convenient," Judd said. "I say put it on the record. If it's a lie, she'll have to own it, answer for it. Sit down, Ms. Mays, and talk to us."

"I want to sit with you," she said. "Not with them."

Qahtani threw up his hands. "How childish is this going to get? Now she's going to dictate where she sits?"

"Again," Judd said, "this is what you call asylum? You tell her where to sit, try to intimidate her into silence?"

"Let her sit where she wants," Harb said. "Let's just get this over with, whatever it is."

Kayla moved to the other side of the table and sat next to Pranav. Harb slid her head covering to her. "Please," he said.

"No," she said, "I want to speak my mind. I came to Dr. Qahtani because I could tell Detective Chakrabarti was closing in on me."

"Closing in on you? I was doing nothing of the sort."

"Oh, come now, Pranav. I could tell from the look on your face and all the rushed phone calls and conversations with Dr. Berman that something was up back home."

"Yes, but—"

"I knew it wouldn't be long before you'd put two and two together and know that Dr. Qahtani was the reason I came here."

"Tell her, Harb!" Qahtani said. "Tell her how seriously we take perjury here."

"She's not on trial!" Bo Judd said. "She's not under oath. Plus I want to know what she's saying."

"She's on the record," Harb said. "So she'll have to answer for anything she says, any charges she levels at anyone."

"Gladly," Kayla said. "Dr. Qahtani contacted me weeks ago in New York and—"

"That's a lie!" Qahtani said. "I didn't even meet you until you got to this country."

"Well, you sure knew a lot about me. You knew where I lived. You knew where I was from. You knew where my family lived."

Qahtani waved her off. "She's dreaming. This is lunacy."

"He said two volunteers for Nicole's dig would soon drop out and that I should apply. At first I was thrilled, because I had always wanted—"

Qahtani slapped the table and muttered something in Arabic.

"I don't know what that means," Kayla said.

"It means 'malarkey,'" Bo Judd said. "And if I may say so, Dr. Qahtani, you're pretty exercised over something you say has been invented out of thin air."

Qahtani repeated the Arabic word.

"Well, you would say so, sir," Kayla said, "but you know what comes next. You want to pick up the story from here?"

"I have no idea where you're going with this, but you're going to regret it nonetheless."

"So you didn't threaten the lives of my parents if I didn't find a way to kill Dr. Berman's mother—"

"That's defamation!" Qahtani shouted. "Tell this liar the punishment for that!"

"A year in jail," Harb said, "and a half million Saudi Riyal. That's more than one hundred thirty thousand U.S. dollars. A trifle compared to what you'll face for murder—in either country."

"A slap on the wrist in the U.S.," Qahtani said. "A beheading here."

"That's what *you* deserve, sir," Kayla said. "You forced me into it."

Bo Judd held up a hand. "This is spinning way out of control. This was intended to be a fact-finding meeting with a bit of diplomacy and decorum. But now I must advise my client to not be confessing to—"

"Oh, she's *your* client now," Harb said. "She's gone from a waif seeking asylum to charging a revered Saudi official with a heinous crime."

"Fine," Judd said. "Let her say on the record if she would like to retain me, in my role as a representative of the U.S., as her counsel."

"I do!"

"It's not that simple," Harb said.

"Yes, it is!" Judd said. "You can sort out all the legalities later, but for now, as her counsel, I'm advising her to be quiet."

"But I want to—"

"Be quiet, Ms. Mays," Judd said.

Again, she pulled a small bottle from her pocket, looked to the ceiling, and applied drops to both eyes. "Okay," she said, sighing.

CHAPTER 60

Near Hebron

By now Abram was a wealthy man with hundreds of servants and workers tending to his vast herds of livestock. His nephew Lot enjoyed a similar existence in the nearby town of Sodom until nine kings in that area waged war with one another. Five cities, including Sodom and Gomorrah, went to battle against four other kingdoms, including Babylonia—which was still ruled by King Nimrod, who continued to refer to himself as Amraphel. Though his failed tower had made him a laughingstock and his wasted body intimidated no one, he had enough of an army to send into battle.

The four kingdoms drove the armies of the five cities into the valley of the Dead Sea, where many fleeing warriors fell into tar pits, while the rest escaped into the mountains. The victors pillaged Sodom and Gomorrah, stripping the towns of valuables and food stores.

Word came to Abram that Lot had been captured and lost all his possessions. Abram immediately assembled more than three hundred trained fighters from among his ranks and set out after the plundering army, finally engaging them at Dan. He separated his men into fighting units and attacked after dark, pushing the enemy north of Damascus. Abram recovered everything Lot had lost and rescued his nephew and all who had been captured.

The king of Sodom met Abram in the valley of Shaveh, and Melchizedek, the king of Salem and a godly priest, presented him with bread and wine. "Blessed be Abram by God Most High, Creator of heaven and earth," Melchizedek said. "And blessed be God Most High, who has defeated your enemies for you."

Abram presented Melchizedek a tithe of everything he had recovered.

The king of Sodom asked for all his citizens who had been taken, telling Abram he could keep all the goods he had recovered.

"No," Abram said. "I swear to the Lord Most High that I will not take so much as a single thread or sandal thong. I will accept only what my men already ate, and I beg you to share the goods with my allies."

After all this had taken place, God came to Abram in a vision. "Do not fear," He said. "I will protect you and reward you greatly."

Abram didn't know what to think. What good would rewards do him when Sarai still had not borne him a son? He told the Lord that one of his servants, Eliezer of Damascus, would inherit his wealth, "because you have favored me with no descendants."

But God told him, "You will have a son to be your heir. Count the stars. That's how many descendants I will give you!"

It sounded ludicrous, especially to someone Abram's age, but remembering the faith of his parents, he trusted God.

The Lord said, "I brought you out of Ur to give you this land."

This land? It was one thing to believe God's promise of offspring, but also all this territory? He asked the Lord how he could be certain.

God instructed him to bring a three-year-old heifer, a three-year-old female goat, a three-year-old ram, a turtledove, and a young pigeon. Abram cut each animal in two, but not the birds. When the sun began to set, Abram fell asleep, and a horrifying darkness enveloped him. The Lord appeared to him and said, "Your descendants will be slaves in a foreign land for four hundred years, but in the end they will become vastly wealthy. And you will die in peace at an old age. Your descendants will return to this land."

A smoking pot and a flaming torch passed between the halves of the animal bodies. God said, "I have given this territory to your offspring from the border of Egypt to the Euphrates River."

CHAPTER 61

Square One, the Mada'in dig

Nicole had to get to Dr. Samir Waleed, that was all she knew. She raised herself to her hands and knees and tried to catch her breath. Her headlamp lay several feet away, and its light flickered dimly. How long had she used it since the last charge?

Trying to clear her head, Nicole forced herself to regulate her breathing and to not panic. She had blasted into the statue on the way down, she was sure of that. It had likely saved her life, keeping her from landing on her head and breaking her neck. But she had to have other damage—there was no way around it. Did she have time to assess herself with Samir buried at his chest and likely struggling to breathe?

Nicole rocked forward and felt a throbbing pull in her ribs. One had to be cracked on her right side, likely more. A deep pain just above her right knee told her a deep bruise would form. Anything else? She didn't think so, though the right side of her face ached too. So striking that effigy on her way down had flipped her so she landed flat on that side.

She crawled to her headlamp and winced as she tapped and shook it, getting the light to hold steady, at least briefly. It was all Nicole could do to slowly stand and wait for dizziness to pass. How does one climb nearly ten feet of sheer wall to a ceiling that had crumbled under her? It was futile to try to get Dr. Waleed to hear her, let alone respond, but still she called out for him anyway. The yelling made her grab her excruciating ribs.

She felt for her phone and her walkie-talkie. Until she could conjure a way to climb, especially injured, others above stood a better chance to get to Samir in time to free him. Nicole herself would be an easy extraction, she surmised, if they could somehow get some sort of pulley system in there where the soil above was solid.

Had Suzie or anyone heard or at least felt the collapse of the ceiling, or had Samir's cries reached them? Her phone shone bright but also showed no coverage that deep. Nicole guessed she was at least eighteen feet from the surface, and she and Dr. Waleed had forbidden anyone to join them until they were beckoned.

Surely her walkie-talkie had more range. Nicole mashed the button and called for Suzie. She could tell from the sound of her own voice and the static of the walkie that little if anything was transmitted. She pressed the gadget to her ear and recoiled. Blood ran down her fingers onto the unit. "Mayday! Mayday!" she tried.

Nicole held her breath and listened for any sound from above. Nothing. Until Suzie finally grew suspicious and realized she and Samir had been down there far too long, Nicole was on her own. She had to find a way up to Samir to dig him out. Maybe then she would be close enough to the surface to be heard.

Nicole mince-stepped toward the wall where she had seen the curved column from above that revealed itself as the statue—of Abraham? She could only hope. Her headlamp revealed a gigantic sculptured leg and some sort of garment hanging from it. How solid might it be after all these centuries? It had to be more dense and compact than the walls, and it did lie at an angle to the ceiling.

Nicole found in her pockets her brush, wood handle still intact, and her handpick. Neither would support her weight on the sheer earthen wall, but maybe she could somehow find purchase on the leg of the statue. If she could find a way to ascend it, she would force herself back to where she had fallen through. Her light would have to hold out so she could avoid the same fate that landed her where she was.

Nicole surveyed the statue and tried to memorize its contours. She turned off her headlamp to conserve its power and steeled herself against the pain of the climb. She had to avoid at all costs slipping into shock, despite that it was her only hope to dull the agony.

"God," she said, "I've been self-sufficient my whole life. Forgive me for always trying to fend for myself when You are my rock and my protector. Now I'm at the end of myself and need You as never before. I'll fight through the pain, but only You can get me out of here. Somehow allow my friend to breathe and hang on until I can get to him."

Gritting her teeth and whimpering with every labored step, Nicole mounted the massive leg of the statue and tried to pull herself up. Her pick gave her a tentative hold on the right, but the handle of her brush proved no help on the other. She pocketed it and tentatively worked with her bare hand, spreading her fingers as far as she could and inching up. The incline was such that her rubber soled boots barely held her in place, despite that her arms and legs soon began to shake and she wasn't sure how long she could hold on.

It seemed to Nicole that she was advancing but an inch or so at a time, and she fought to keep her boots connected to the structure. More than once, as she paused for breath and to ease the agony in her ribs and thigh, she felt herself slipping and hugged the statue with all her might. She had no idea how long it took her to reach about halfway up, but she couldn't imagine mustering the strength to make it all the way.

Hanging on and panting for several minutes, Nicole prayed for just enough strength to reach the top. She stole a glance at her watch. Nearly noon. Surely someone would come looking for them when she and Samir missed lunch. She didn't want to think about what she would do if she reached the ceiling of the vault, only to find nothing solid enough to get her past where she had fallen through.

Nicole chastised herself for not having listened to Samir's warnings. She knew all along that his counsel was the better part of wisdom. He had a lifetime of experience on her, but even she had seen dangerous collapses at various digs, lives endangered, colleagues badly injured. In short, she knew better. Sure, this was the find of a lifetime and worth certain risks—but not their lives.

Several minutes later, quaking with fatigue, Nicole paused again. Her walkie-talkie rattled with static and she instinctively reached for it, dropping her pick and having to scramble to keep from sliding down. With her face pressed against the stone of the statue and her left hand pressed as hard as she could manage, she shouted into the talkie, "Suzie! Suzie! Mayday! We need help!"

More static. Had she been heard?

Nicole had to continue. When finally she reached the crumbled ceiling, she hoisted herself up and turned on her headlamp, delicately felt around for any surface that might support her. The light flickered, and the first few places she fingered disintegrated to dust. Surely she hadn't come this far only to fail. The statue seemed to have been sheered off where its top met the ceiling. And while the ceiling itself was anything but solid, if Nicole could somehow reach the top of the sculpture, she ought to be able to see how Samir was doing.

Getting atop that structure exhausted Nicole, and all she could do for a minute was sit there, legs crossed, gasping. "Samir!" she called out, the bottoms of his boots in the beam of her lamp. She checked her phone again—still no signal—and also tried the walkie. More static.

Nicole stretched her legs and tapped with her heels on the top of the ceiling. It wasn't far from where she had plunged in, but it felt like it might support her. What did she have to lose? Only her life. But if there was any chance to save Samir...

She crawled toward his feet, expecting any moment to be hurtling through the air once again. If that happened, Nicole decided, she sincerely hoped it would be the end of her. She wouldn't want to live as an invalid, and there was no way she could endure a second fall from that height without serious damage.

The top of the vault's ceiling didn't feel as secure as she might have hoped, but it held. When she stretched to reach Samir's feet, she cried out in pain but tugged them hard. "Move if you can feel me! Let me know you're alive!" The earth lay on his back and she detected no movement.

Nicole used her brush handle to poke at his shins, just above his socks. She drove the point in deep enough that he should have recoiled in pain. Nothing. She removed his boot so she could feel for a pulse near his ankle. "Oh, no, Samir!"

Nicole dragged herself to where the soil wall had dropped onto the man's back and began digging with her hands. Believing he was gone and pierced too by the pain in her body, she sobbed as she cleared the debris. Would she cause only a further collapse? It was far too late to start heroic resuscitation efforts even when she could reach his head. If he was gone, she still had to break through to where she could communicate topside.

It took Nicole nearly an hour to break through enough earth to crawl through. She felt for a pulse at Samir's neck but knew it was futile before she began. She sat next to him and lifted his head into her lap, weeping.

Her walkie-talkie crackled. "Nicole, do you read? Nicole? Dr. Waleed?"

CHAPTER 62

Canaan

Despite all God's promises and what Abram believed with all his heart was a covenant between him and the Lord, ten years after he had settled here, he had reached his mideighties and Sarai still had borne him no children. She seemed to grow more and more despondent with every passing day, yet Abram didn't know what to tell her, other than that God had assured him he would have many offspring. It pained him to see her in such turmoil, and he wanted answers as much as he knew she did.

"I want to be the one who bears your children," she said, "but at seventy-five, my time is long past. What if I gave you my servant? Maybe through her I can have children…"

"Hagar the Egyptian?" Abram said. "You must think this through. Are you certain this is what you want?"

"I assure you it is."

"Should we not trust God?"

"We have trusted Him all along! Who's to say this isn't His plan for us, the way He wants it to come to pass?"

So Abram took Hagar as a second wife, and soon she became pregnant. But the moment she began to show, she said, "Look at me, Sarai. And look at you. I did what you could never do."

Such boasting and contempt went on for days until Sarai told Abram,

"This is on you! I gave her to you, but now she treats me with disdain because she is going to be the mother of your child. I can no longer stand the sight of her. I will beg God to show me who was wrong—you or me!"

"You gave her to me as a wife," Abram said, "but she works for you. Do with her as you will."

Sarai accepted no more sass or mistreatment from Hagar and forced her to do so many chores for her that eventually she stormed off and disappeared.

Hagar found a spring in the wilderness on the road to Shur, where she collapsed to rest. A strange man appeared to her, whom she quickly recognized as an angel because he called her by name. "Hagar, servant of Sarai, where are you coming from, and where will you go?"

"I'm escaping my mistress."

"Return to Sarai and obey her, and you will not be able to count the descendants I give you. You will bear a son and name him Ishmael—which means 'God hears.' He will be wild as an untamed donkey, will fight everyone, and they will all oppose him. He will even raise his fist to his own family."

Hagar found herself nearly speechless, but finally said, "Have I truly seen God, the One who sees me?"

She returned to Sarai and served her, then gave birth to Ishmael when Abram was eighty-six years old.

CHAPTER 63

Al-'Ula

To Detective Pranav Chakrabarti, Dr. Nasim Qahtani appeared eager to escape the meeting. "Let's wrap this up," he told attorney Fares Harb. "I don't intend to sit here and listen to more fantasies from a—"

"That won't break my heart," Beauregard Judd said. "As long as you let me take my client back to the embassy, I think we're done here."

"She's going nowhere," Qahtani said.

"Now hold on a second, Nasim," Harb said. "She's on the record that she wants Mr. Judd to represent her and that she no longer seeks asylum here, so—"

"You're going to let her return to America and level all sorts of ridiculous charges against me, without my having a chance to—"

"The Saudi government will protect you, Nasim," Harb said. "We're not about to allow *you* to be extradited—"

"I want her formally charged with defamation. She must face—"

Judd stood. "File all the charges you care to. You'll know where to find her. You want her to risk a fine and a year in prison here or stand trial for murder in the U.S. Your call."

"Those are my only options?" Kayla said.

"Just giving you the realities," Judd said. "And believe me, you'll have a lot more protection at home than here."

"But I—"

"I really need you to keep your tongue, young lady," Judd said. "Now, Mr. Harb, we need to close and get going."

"Thus ends this meeting," Harb said, turning off his recorder.

"You're going to let her go with them?" Qahtani said.

"Leave it alone, Nasim. Her frivolous claims will be seen for what they are."

"Hey!" Judd said, staring at his recorder. "What's the deal?" He showed the LED readout to Pranav. "You saw me turn this on, right?"

"Of course."

"Nothing! There's nothing on it. I'm going to need a copy of your recording, Mr. Harb."

"Why, certainly. If your batteries failed—"

"My batteries were fresh. There's been a glitch somewhere."

"We have nothing to hide," Harb said. "Oh, would you look at that! It appears mine failed too. We're both going to have to go from memory."

Pranav snatched up his camera and turned it on. "Oh, no."

"What?"

"My memory card has been erased."

"How unfortunate," Mr. Harb said. "Nothing crucial, I hope."

Pranav felt the blood drain from his face. "Only irreplaceable shots from the find—from the dig."

"Surely you backed them up or transmitted them somewhere," Harb suggested. "You were to keep Dr. Qahtani informed. Had you not sent them to him?"

"I have seen nothing," Qahtani said.

CHAPTER 64

Canaan

By the age of ninety-nine, Abram had settled into a comfortable life of wealth and devotion to God, despite his and Sarai's disappointment over not having a child of their own. Puzzled at the apparent mistake his parents, and he, had made—believing that God had promised him unlimited progeny—he could not complain. Their vast dwellings sat amidst acres and acres of rich pastureland for thousands of head of livestock, requiring the assistance of hundreds of servants and household staff.

One day the Lord appeared to Abram and identified himself as El-Shaddai, God Almighty, and told him to "serve Me devotedly and live blamelessly, and I will establish a covenant guaranteeing you progeny too numerous to count."

Abram dropped to his knees and lowered his face to the ground. And God said, "Here is my promise: You will become the father of nations. Your name shall no longer be Abram. Rather, you will become Abraham, for you will be enormously fruitful. Kings will arise from among your offspring. I will reaffirm this with you and your descendants everlastingly. I will bestow upon you all of Canaan forever, so those who come after you may possess it forever, and I shall be their God.

"You must obey the covenant from generation to generation by having every male among you circumcised as a sign on the eighth day after his birth, not only family members but also servants born in your household or ones you have purchased. Any who fails to be circumcised will have broken this covenant.

"Your wife's name will no longer be Sarai. From now on it will be Sarah. I will bless her and give you a son through her. Kings of nations will be among her offspring."

With his face in the dirt, Abraham laughed to himself. *I, a father at one hundred? And Sarah a mother at ninety?*

"Lord, may my son Ishmael also live under this blessing?"

"No. Sarah will bear a son you will name Isaac, and my covenant shall abide forever with his descendants. I will bless Ishmael also, making him exceedingly fruitful, multiplying his offspring. He will beget twelve princes. But my covenant shall be confirmed with Isaac."

That day Abraham took thirteen-year-old Ishmael and all the other males in his household and circumcised them as God had instructed. Thereafter, every male born in the family or among those in the household were circumcised eight days following their birth.

One day Abraham sat at the entrance to his tent near the oak grove during the hottest part of the day when three men appeared nearby. Recognizing them as heavenly visitors, he ran to them and welcomed them, bowing low. "If you wish, please stop and rest here in the shade and allow us to wash your feet. And let me prepare a meal for you before you continue on your way to wherever you are going."

When they agreed, Abraham rushed to Sarah and urged her to bake bread while he hurried out to find a tender calf and had a servant roast it. When the food was ready, Abraham served it to his visitors with yogurt and milk.

"Where is your wife, Sarah?" one of the men asked.

"In the tent."

"I will return about this time next year, and she will have a son."

Sarah overheard this and laughed silently. "How could a used-up woman like me win such pleasure, especially when my husband is as old as he is?"

The angel of the Lord said, "Why did Sarah laugh? Is anything too hard for God? It shall come to pass as I have said."

Sarah called out, "I did not laugh."

But the man said, "Yes, you did."

As the men left, Abraham walked with them a short way. One said, "I am going to Sodom and Gomorrah to see if they are as evil as I have heard."

Abraham said, "Will you destroy both the righteous and the wicked? What if you find fifty righteous people there?"

The Lord said, "If I find fifty righteous people there, I will spare Sodom for their sake."

"Though I am nothing but dust and ashes," Abraham said, "suppose you find only forty-five righteous people? Would you destroy the city?"

"I will not."

"Suppose you find only forty?"

"I will not destroy it."

"Please don't be angry, Lord," Abraham said. "Suppose you find only thirty righteous people?"

"I will not destroy it for thirty."

Abraham said, "Since I have been so bold, may I ask—suppose there are only twenty?"

"Then I will not destroy it."

"Lord, please don't be angry if I speak once more. Suppose only ten are found there?"

"Then I will not destroy it."

CHAPTER 65

Square One, the Mada'in dig

Nicole lay next to the body of Dr. Samir Waleed, too spent even to move. She prayed she would awaken from this nightmare, but would that mean the inscription she had found had all been a dream too?

Suzie continued to beckon them both on the walkie-talkie, but Nicole's every effort to reach it, to plead for help, made her fade only faster.

"On our way down!" Suzie transmitted.

No! Nicole thought. *It's too unstable! Don't risk more lives!*

But excited voices wafted to her from the ladder and strong beams of light crossed and danced.

"Dr. Berman! Dr. Waleed!"

"Over here!" Nicole rasped, reaching for what or whom she had no idea. But the effort drained the last of her strength. In the dim light of her own flickering headlamp, the crumbled devastation of the ruins swam before her and she could no longer keep her eyes open. Somehow sleep seemed welcome, as welcome as any respite had ever been.

Nicole was only vaguely aware of being hoisted out of Square One into bright sunlight, someone shielding her eyes. Suzie?

How long had she been out? How long had it taken them to get to her, to find a stretcher, to arrange a pulley system and hoist her up? Was Dr. Waleed's body still down there? Many around her spoke excitedly in Arabic, others in subdued tones. English words floated and jumbled. "Superficial." "Acute." "Broken." "Punctured." Who could they possibly be referring to but her?

Nicole listened closely for "grave," "life-threatening," or other dire pronouncements, comforting herself that she heard none. But neither did she feel confident she would survive. If Samir was dead, was she close? It certainly could have gone either way. She wanted to grab Suzie, pull her close, and tell her what more she'd found. The priceless artifacts must be protected at all costs.

Sure, Saudis were here now, due to one of their own having perished in the hole. She couldn't keep them from the proximity of the inscription or the statue, but neither could she stand guard over it. Had the collapse damaged the otherwise pristine halves of the inscription? Fortunately, she had pictures. And her memory. She hoped.

Nicole tried silently reciting the translation she had made of the ancient language. She believed it contained *Abraham, Isaac,* and *Ishmael,* but the rest eluded her. It had been a prayer or an oath or a blessing. A blessing, yes! Abraham blessed his sons, and someone thought to memorialize it for the ages.

But again she felt herself drifting toward unconsciousness. That was dangerous, she knew. She had to survive, had to document all this, tell of it, explain it, force the world—even the Muslim world—to acknowledge its significance. But her eyes closed. Nicole could not focus enough to keep them open. Yet she was shaken by rumbling and *thwock-thwocks*— from what? Helicopter rotors? The last she remembered, her stretcher had been placed on the ground, protected by one of the sunscreens.

Saudi accents barked flight lingo in English. They were clearly in the air! How could she have been laded aboard and the craft take off without her having been aware? Where were they taking her, and who had come with her?

"Suzie?" she tried.

"I'm here," the Square One supervisor said, her broad, sun-reddened face looming. "Keep still, but stay awake."

"Can't," Nicole said, letting her eyes close again.

Suzie massaged her cheeks. "No, Nic! Sleep is not your friend right now."

"Where we goin'?"

"Hush. Medina."

"What's in Medina?"

"Please don't try to talk, Dr. Berman. Apparently there's a trauma center at Faisal Specialist."

"Trauma?"

"Just like you not to feel traumatized, but you got pretty banged up."

"Was I just dreaming or is Samir dead?" Suzie's hesitation told Nicole all she needed to know. "Hope he didn't suffer," she slurred.

"Just keep your eyes open and stay with me, Nic."

"Um-hmm. How long?"

"We left about twenty minutes ago, so another forty."

"Can't stay awake that long."

"You have to, hon. Show me what you're made of."

Nicole gave it everything she had in her but felt herself fading. Suzie continued to prattle on, apparently trying to keep Nicole engaged, but her very cadence served as a lullaby. Despite the bouncing of the craft and the noise of the blades, Nicole glided ever so slowly into unconsciousness, awakened again every few minutes when Suzie apparently noticed and prodded her.

"You've got a lot to tell me," her old friend said. "Not right now, of course, but be thinking about it. I need to know what you found down there and what happened. Whatever crushed Dr. Waleed seems to have missed you, but you couldn't have gotten all your bruises from just lying there, could you? Did you fall through the ceiling into that burial vault? Just nod if you did."

"I did."

"I'm not trying to get you to talk, Nic. I'm trying to keep you awake.

Just think about telling me how you got back up out of there and what made you both venture that far in to start with."

Nicole nodded and mouthed, "I'll try." She struggled to sit up, but Suzie gently stopped her. "Does Pranav know?"

"Shh! We've been trying to call him. Max'll find him."

Max? No.

* * *

Al-'Ula

Detective Pranav Chakrabarti wracked his brain. Where else might those images be? Transmitted to Nicole, to Max? Anywhere or anyone else? He reached into the basket for his phone, just as every device in there began to ring, ping, or vibrate. Everyone grabbed theirs, some staring at the screen, others answering.

Pranav received a text from Max:

Where are you? Ck previous texts! Collapse in Sq 1.
Waleed gone. Nic airlifted to Faisal/Medina. Hurry.

Dr. Nasim Qahtani bolted as soon as he'd peeked at his phone, and what Pranav could only assume was the squeal of the man's tires reached the conference room.

"Oh, no," Fares Harb said, gathering his stuff.

Beauregard Judd swore. "Let's get Ms. Mays to the consulate, Detective. Then we've got to get to the dig."

"Wait!" Pranav said.

"What! We've got to go! There was a Saudi death, man! This is going to be a royal mess!"

"I've got nothing else on my phone! No previous texts, no contacts, no pictures, nothing! What's going on here, Harb?"

"How would I know?" the Saudi lawyer said, heading out as if in shock.

"Hey!" Judd said. "My phone too! It's like it's brand-new! What in the world did you do, Harb?"

Harb stopped at the door and sounded flat, emotionless. "Ms. Mays is not to leave the country without our knowledge."

"We'd better get going," Judd said. "We can talk in the car."

"I've got to get to Medina," Pranav said. "Dr. Berman is at Faisal Hospital there."

"There's nothing you can do for her," Judd said. "Anyway, Medina is another two hundred miles south of here."

"Can you get me a plane? I need to talk to her before anything happens to her."

"No, I can't get you a plane! You'll not likely be allowed to see her right away anyway, man! The consulate, then the site, okay? Maybe you can reach Medina by phone in the meantime."

CHAPTER 66

Sodom

Abraham's nephew Lot sat at the city gate the evening after the angels had visited his uncle. When he saw two angels approach, he rose and greeted them, bowing low. "Wash your feet at my home and stay the night."

"No, we can stay in the city square."

"Please! I insist! I'll have a feast prepared, even bread without yeast!"

And so they relented and followed him home. After they had finished their meal and conversed awhile, Lot stood to show them to their quarters. "What's that racket outside?" one said.

"I don't know," Lot said, moving to his front door and peeking out.

It seemed every male in the city—young and old—had encircled his house. "Where are your guests!" they shouted. "Send them out so we can have our way with them!"

Lot stepped outside and shut the door behind him. "Please, no!" he said. "Refrain from such wickedness! Let me bring my two virgin daughters out, but leave my guests alone. I must protect them."

"Get out of our way!" they shouted. "You can't move to our town and then act like our judge! We'll do worse to you than to your guests!"

They rushed Lot, clearly intending to break down his door, but the two angels quickly opened it, pulled him inside, and slammed the door, bolting it. They stood before the door and lifted their hands. From outside came wailing.

"I can't see!"

"What's happened?"

"I can't either!"

"Me either!"

Soon the place fell silent, and Lot knew the men of the town had staggered away.

"If you have other relatives in the city," the angels told him, "any at all, you must get them far from this place before we destroy the entire region."

Lot ran to warn his daughters' fiancés, but they just laughed at him. "You're joking!" they said.

At dawn the angels insisted Lot hurry. "Get your wife and daughters out of here now so you're not all lost in the destruction!"

Lot hesitated. "I don't know," he said.

The angels took him and his family by the hands and dragged them away from Sodom. "Now run! And don't look back! Escape to the mountains, or you will die!"

Lot pleaded with them not to send him and his family to the mountains, believing he would die there. "Please let me stop in the small village Zoar, where I can be safe."

The angels agreed and promised not to destroy Zoar, but urged him to hurry, "for we cannot wipe out these evil cities until you are safe there."

Lot arrived in Zoar as the sun rose, and in the distance God rained fire and burning sulfur on both Sodom and Gomorrah, obliterating them and other cities and towns of the plain, including all the inhabitants and vegetation.

When it was all over, Lot took stock of his situation and was horrified to find that his wife must have disobeyed the angels and looked back. She had become a pillar of salt.

That morning Abraham rushed to the spot where he had negotiated with the Lord to save Sodom if He found even five righteous people there. Smoke rose in the distance as if from a furnace.

* * *

Eventually Lot left Zoar, fearing the people there, and took his two daughters to live in a cave in the mountains. There the daughters determined that because there were no men available to them, they would be unable to preserve their family line. So they conspired to get Lot drunk and sleep with him.

Both became pregnant by their own father, and their sons begat the respective nations of the Moabites and Ammonites.

CHAPTER 67

King Faisal Specialist Hospital, Medina, Saudi Arabia

Nicole Berman was devastated that so much of the trip to the hospital had eluded her. It scared her. How was it possible the medevac chopper had delivered her to personnel who ferried her to the trauma center's intensive care unit, hooked her up to all manner of machines, lifelines, and drips, and fitted her with an oxygen mask, yet none of this—not even the landing—had registered with her? She could live with physical injuries—even debilitating ones, if necessary—but if she'd suffered brain trauma…

"Suzie?"

Her friend quickly stood. "Good morning, sunshine!"

"Tell me it's not morning. If it is, I'm seriously—"

"It's not, sorry. Just me implying how long you've been out. You fought hard until the last ten minutes of the flight."

"How long have I been out?"

"Coming up on two hours. Though you arrived unconscious, they stabilized you and let you sleep."

"I musta hit my head something awful."

"Should know soon," Suzie said. "You've already had a scan."

"Seriously? I was in one of those tubes?"

Suzie nodded. "The best way you could be. Totally out. They scanned your whole body, but they're most worried about your head, of course."

"So am I. Foggy. Everything's foggy."

"Your father's on his way from the States."

"Oh, no! He must be worried sick."

"Of course, but wouldn't you have wanted to be told if something like this had happened to him?"

"Well, yeah, but—"

"He's flying private and said he should be here by late tomorrow morning."

"Mm-hmm…"

"Max is on his way too."

"Wait, what? No."

"What'd you mean? You don't want—"

"Make sure he checks in with Pr-Pran—"

"Detective Chakrabarti?"

"Yes. He needs to, I don't know…something…"

"Get some rest, Nicole."

"But…"

* * *

Al-'Ula

Detective Pranav Chakrabarti sat in front with Beauregard Judd on the way to the consulate office, with Kayla Mays directly behind him. He called Faisal Specialist and was transferred to the trauma center's nurses station, where he was told that Dr. Berman was sleeping and could not be disturbed.

Pranav tried calling Max—whom he knew, of course, was not really Max. Whoever he was, he looked more and more like another suspect in this whole debacle. Chakrabarti had been about to involve Saudi authorities in a search for him, but clearly Max was back, as he had been the one to inform Pranav about the disaster in Square One. But where had he been? What was he up to? He wasn't answering his phone, but a text came through.

Can't talk now. Call you later?

Sure, **Pranav texted back,** but just tell me where you are.

Square One, but the Saudis aren't letting any of us down there. They're hauling tons of stuff away.

Stay put. I'll come to you. Talk later.

Pranav had been trained not to jump to conclusions, but it wasn't easy. Max had seemed so cooperative, so congenial. But with his unauthorized visit to Square One after hours, the phony name, going AWOL—at least temporarily—could he have any kind of a rational explanation? Pranav could not imagine.

"Finished?" Bo Judd said.

"Sorry?"

"We need to work together on Ms. Mays here."

"Work on me?" Kayla whined. "What does that mean? You don't have to talk me into anything. I know I'm better off in the States."

"Better off than here, sure," Judd said. "Except you didn't murder anybody here. Exposing a Saudi official wasn't the brightest move—"

"But he gave me no choice!" She laid her head back and applied another drop to each eye.

"That's going to be your defense? He made you do it?"

"You tell me, sir. You're the lawyer."

"You're not going to like what I have to say, ma'am. In essence, you're telling me you committed a murder under a forced motive."

"Exactly! It was either a very sick old lady or me and my family."

"So you did it under the stress of threat."

"Yes!"

"Well, take this with a grain of salt, because I'm no criminal defense attorney. But I do know the law. What you're claiming here is called the defense of duress."

"I wouldn't have known what to call it, but I agree."

"The problem is that in virtually all jurisdictions, that defense is not allowed for murder. A judge might consider it a mitigating circumstance during sentencing, but there's no guarantee."

"It's my only defense. I never would have done something like that otherwise."

"Assuming you have no criminal record—"

"I don't."

"—that's another mitigating factor. But the fact that you didn't confess until you'd been found out would likely outweigh your otherwise clean record."

"So I'm in a bad way…"

"You could say that."

Bo Judd squinted into the rearview mirror. "Are you drinkin' that stuff?"

"Nah," Kayla said. "Just pulling the cap off with my teeth."

She fell silent for the next several minutes, and Pranav heard her eyedrop container hit the floor. "Can I reach that for you?" he said, but refrained when she didn't answer. Soon she leaned forward and lay her head on his shoulder. He hadn't felt that close to her, and she'd never acted so familiar with him. But if the full weight of the killing and what it boded for her now was finally washing over her, naturally she needed a friend.

"Remember what I told you," he whispered. "Jesus loves you. God can forgive you. You'll still have to pay for what you did, of course, but…"

Kayla's breathing sounded labored, gruff, croaky. Pranav pulled back to see her better and found her drooling, eyes rolled back, eyelids raw and red. "What the devil?" He unclasped his seat belt and wrenched around onto his knees to face her. He gently laid her back, and she appeared to stop breathing. "Pull over, Bo! She's in trouble! What's 911 here?"

"Ambulance is 997."

"Call 'em!"

CHAPTER 68

Canaan

Over the next few years, Abraham and his entire household and comple-
ment of animals became nomads, traversing south and settling in various
spots in the Negev before moving to Gerar. There, because he was an outsider, he again introduced Sarah as his sister. Eventually word reached the
king of Gerar, Abimelech, of the beautiful foreigner. He had her delivered
to the palace.

Two days later the king sent for Abraham, who found the entirety of
Abimelech's court looking as if they'd seen a ghost. "Let me tell you what
has happened here, Abraham," the king said. "Last night God came to me
in a dream and told me He would slay me because the woman I had summoned is married! But I had not touched her, and so I pleaded with the
Lord not to destroy me or my nation for a sin I had not committed. You
told me she was your sister! She told me that was true! Why would you
deceive me in such a way?

"God assured me He knew I was innocent and that He had kept me
from wickedness. But He also told me to return her to her husband and
that you would pray for me because you are a prophet. Otherwise I would
die, along with all my people. Abraham, I must ask, what did I ever do to
you that warranted such evil as this? How could you do this?"

"I confess I believed this was a godless kingdom," Abraham said. "I feared you would want my beautiful wife and might kill me for her. But in truth she *is* my sister, our having the same father but different mothers."

"I want no trouble with your God," Abimelech said. "Or with you." He gifted Abraham with sheep and goats, cows, and servants, and also returned Sarah. "Choose anywhere in my realm you want to dwell. And Sarah, I give your 'brother' one thousand pieces of silver for any wrong I did to you. Your reputation is restored."

When Abraham was one hundred years old and Sarah ninety, she miraculously bore a son, just as the Lord had promised, and they could not have been more thrilled. "We should be ashamed of ourselves for doubting God," Abraham told her.

"We both laughed when the prophecy came to us," Sarah said. "We should name him Isaac, for it means 'laughter.'"

When the lad reached weaning age, Abraham planned a feast to celebrate.

"I don't want Hagar or her son at the celebration," Sarah said.

"But why?" Abraham said. "Ishmael is also my son." By now he was nearing his fourteenth birthday.

"He and his mother ridicule Isaac and make fun of him, calling him a worthless second-born. Well, he is *my* firstborn and he is the promised one of God. He should not have to share his inheritance with anyone, especially that woman and her son. I will not stand for that. I want you to banish them from this household."

Abraham was deeply grieved by this, but God told him, "Do what Sarah says, because she is right about Isaac. He is the one through whom your lineage will come. But because Hagar's son is also yours, I will also bless him with a nation of descendants."

Early the next day Abraham gathered food and water for Hagar and Ishmael. "Where are you sending us?" she asked. "Where are we to go?"

Abraham remembered his own mother telling him the story of his father banishing them to a cave when he was an infant. "God will lead you," Abraham said.

"Where will we live?" Ishmael said, trudging with his mother into the Beersheba wilderness. They wandered aimlessly for days until their water ran out.

"Find shade, my son," she said, leaving him beside a bush. Though he was out of direct sunlight, he sat panting and sweating—and crying.

Hagar did not want to see him die and moved about a hundred yards away, where she sat sobbing.

"Hagar," God said from heaven, "fear not, for I have heard the boy. Go comfort him. I will make a great nation of his offspring." The Lord showed her a well, where she filled her jar and took it to Ishmael. God blessed him and he grew to become a skillful archer, settling in the wilderness of Paran and eventually marrying an Egyptian.

"What affords me this privilege?" Abraham asked when King Abimelech visited his vast dwelling.

"It has become obvious to me over the years that God favors you," the king said. "He seems to help you, whatever you do. I beseech you to swear to me in His name that you will never deceive me or any who come after me in my family. I have been generous with you, so covenant with me that you will remain loyal to me and to this kingdom, to which you came as a foreigner."

Abraham swore to it, then said, "But we do have a problem."

"Tell me!"

"Some of your servants commandeered a well from my servants, taking it by force."

"This is the first I've heard anything about this."

Abraham suggested a treaty, offering the king livestock plus an additional seven she-lambs. "Accept these to show you agree that the well is mine."

One day several years later, God called out to Abraham.

"I am here, Lord," he said.

"I want you to take your only son, who you love deeply, to Moriah and make of him a burnt offering on one of the mountains I show you."

Abraham felt deeply vexed, shocked that he was to lose his son. How would God fulfill His covenant with Isaac gone? And how would he and Sarah survive such a loss? But Abraham loved God and believed Him sovereign. He could not, would not, disobey the Lord's direct order. Early the next morning, he saddled his donkey, chopped kindling for the fire, took two servants and Isaac, and set out for Moriah.

Three days into the trip, Abraham saw in the distance the mountain God had led him to. "Stay with the donkey," Abraham told the servants. "Isaac and I will journey farther to worship there, and then we will return." He said this with more confidence than he felt. Having no idea what the Lord would do, he simply believed.

So Abraham stacked the wood onto his son's shoulders, and he carried a flaming pot and a knife. As they walked together, Isaac said, "Father, we have the fire and the wood, but where is the sheep for the offering?"

"God will provide."

When they arrived at the place God had led him, Abraham built an altar and arranged the wood on it. He bound Isaac hand and foot and laid him atop the kindling, unable to look away from the shock and fear in his son's eyes. But when he raised his knife, God called out, "Abraham! Abraham!"

"I am here."

"Don't hurt him, for you have proven you truly fear Me and have not withheld even your only son."

Flooded with relief and almost too weak to stand, Abraham found a ram in a thicket nearby, which he burned as a sacrifice in place of Isaac. And the Lord spoke again. "Because you have obeyed Me, I will multiply your offspring beyond counting, as plentiful as the stars and the sand. Your progeny will conquer their enemies. And through them all the earth will be blessed."

CHAPTER 69

Al-'Ula

Detective Pranav Chakrabarti found himself astounded at U.S. Embassy attorney Beauregard Judd's callousness while they waited for an ambulance. While Pranav frantically performed artificial resuscitation on Kayla Mays, the lawyer actually said, "So much for U.S.–Saudi dialogue."

"A little help here, Bo!" Pranav said.

"I know better'n that!" Judd said. "Leave me outta this."

"What's the matter with you? This girl's about to die!"

"I don't know CPR, for one thing. And I don't need what might come of it legally."

"That's what you're worried about?"

"Look," Judd said, "I don't wanna sound cold, but if this girl lives, it sets our relationship here back several years. Both governments just announced bilateral working groups to strengthen cooperation."

"You beat everything, Bo. Google what's in eyedrops that could cause this reaction. And is it fatal?"

* * *

King Faisal Specialist Hospital

"I need to sit up," Nicole Berman said.

Suzie Benchford appeared at her side. "No, you don't. You need to rest."

282

"Suzie, listen to me. I know I'm hurt, and I'm not going to do anything stupid. But I need to tell you what we found down there so you know how important it is to protect it."

"The team will protect it."

"From the Saudis? Are you serious? You're my square super, and you're not even there!"

"Max will—"

"Help me sit up, will ya? I have to tell you about Max."

"Tell me from where you are. Until that CAT scan comes back, I'm not helping you sit up."

"Bring me my phone."

"Neither of us have phones, girl."

"What?"

"Yours was in pieces, and mine was confiscated on the helicopter."

"Confiscated?"

"The pilots told me they'd been ordered to take it but that I would get it back later."

"Fat chance."

"I made 'em let me call your dad and Detective Chakrabarti first, but, yeah, my guess is that phone's history."

* * *

Al-'Ula

Bo Judd studied his phone and swore as Pranav Chakrabarti continued CPR on Kayla Mays. "It *is* fatal, Detective! In fact, she's probably gone already. I saw her drinkin' that stuff, man, and according to this, if she took as much as it looked like, you're not gonna revive her."

"Well, I'm not about to give up. What's the poison?"

"Tetrahydrozoline. Great for the eyes and maybe the nose, but taken by mouth, it's an immediate blood vessel constrictor. You're not even supposed to put more'n two drops in your eyes every four hours. This Tetra-stuff gets absorbed fast, and as soon as it's in your circulatory system, it moves to the heart and the central nervous system. Slows your pulse and blood pressure drops. Lemme see here—temperature falls, coma, death. Best-case scenario, she's in a coma and the EMTs can save her. Worst-case, she's already gone."

"No pulse," Pranav said. "No breath. And she feels cold already." He pried open one eye. "Pupil dilated. Lips and nails blue."

"It's over, man."

* * *

King Faisal Specialist Hospital

Gradually, Nicole felt she was regaining her faculties. And when a resident evaluated her body scan and determined she was "very fortunate to have suffered no brain trauma," she became determined to get herself up and around in record time. She had to get back to the site, to document and protect the find of a lifetime. Not even all the trauma she'd suffered could diminish her excitement.

The resident surveyed her scan from top to bottom. "Whatever issues you're having with memory or—"

"—fogginess?"

"Yes. That should pass soon. Your brain was clearly jostled, but there appears no swelling or bruising, at least that we can see. The contusions on your face will scab up and should heal without scarring. You can see some trauma to your right shoulder, but it remains in the socket without damage to the rotator cuff. It may be weak and sore for a few weeks, but you'll be able to use it.

"You do have three cracked ribs, which will have to heal on their own, and ribs are good that way. You'll feel that for a few weeks too, laughing, sneezing, coughing, rising, sitting, reaching. With the deep bruising on that right hip and just above the knee, we were surprised to find no internal damage. You'll just have to take it easy. All in all, you were extremely lucky. Any idea how far you fell?"

"About three meters."

"Something must have broken your fall."

Nicole nodded. "I hit and flipped." She couldn't wait to get back and take pictures of the statue she'd bounced off. Could it have been of Abraham himself?

"Had you not, we would not be having this conversation. Unimpeded impact from that height could easily have killed you."

* * *

Al-'Ula

Pranav Chakrabarti sat at the side of the road with his back to the grille of Bo Judd's embassy-issued car. Exhausted from several minutes of CPR, he buried his head in his hands and wept as Saudi paramedics informed him they would be taking Kayla to the morgue rather than to an emergency room.

"Sorry for your loss, man," Bo Judd said. "I didn't realize you were that close."

"We weren't really, but I knew her. Thought I did anyway. I cared about her at least."

"Well, you did your best, I'll say that for ya. More'n I would'a done for a murderer. Not a huge tragedy though, right? I mean it *was* self-inflicted, and you gotta admit, she got what she deserved."

Pranav stared at the man. "She got what we all deserve, friend. And I fear she never came to faith."

"Faith in what?"

"In God, sir. It's a terrible thing to enter eternity without Him."

"Believe that, if it gives you comfort, Detective. I say when we're gone, we're gone. Eternity is just that. Eternal sleep, unconsciousness. I'll be gone, yeah, but I won't have gone anywhere."

"You'd better hope that's true."

"Why? 'Cause the alternative is hell? I heard all about that, all the time, growing up in Baton Rouge. Didn't make any more sense to me than voodoo."

"It's not superstition, Bo. Heaven and hell are real, and I'd want to be sure I'm headed in the right direction."

"Like I say, Chakrabarti: if that makes you feel better…"

CHAPTER 70

Kiriath-arba, Northern Negev, Canaan

When Abraham was 137 years old and had moved his vast compound for the last time, Sarah fell ill. He worried and prayed over her and wept bitterly when she passed away. During the customary grieving period, he went to the Hittite elders. "As a foreigner here, could I prevail upon you to sell me a portion of land so that I may properly bury my wife?"

"Oh, sir," they said, "we consider you a prince and urge you to select from our best burial sites. Not one of us would deny you this."

Abraham bowed low. "As you are agreeable to favor me this way, might you ask Ephron to allow me to purchase the cave at the far end of his field? I would be happy to pay the full value to have permanent burial places for my family."

Ephron said for all to hear, "Abraham, please. Allow me to give you both the land and the cave."

"No," Abraham said. "Let me pay you the full value."

"Well," Ephron said, "it is worth four hundred pieces of silver, but we are friends! Go bury your dead."

But Abraham paid the amount Ephron suggested, and the elders witnessed the transaction.

* * *

As Abraham continued to age, God continued to favor him. One day Abraham asked the longtime servant in charge of his entire household to take an oath in the name of the Lord of heaven and earth that he would never let his forty-year-old son Isaac wed a Canaanite woman. He told the servant, "Rather, go to my homeland and find a bride there for Isaac from among my relatives."

"But if I find no woman who is willing to travel this far, should I take Isaac there?"

"No! Never! God vowed to give this land to my offspring. He will make sure you find a wife for my son. If she won't return here with you, I will free you from this oath."

The servant laded ten of Abraham's camels with gifts from his master, and he and a small band of men made the long journey to where Abraham's brother Nahor lived. He arrived at a well just outside town one evening as women were coming to draw water. He prayed, "Lord, show favor to my master. I will ask one of these young women for a drink, and if she agrees and also offers to water my camels, allow her to be your choice for Isaac."

A beautiful young woman, clearly of age, filled her jug. The servant hurried to her and asked for a drink.

"Of course," she said, lowering the container from her shoulder. "And allow me to draw water for your camels as well." She poured the rest of her jar into a trough and then spent several minutes drawing enough water for all ten animals.

The servant watched, amazed, and when the camels had their fill, he asked whose daughter she was. "And might your father have room to put us up for the night?"

"I am Rebekah, the daughter of Bethuel," she said, "granddaughter of Nahor and Milcah. And yes, we have straw and feed for your camels and room for visitors."

The servant gifted her with rings for her nose and wrists, and he worshiped God, praying, "You have shown unfailing love for Abraham and have led me directly to his own family."

At her home, Abraham's servant sat for a meal with her whole family. But he told Rebekah's brother Laban and her father Bethuel and her grandmother Milcah that he didn't want to eat until he had explained why he had come. And so he told them everything, from the vow he had made to Abraham to his prayer for God to show him to the right woman. "So, what do you think?" he said finally. "Will you also show favor to my master? Give me a yes or no so I know what to do."

The men nodded, and Bethuel said, "This is obviously of God, so there is nothing else to say. Take Rebekah and allow her to become the wife of Abraham's son, as the Lord has willed."

Abraham's servant bowed low and worshiped, then presented to Rebekah silver and gold jewelry and clothes, and also lavish gifts to Laban and Milcah.

The next morning, the family prepared to send Rebekah on her way along with her childhood nurse and several servant girls. As she was leaving, they offered a blessing, praying that she would become the mother of millions and that her progeny would be mighty and defeat their enemies.

Several days later at his dwelling in the Negev, Isaac walked the fields in deep thought. In the distance a cloud of dust arose, and Abraham's servant's caravan slowly came into view. A beautiful young woman dismounted from one of the camels and seemed to peer at him. Abraham's servant must have told her who he was, for she quickly covered her face.

The servant introduced Rebekah to Isaac and told him the whole story. Isaac was immediately smitten with Rebekah and they were soon wed. They moved into Sarah's tent, and Isaac loved her with all his heart. He found her especially comforting as he grieved the loss of his mother.

Isaac's father Abraham married again and even in his very advanced age begat six more sons and countless grandchildren. As he neared his 175th birthday and knew he was dying, he bequeathed everything to Isaac while also bestowing gifts upon the sons he had produced through his concubines. He sent them east, far from where Isaac had settled.

While he had enjoyed a long and fruitful life, Abraham did not want to die without blessing his sons, Isaac and Ishmael, and making certain they were reconciled to each other. Isaac was clearly the descendant of promise, through whom the Lord would accomplish all He had vowed to Abraham—and indeed God had already abundantly blessed Isaac. Abraham had once asked the Lord if Ishmael could not also live under their covenant. But God had told him in no uncertain terms that the promise would forever abide with Isaac's descendants. And while He promised to also bless Ishmael and exceedingly multiply his offspring—including bestowing upon him twelve princes of vast tribes—Abraham also knew that God had told Ishmael's mother Hagar that her son would be wild as an untamed donkey, would fight everyone, and that he would raise his fist even to his own family.

So Abraham summoned Ishmael from more than 250 miles away in Egypt to visit him and Isaac so he could bless them before he died. He only hoped his younger son could make it before he passed. The old man was thrilled when Ishmael finally arrived, and he prayed and meditated for days, asking a servant to serve as his scribe. It also warmed Abraham to see his sons greet each other heartily and bring each other up-to-date on their families.

After feeding Isaac and Ishmael a lavish feast, he forced himself to read slowly through dim eyes what he had composed with the help of the scribe:

"My sons, hear the words of your father, hear them and obey them. May Yah, the Lord God, judge between the two of you and may he bless me in my old age. May he bless you and multiply you in your days and may your days be long; may you have many sons and daughters; and may you live in this land that he has given to me and you forever. May your land blossom with fruit, may it flow with milk and honey, may your sheep and your cattle multiply. I admonish you, my sons, that you live in peace, that you love one another, that you never raise your hand against the other, that the sword is never taken up. If you heed my words, my sons, you will be blessed and you will live in peace forever in this rich land that Yah has given me and you.

"The words of Abraham, friend of God, to my sons, Ishmael and Isaac."

CHAPTER 71

June 15, 2019
King Faisal Specialist Hospital, Medina, Saudi Arabia

After having been awakened several times in the night so nurses could check her vitals, Nicole awoke before dawn famished. Suzie Benchford, who had slept in a recliner nearby, asked an aide if was too early for breakfast.

A nurse helped Nicole to the bathroom, then told her she could have dates, bread, and cheese, which sounded heavenly. "And would you like *qahwa*?"

"Oh, yes," Nicole said. "Got to have my caffeine." She had long loved Saudi coffee, yellow from the saffron.

As soon as she'd eaten, she asked Suzie to help her walk the corridors. She felt stiff and sluggish, and every movement aggravated her tender ribs. The deep bruises on her hip and knee slowed her too, but she wanted to become as mobile as possible as soon as she could. And she didn't want to be in bed when her father arrived.

A nurse intercepted the pair on their second loop of the halls and told Nicole a call awaited her at the nurses' station. "A detective."

"We've got to get phones fast, Suzie," Nicole said, painstakingly making her way to the counter.

"They tell me you are not in danger and will heal, albeit slowly," Pranav said. "Thank God."

"I'll be fine," Nicole said. "Tell me about yesterday."

"I need to start with bad news," he said.

"How much worse can it get?"

"More tragedy, I'm afraid," Pranav said, and Nicole reeled from the news of Kayla's suicide.

"I don't understand it," she said. "Despite what she did to my mother, her death doesn't make me feel any better. What a tortured soul Kayla had to be."

"It appears Qahtani forced her to do what she did in New York."

"Oh, no."

"It gets worse. I'll tell you all about it when I get there. I'm about three hours away."

"I need you at the dig site, Pranav. I need to know—"

"That ship has sailed, Dr. Berman. I'm sorry."

"What do you mean?"

"I'm not allowed on the premises. I was allowed no farther than the guard shack. Everyone's visas have been revoked—every member of the team. Saudis have swarmed the place, confiscating everything. They're hauling truckloads out of there and filling in the squares."

"They can't do that! What of all our documentation and artifacts?"

"Nicole, I'm telling you, it's all in Saudi hands now."

"I was about to have Suzie rent us a car so my father and I can head that way when he gets here. He should be here about the same time as you."

"The site is closed, except to the Saudis."

"Were you able to find Max? What's his role in this?"

"I've been texting him, and it doesn't look good. The UN guard let me look at his log, and when Max was down in Square One, it looks like Qahtani was too. He wouldn't let me get a picture of that and says he'd never testify to it."

"Max and Kayla were *both* working with Qahtani? How could I have been so blind?"

"I was too, Doctor. And I should have known the local guards weren't telling me everything."

"Yeah! How could they have seen Max and not Qahtani if they were both on-site at the same time?"

"I tracked them down and confronted them, and actually they did see Qahtani. They say he told them to record only Max's presence. And they'll also deny telling me that. They're scared to death of him."

"What in the world have I gotten myself into, Pranav? I thought I came into this with my eyes wide open, but I didn't know the half of it."

"I'll see you in a few hours, Nicole. Max is on his way to you too, and I have no idea what he's up to. The NYPD, the U.S., and Interpol are trying to figure out his real identity. All I know is, he has to be in bed with the Saudis."

"I've been so stupid," Nicole said.

"I don't know how much more careful you could have been."

"I should have been suspicious of the late dropouts, but Kayla seemed like a no-brainer. How could I have ever put that together?" Nicole suddenly felt dizzy. "I'd better get back to my room. Be safe, Pranav."

"Oh, believe me, I'm being careful. If I give the Saudis any reason at all to pull me over, they could deport me on the spot."

"No one's come after Suzie or me yet. Hope they'll let Dad in the country."

"Every time I've mentioned his name here, it's obvious he's revered. If they allow anyone in, it'll be your dad."

"I don't care what it takes, but we have to let the world know what Dr. Waleed and I found."

The detective went quiet.

"You still there, Pranav?"

"I am," he said. "But you have an even higher priority than that. Your life may be at stake. I've spoken with the hospital security staff, and if Max gets there before I do, I've asked them to be sure he's not armed and hold him till I get there. I don't want him anywhere near you."

"Well, neither do I. But if he's as tied in with Qahtani as you say, can you trust the Saudis to protect me from him?"

CHAPTER 72

King Faisal Specialist Hospital

Nicole couldn't seem to process Detective Chakrabarti's answer and felt herself wobbling.

"You don't look so good, Nicole," Suzie Benchford said.

As Nicole dropped the phone, Suzie grabbed her and a nurse ran around from the other side of the counter. "Wheelchair!" she shouted, and someone came running with one.

"I'm okay, I'm okay," Nicole said, as they lowered her into the chair. "Just a little dizzy."

"Back to bed with you," the nurse said. "You just overdid it a bit."

"Wanna be sitting up when Dad gets here."

"Depends," the nurse said. "Recline a few minutes first."

Suzie and the nurse helped her back into bed, making her cry out at the pain. But as soon as she lay back she felt better, though she could also barely move. And much as she fought it, drowsiness overtook her.

It was nearly noon when Nicole finally roused. She found herself on her left side, everything throbbing—her right knee and hip, her ribs, the side of her face, and her head. As she stirred, Suzie rushed to her, blocking her view of anything—or anyone—else. She had to still be dreaming, Nicole told herself, because the room felt full of people whispering.

"Wha's goin' on?" she managed.

"Visitors," Suzie whispered, "but we have to make sure you're up to it."

"Dad here?"

"I am," she heard.

"Come to me!"

"Not allowed yet. Take your time."

"I'm okay! Come!" She tried to rise.

A nurse appeared. "Dr. Berman, I need to be sure you're stable enough to sit up before these people talk to you."

"Hurry. I haven't seen my dad for weeks, and—"

Still blocking her view, the nurse took Nicole's temperature and blood pressure and peered at the readouts on the machines. "I'm going to help you sit up, but tell me if you suffer any more vertigo."

"I want to sit in a chair."

"The bed is going to have to do."

The nurse lowered the railing, and she and Suzie helped Nicole up and swung her legs over the side. Both hung on as Nicole forced herself not to whimper at the agony in her ribs, and she took deep breaths as the blood seemed to rush from her brain.

"I'll be right outside," the nurse said.

Suzie stepped aside, and Nicole reached for her dad, who gently embraced her and held her head to his chest.

"I was so worried about you," he said.

"How long have you been here?"

"A little over an hour."

"How long did I sleep?"

"Several hours," Suzie said. "You needed it. Now hush."

Nicole didn't recognize a Saudi in uniform and an Anglo man in a suit and tie sitting to the left of Pranav. She was dumbfounded to see Max to Pranav's right, a manila envelope in his handcuffed hands.

Nicole bore into Max's eyes. "I can't wait to talk to you."

"Same here," he said, appearing to try to look confident. But she saw fear in his eyes.

"Who are these others?" she said.

"This is Beauregard Judd," Pranav said. "An attorney with the U.S. Embassy. He's going to walk us through our options. And this is the hospital security chief."

"What do you mean, 'our options'?"

"Let me explain," the chief said. "All your visas have been suspended and you must leave the country as soon as Ms. Berman is cleared to travel."

"I can't leave!" Nicole said. "I have a ton of documentation to finalize, and—"

"To stay in-country you'd have to sign a document wherein you confess your involvement in the death of the Saudi statesman on your dig site in Mada'in Saleh."

"Involvement? I was nearly killed myself!"

"And such a confession would get my daughter sentenced to death here," Ben said.

The security chief handed a folder to Attorney Judd and moved to the door. "Dr. Berman," he said, "I wish you a speedy recovery and safe travels, on behalf of Saudi Arabia."

Nicole furrowed her brow, unable to respond after having been accused of playing some role in Dr. Samir Waleed's demise.

Judd opened the folder, but Pranav said, "Bo, I'm going to ask you to give us a moment."

"Are you sure, because there are some serious matters that have to be dealt with here, and—"

"It sounds to me like Nicole has already decided she's not going to sign. Please. Stay close and I'll ask you back in as soon as we've dealt with a personnel issue."

"I haven't got all day, you know."

Pranav smiled at him. "Of course you do. You're here to keep us from embarrassing the Saudis, and that's not going to be easy."

"Don't be long."

"We'll be as long as we need to be."

With Judd gone and the door shut, Pranav said, "Max showed up unarmed and pleaded with me to let him explain himself to you. First I required him to justify his actions and his whereabouts at critical junctures. You may or may not be any more persuaded of the veracity of those claims than I am, but he swears he can convince you of his good faith."

"You can try, Max," Nicole said, "but you haven't even been honest with me about who you are."

"I can explain that too."

"I'm all ears," Nicole said.

Max leaned forward. "I mean you no harm," he said.

"Try anything," Benzion Berman said, "and it'll be the last thing you ever—"

"You have zero to fear from me, sir," Max said, "as you will soon learn. Nicole, I have been planning to join you on a dig for years. In fact, your father is one of the main reasons I chose to study archaeology."

"Many try to flatter me by praising Dad, Max—or whoever you are. I know he's a legend. So what's your point? Why my dig and not one of his?"

"I had read of his exploits forever, and I longed to meet him, to work with him—"

"Fine! Can we get to the point of all the deceit, your connection with Dr. Qahtani, whatever you did in Square One that led to the death of Samir—"

"All right, listen to me. I was aware of Qahtani before I arrived in-country, yes, but only because he's head of the national museum. Before you introduced him at Mada'in, I'd never met him, corresponded with him, talked with him, or even knew he would be assigned as your overseer on this dig."

"Then what were you doing with him in Square One?"

"Exactly what I told you I was doing. I was curious. I wanted to see what I'd face when I started surveying down there. I didn't touch anything, didn't use a tool, nothing. I just looked around, trying to determine where I'd place my equipment when the time came. I was surprised when

Dr. Qahtani showed up. He was the one carrying a mattock, even though he was in a suit and tie and wearing dress shoes."

"You're trying to tell me Qahtani was the one digging around down there before Samir and I discovered what we did?"

"I didn't see him do anything, but I left before he did, and he was equipped."

"So you admit you were down there, but you say you had nothing to do with any digging."

Max nodded. "That's the truth."

"But what is not the truth is that your name is Max."

"Actually, I go by Max, even in my home country."

"How comforting that you didn't lie about your nickname. But you did lie about your real name."

"I did."

"You told me you were Rith Sang from Cambodia and that you graduated from International University in Phnom Phen. But you didn't."

"No, I didn't."

"You may not believe this," Nicole said, "but I frankly always suspected your accent. It didn't sound precisely Cambodian to me."

"A true linguist."

"So spill. Who are you really, and why all the dishonesty?"

"My degrees are real. But they're from the University of Da Nang."

"Vietnam?" Ben Berman said. "I'm a Vietnam vet."

"I know. I told you, I'm a fan. Have been all my life."

"Surely not *all* your life," Ben said.

"For as long as I can remember."

"You've wanted to be an archaeologist since childhood?"

"No. But I knew of you. My mother told me all about you. She even named me after you. I have to be the only Vietnamese named Benzion Nguyen. My mother's name is Bian. People call her Charm."

Nicole felt woozy again. "Wh—?"

"I'm your half brother, Nicole."

"Dad!" she cried. "You never—"

"I didn't know! Is this some kind of a trick?"

"No trick, sir. I even sent off for one of those genealogy DNA tests, because I knew you'd want proof." Max stood and extended the envelope to Ben with both hands.

Nicole's father ignored it, shaking. "She never told me…"

"And she never heard from you again either. Why was that?"

"She got the grant from our foundation and I assumed she used it to get her teaching degree."

"She did, and she taught for years. But it's as if you fell off the face of the earth. She told me you didn't even know about me, but that didn't make it any easier. For years all I wanted was the chance to confront you. This was my chance. I get it that you couldn't be expected to ask after a son you didn't know you had, but how do you abandon someone who loved you so much…"

"Any excuse sounds lame now," Ben said. "Parting had been too painful, but we both agreed I couldn't stay in 'Nam and she couldn't come to the U.S. I had to move on to keep from losing my mind. We didn't have a name for PTSD back then, but I had it in spades. I lost a lot of people there, and the last thing I wanted was to hear that anything had happened to her. I absolutely believed I'd never see her again. How is she?"

"She's well. Retired. Never married. She turns sixty-five this week."

"Do you have a picture?"

"Of course." But Max couldn't reach his pocket with his hands cuffed. Detective Chakrabarti quickly freed him and he dug a photo from his wallet.

"That's her," Ben said, showing Nicole.

It was clearly the same woman whose picture had been among her dad's effects for years. She was gray now, with luxurious long hair, and though age lined her features, she retained the high cheekbones and pearly teeth, the ebony eyes. "Beautiful," Nicole said.

"Does she hate me?" Ben said.

"Idolizes you, if the truth be known. I never heard a bad word from her about you ever. I had a few of my own though. How does a former lover, a father, never make contact?"

"I never knew. She never t—"

"You never asked. She was out of sight, out of mind."

"She has never been out of my mind," Ben said. "Not for one day. She was the first true love of my life. I'd love to be able to tell her so."

"I might be able to arrange that," Max said.

"But first, may I embrace you and ask your forgiveness?" Ben said, gathering him in. "I swear had I known about you, I'd have made contact. I can't believe I have a son."

"I can't believe I have a brother," Nicole said, reaching to get in on the hug. "Why didn't you just tell me or write directly to Dad? Why go through all this?"

"Truthfully, I didn't know what I'd do or say if I ever met either of you. Or how you'd react. I had to keep my options open in case I wanted nothing to do with this family."

"You've got no choice now," Ben said. "There's no turning back. And as soon as we can get out of this country, I want to go see your mom."

"Me too," Nicole said, "but aren't we going to be under investigation here? I have a lot to prove."

"I'd better get Mr. Judd back in here," Pranav said. "He's convinced we have to get out of here fast, and I can't say I disagree."

"You think I'd leave evidence of the greatest find of any archaeologist's lifetime? Not on your life. Any self-respecting professional with a brain will be able to see what we found here. This will be the noisiest thing in our business since the Dead Sea Scrolls."

CHAPTER 73

King Faisal Specialist Hospital

Nicole rehearsed that very argument again when Bo Judd returned. "I hear what you're saying, Dr. Berman, but we have to look at the bigger picture. You had to know the Saudis would never allow this to come to light, no matter what you found or how you tried to prove it."

"They won't be able to deny it!"

"They're already denying it!"

"Meaning what?"

"I can show you on my phone the official pronouncements coming out of Riyadh."

"Just tell me."

"The government's saying publicly that you murdered Samir Waleed, that your injuries are inconsequential and mostly fake. Your claims of having found evidence of something that would corroborate the Bible's western view of history and reflect poorly on the Qur'an are bogus. They have already meticulously combed through everything found at Mada'in Saleh and say uncategorically that there is no evidence supporting your claims. They were wrong to even grant a dig permit to a female, especially one so young, so inexperienced, who identifies not only as a Christian but also a Messianic Jew. Everyone associated with you is being deported, and—"

"I'm not going anywhere! I'm staying, and I will fight this and prove my case!"

"—and anyone who refuses to leave will suffer the full weight of Sharia law."

"Without even a day in court?"

"You don't want your day in court here, Ms. Berman."

"Of course I do! I have evidence that pr—"

"Let me guarantee you something, Doctor. If you're foolish enough to stay here, you will be imprisoned for as long as they want in conditions you wouldn't wish on your worst enemy. The entire case would be stacked against you, not to mention the entire country and its religion and adherents. If you ever got to trial, you would lose, and your punishment would be beheading."

"It would be a privilege to die for the truth. Isn't that what we're called to?"

"I'm not," Bo Judd said. "And I don't recommend it. You'd have a much better chance to convince people of the truth if you did it outside this country, where you'd be free to present your evidence—what little of it is left."

Nicole held her head in her hands. "I'll commit the rest of my life to this cause," she said. "Where and how can I best do that?"

"Not here," Judd said. "No matter where you decide to do it from, anyone who supports you in this will become an enemy of Saudi Arabia, and you'll have a price on your head."

"I won't quit," she said.

"I'll make a public statement," Max said.

"So will I," Pranav said.

"Me too," Benzion Berman said.

"Nobody knows me or cares what I say," Suzie said. "But count me in. And there'll be a lot of others—especially Square One volunteers."

"So much of the evidence is gone though," Pranav said. "Gone from my phone by whatever super magnet Qahtani and his lawyer used in our meeting."

"And from my phone," Nicole said. "Which I'll never see again."

"Mine too," Suzie said.

"We have our memories," Nicole said. "I can recite the blessing word for word, I obsessed over it for so long."

"Even with the blow to your head?" her dad said.

"I think so."

"Guessing is hardly evidence."

"I'll devote the rest of my career to this," Nicole said. "I'll take depositions from everyone who was at the site, anyone who ever saw the inscription in any form. I'll organize a task force to tell every detail of what happened."

"Can I be on it?" Max said.

"Of course."

"Me?" Pranav said.

"Yes!"

"I suppose I get to finance it," Ben said.

"I hope so!"

"Let's stay on point," Mr. Judd said. "When Detective Chakrabarti and I met with Qahtani and his lawyer and Ms. Mays yesterday, our end game was to trade information on what you'd found for Ms. Mays's freedom. But they already knew what you'd found, and though we were allowed to take her anyway, we all know how that turned out. Before the Saudis change their minds and just execute you all for crimes against Islam, I suggest you get out while the getting's good."

"I can fit on my plane everyone here who wants to go," Ben said.

"Back to the States?" Suzie said.

"Of course. But the long way. We'd be dropping off my son in Vietnam and paying a social call on his mother first."

"On one condition," Nicole said. "Everyone on that plane commits to telling the truth to the whole world about everything that happened here."

"You won't accomplish a thing," Bo Judd said.

"Maybe not," she said. "But we'll never give up."

POSTLUDE

While *Dead Sea Conspiracy* is, of course, a work of fiction, I made every effort to reflect the reality of archaeology. That was made easier by my consultant, the renowned Dr. Craig Evans, who—besides his many other scholarly gifts—is himself an archaeologist. He reminds me often that archaeology done right is painstaking, requiring careful planning, a host of volunteers, technical expertise, and a director with years of experience. The work can be rewarding but also dangerous.

The excavation I imagined for my story is set at Mada'in Saleh, an actual location in northwest Saudi Arabia. Years of real archaeological work has been undertaken there, and Dr. Evans tells me that many believe Mada'in Saleh was, in antiquity, known as Dedan, which happens to be the name of one of Abraham's grandsons. An Islamic legend links Abraham to Dedan, and it made sense to have my main character eager to excavate at this intriguing, beautiful place. And naturally, any such effort in Saudi Arabia led by a woman—and Jewish at that—would create controversy.

The great colorful rock cliffs of Mada'in Saleh resemble the cliffs of Petra in Jordan and were once part of the Nabatean kingdom, a thorn in the side of imperial Rome. This was part of the world in which T. E. Lawrence (Lawrence of Arabia) caused trouble for the Ottoman Empire during World War I.

Not all scholars know what to make of the Old Testament records of some of the great patriarchs living hundreds and hundreds of years. Some refer to this as "Babylonian algebra." I accepted these numbers at face value, allowing for what I hope you found interesting patriarchal conversations.

ACKNOWLEDGMENTS

Jeana Ledbetter, my champion at Worthy.

Dr. Craig Evans, the smartest guy in the room, no matter the room.

Leeanna Nelson, my editor.

James Scott Bell; thanks for legal input.

Lynn and Debbie Kaupp, backbones of my day-to-day for more than fifteen years.

Sarah Helus, my new assistant.

David Loy and Chase Neeley and my team at Leverage Creative Group, Franklin, Tennessee.

Alex Field, my stellar agent.

Dianna Jenkins, my lifetime one-and-only.

ABOUT THE AUTHOR

Jerry B. Jenkins's books have sold more than 72 million copies. Twenty-one of his titles have reached the *New York Times, USA Today, Publishers Weekly,* and *Wall Street Journal* best-seller lists. The phenomenally best-selling Left Behind series inspired a movie starring Nicolas Cage. Jenkins has been featured on the cover of *Newsweek* and his writing has appeared in *Time, Reader's Digest, Guideposts,* and dozens of other periodicals. Jenkins owns the Jerry Jenkins Writers Guild, coaching thousands of aspiring writers in both fiction and nonfiction. He and his wife, Dianna, have three grown sons and live in Colorado.

www.JerryJenkins.com